Cherry Blossom Girls 2

-Harmon Cooper-

Chapter One: Biker Feast

It was the best of times, it was the worst of times. It was the most fucked of times.

All this to say, a tiny bar in Chattanooga, Tennessee, wasn't a place I would normally end up. Sure, there was Shakespeare's Pub in Hamden and a few other small Irish joints back in New Haven, but a bar that came with the prerequisite that you would likely have to fight your way in and fight your way out?

My, how things had changed.

A thin man with a wiry mustache and a black leather vest pointed a grimy knife at Veronique.

It was almost comical how fucked he was, but I didn't feel bad for what was going to happen to him. True, we came here looking for a fight, but we would have also left without one.

However, knife guy just happened to be stupid enough to grab Veronique's ass, which led to her slapping his hand away, which led to him pulling a knife.

Knife man's biker friends were already backing him up – four of them, all dressed in leather and denim and each with their own collection of prison tattoos and violent backstories.

Grace and I sat at the bar, Yours Truly nursing a margarita and Grace sipping a glass of water. I'd recently learned not to get a shifter drunk.

"Are you ready?" I asked her.

The bartender, who was just about to call the police, put the phone back down, his eyes flashing white. He grabbed a rag and began cleaning the back counter, completely oblivious to what was happening before him.

"This is your last warning," I told the man with the knife. "Scratch that, this is your first *and* last warning. You made a mistake by assaulting her, and the mistake could cost you your life. Run now. That's my suggestion."

"The fuck it is," Knife Man slurred, "coming here with two hot bitches thinking you own the goddamn place. This is *our* bar! Right, boys?"

The men that had gathered around grunted in agreement.

"Well, I warned you." I looked at Veronique. "They're all yours."

The blade of the man's knife began to bend backward until it was aimed at his wrist. The metal thinned, elongated, and lightly pricked his skin.

He dropped the blade. "What kind of goddamn witch are you?"

The answer to his question came when Veronique used her abilities to pull the fillings from his teeth.

Hunks of metal and enamel burst out of Knife Man's mouth, carrying blood and saliva with them. The fillings hovered in the air before his face, and about the time he realized what had just happened, they cut him down like bullets.

His friends were quick to react.

A bald biker with several piercings swung his pool stick at Veronique. Grace stopped him mid-swing, and the towering brute turned to his compadres, his mind now hers.

"Gary? What the hell are you doing?" one of the men cried as his former friend swung his pool stick at the shortest guy in the group.

With three engaged or down, one of the last members of the biker gang pulled a gun. "I don't know what the hell you two are, but this ends now!"

Except it didn't.

The tiny screws holding the gun together unraveled, and his weapon fell apart in his hands. He started to back away, but Veronique pulled him over to her using the metal on his belt and the buckles on his boots.

The final biker still standing turned to the door, a fire lit under his ass.

"Grace." I nodded at the man trying to escape and he stopped, turned toward a pool table, and lay down on it.

"Make sure he isn't drunk," I reminded Veronique as she stood before the gunless man, who was now on his knees.

I'd seen what happened if she took the life force of a drunk person.

Not that I wouldn't mind another shower encounter, especially after two days of traveling with her and not quite getting the cold shoulder … yet not getting the warm shoulder either. But I wasn't ready to handle her, nor Grace, in a drunken state.

"He isn't drunk," Grace said, her eyes blazing white. Damn, she looked beautiful. She was in her Asian form, her thick, bleached blonde hair pulled into a tight ponytail. But rather than go with the Asian's body, she had her normal voluptuous shape, with more curves than a Fibonacci spiral.

The guy who'd had his fillings ripped out earlier grabbed my ankle.

Bad idea, I thought as I kicked him in the chest with my other foot, adrenaline surging through me.

I'd never actually attacked someone before.

Sure, I'd wrestled once or twice, but that was just horsing around with friends. I'd never punched anyone, and I'd definitely never kicked a person in the stomach.

But this was Gideon Caldwell reborn, Gideon stripped from his past. As Nic Pizzolatto wrote in one of his earlier books, before *True Detective* became an HBO hit, "The past isn't real."

And with each action I took that was foreign to the old Gideon Caldwell, I gave the new Gideon strength, separating him further from the past. Not that I wanted any of this to go to my head, and not that I truly agreed with Pizzolatto's quote; I really just wanted to be hardened, ready for what lay ahead.

But as it would turn out, I'd never be quite ready for what was to come.

Veronique placed her hand on the now gunless biker's throat and began the devil's work, red energy swirling around her wrist as she fed, her skin turning radiant almost instantly.

That's what this was about.

I knew we were out of place at the biker bar and that our appearance would stir up trouble, but Veronique needed to feed, and regular food just didn't seem to do it for her.

It really was like being friends with a vampire, and I didn't know if she suffered some type of hunger that would turn her against me if she didn't feed regularly. That was also on my mind: *Let the predator feed or be fed upon.*

"Don't do it all the way," I said quickly. "No killing if it can be avoided."

So maybe I wasn't that hard yet. I still had a moral compass, even if it was cracked.

"How's toothless?" I asked Grace.

"He's drunk."

"What about the guy you turned, the one with the pool stick?"

"He's sober."

I placed my hand on Veronique's shoulder, which sent a spark of fear down my spine. After a moment of hesitation on both our parts, she let go of the gunless man and turned.

"Yes?" she asked, her dark eyes narrowing on me.

"Remember, feed on them, but don't kill him. We don't want to leave a trail. Grace is going to wipe everyone's memories anyway."

She sighed, blowing a bit of the hair out of her face. "As you wish."

Veronique fed on the biggest biker with the pool stick first, then the one that had lain down on the table, and finally the bartender.

It was a big meal.

Chapter Two: Stranger Danger

It had been two days since we left the East Coast, two days of driving, swapping out vehicles, staying in posh hotels, and just trying our damndest to keep on the run.

I wasn't the type that could drive all night, and even though Grace could technically take over my mind and have me drive for us, I wasn't keen on that idea either.

I also wasn't stupid enough to think they weren't somehow tracking us.

I didn't know enough about Grace and Veronique's drives to know if they could give off GPS signals – or even scarier, if they could be taken over somehow by an unseen force.

But they hadn't yet, so I tried not to think about it.

I'd continued communicating with David Butler in Texas, and we were set to meet once we arrived.

I wasn't nervous about this, considering I had Grace and Veronique with me, but maybe I should have been.

Because of the success of *Mutants in the Making*, I'd received tons of messages, and as I'd predicted, the tinfoil hat crowd had made their presence known.

I stopped replying to most emails unless I saw pictures or some type of photo evidence. Nothing compared yet to the pictures the man from Texas had given us, and the fact that Mother was in them only made me want to get down there even more.

Whoever the mysterious 'Mother' was, Veronique and Grace had her on their hit list.

I hadn't been able to discover much more about her through their drives, and I'd definitely probed around, at least in Grace's. Neither were very forthcoming about Mother either.

Veronique had let me plug in only once, for just a moment yesterday morning, but she was hesitant to let me play with her stats; I was still working on gaining her trust. While it would have been easier to have Grace simply take over her mind, I was opposed to that strategy.

Still, the sooner I could understand what she was capable of, the better.

I had seen a glimpse of their combined abilities back at the Rose-Lyle facility. Veronique had drained Angel and was able to externally transfer his life force energy into the air, where Grace used her telepathic abilities to keep it in a sphere, which she used to destroy the facility.

12

So, there were ways forward, and I was pretty sure one of these ways was through adjusting Veronique's skills.

But that could wait. MercSecure and whatever federal authorities were after us could find us tomorrow or they could find us in a week; there was really no telling when they would attack.

But they would attack. Of that I was certain.

Then there was my personal life, and how much it had changed since Grace showed up on my doorstep.

The fact that my picture was on her drive was still a mystery. I hadn't been able to find it again, which was odd, because it didn't take me much clicking to find it the first time.

The first installment of *Mutants in the Making* had become a number one bestseller and had already garnered over two hundred reviews. Many were positive, but an increasingly high amount were not. Other authors had started to dig in, claiming my story was bullshit, and I knew that my writer buddy Luke had come to my defense several times.

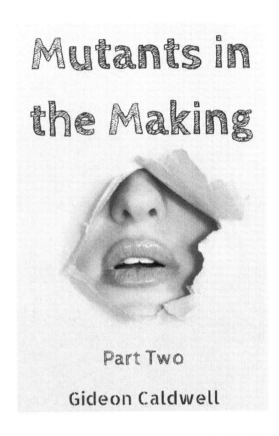

Mutants in the Making

Part Two

Gideon Caldwell

The cover of the second installment was ready, but I still needed more time to flesh out the book and edit it. I guess calling it a 'book' was somewhat of a misnomer because it was shorter than that – barely a novella – but it made more sense in my mind to call it that.

"Grace, what do you think of the second cover?" I asked as I moved over to the bed with my laptop.

It was a couple hours after the bar incident, and we were at the Hyatt in downtown Chattanooga. Grace and Veronique were both on the bed, watching another home makeover show, as they had been since we arrived.

"I like it," she said, her eyes flashing white.

"You didn't even look at it …"

Grace had done this a couple times over the last two days, briefly taking over my psyche and then giving it back to me. It was at the point where oftentimes, I didn't know if I was thinking my own thoughts or if it was Grace thinking them with me. Sometimes I thought I was thinking Grace's thoughts, and sometimes I thought we were a collective mind, thinking together.

It was definitely eerie.

"Veronique?" I asked. "Do you like the cover?"

She simply nodded, still glued to the television.

The plan was to get to Shreveport, Louisiana, tomorrow and arrive in Austin the next day.

As we had done thus far, we would probably change vehicles at least twice on our way south tomorrow. This had proven easiest to do at a gas station, but it was also fairly simple at a WalMacy's or a mall along the highway.

Anywhere there were people, we had vehicles.

"Well, I'm glad you both approve," I said as I closed my laptop, ready to take in the views outside.

I went to the balcony and leaned over the edge, looking down at the city of Chattanooga. The sun was setting in the distance, casting orange stripes across the Tennessee River. There was something about the city that I liked; it was small like New Haven and filled with shadowy corners, which gave an air of intrigue to the location.

I wished we could have stayed longer in Tennessee, as I heard Nashville was pretty sweet, but our destiny was farther south, in the Lone Star State, and from there possibly west.

Of all the quacky emails I'd gotten, I still hadn't received one from the West Coast.

I knew there was something out there, though; I'd seen some information about it on Grace's drive. I had also received another message from the scientist who worked at the Rose-Lyle facility.

Still hadn't replied to that one.

"Choices, choices, choices," I mumbled as I stared out at the river. Cars moved in the streets below and I watched a particularly aggressive driver in a large car swerve around an SUV, narrowly missing a Kia hybrid as the big vehicle twisted onto the highway.

Damn, if there weren't bad drivers everywhere.

"Enjoying the view?" Veronique asked, startling me.

Just hearing her voice caused the hairs on my neck to stand at attention.

She walked up next to me and placed her arms on the rail. She was dressed like a country singer now, with her pearl snap collar shirt and an extra tight pair of Wranglers. It had been her choice, and there weren't many options at WalMacy's that were her size.

"It's nice, right?"

She nodded. "Grace is tired tonight; I think she's going to bed."

"Oh?"

I had a feeling she was hinting at us spending the night together, but I couldn't be sure, and I didn't want to project those thoughts onto her. So I just shrugged and tried to change the subject.

"I'd really like to plug into you soon and play with your stats and skills."

"Plug into me? I'm sure you would," she said as she moved closer to me and leaned on the balcony.

"You know what I mean."

Grace didn't mind if I plugged in and searched through the files and subfiles on her drive. I had played with her Opacity a number of times, and last night, she'd asked me to turn her clear while we banged.

Which was ... like having sex with a ghost? I don't know. It was cool, though. Still, I hadn't been able to discover more as to why my photo was on her drive, and I was no longer able to find the photo.

Weird.

Yesterday morning, when Veronique had let me plug in, she'd quickly decided against it and told me we could do it later.

The thing was, I wanted to see what was actually modifiable with her skills.

Plus, there was information on her drive that wasn't on Grace's – like the snuff videos. And who doesn't like a good superhero snuff video? The last time I checked Veronique's skills, back at the hotel in Stamford when she was unconscious, portions of them had been grayed out.

I knew there was more to what she could do; I'd seen it firsthand back at the Rose-Lyle facility.

Just as Veronique moved a few inches closer to me, so that our bodies now touched, my phone buzzed.

"Are you going to answer that?"

But I was no longer focused on the flirty way she asked the question, I was legitimately freaked out.

No one had this number.

When Luke and I spoke, we did so over GoogleFace. And he never called me, so I was unaware of what the phone's ringtone even sounded like.

"It's an unknown number," I told her as I looked at the anonymous face icon flashing on my phone's screen.

"Answer it," she said.

I took a deep breath and decided to go with Veronique's advice.

"Hello?"

"Please, do not hang up the phone," a man said on the other end. "My name is Ken Kim, and I'm the scientist at the Rose-Lyle facility who sent you the email. Two emails. And do not worry, I'm not tracking this call or anything. I need to talk to you. I need to tell you what's to come. Your life and the lives of Subject S and Subject V are in danger. Please, do not hang up the phone!"

"You have fifteen seconds," I told him as I turned my back to the balcony. My knees suddenly shaky, I sat down and crossed my legs. Veronique crouched next to me, her hand on my shin as I put Ken on speakerphone.

"Again, my name is Ken Kim, Dr. Ken Kim, and I'm not your enemy, Gideon."

"Yeah? How the hell am I supposed to know that?"

"For starters, I'm guessing you found the ports on both of their necks, otherwise you couldn't have done what you did back at the facility. Well, I'm the one who put all that information on their drives; I put it there with the hope that someone could possibly uncover and unravel a little bit of this mystery. Far-fetched at the time, but then Sabine got out."

It didn't add up. How could he have possibly known Grace would escape and that Veronique would come looking for us and later switch sides? It was too hard to believe, even for a fiction writer like myself. But there was something about the way he spoke that seemed genuine.

"You have thirty more seconds," I finally said.

"Please believe me, I cared about ... Sabine. Has she told you her backstory by now?"

"Yeah, being kept in isolation all her life and escaping after tricking two scientists."

"I was one of the scientists that interviewed her every day. My colleague, Bobby, was the one she used to escape. Is Sabine there? I'd love to talk to her."

"You're never going to get to talk to her again," I said with a growl. "But you can talk to me. You have one minute now."

"If I only have one minute, then I'll explain how I gained access to your phone number. I'm a bit of a hacker, which was why I was able to put all that information on their drives. The code Sabine gave you to access the drives? I gave her that code."

"How? From what I recall, you were knocked out by the other scientist."

"Before that." He cleared his throat. "And yes, Bobby did knock me out. He's since been fired and … disappeared. He's disappeared. I can't talk about that right now, though. And there's nothing we can do about it anyway. Ask her about it when you speak to her again. She'll tell you the truth."

I looked at Veronique, who quietly stood and walked back to the room. She returned seconds later with Grace, who locked eyes with me and instantly transferred what she knew into my brain.

"So if you are the one who gave that code to her, what is that code?"

"1QAZ2WSX3EFV4321QWEASD," he said. "That's the access code."

Grace nodded.

"And how did you gain access to my number?"

"They're following your trail – 'they' being MercSecure and the federal government. Why aren't you sending encrypted emails? Let's start there. You know they can track that, right? I mean, you've been wise to do some things like change cars and change rooms, but you give them a crumb every time you send an email."

I bit my lip. I had no idea if he was right, but it did seem possible. "How'd you get my number, then?"

"Remember when you bought a phone in Stamford?" Ken asked.

"Yes."

"That's how I gained access to your info. You see, the analysts they've got on your case have gone about this the wrong way: Rather than check the employees at the Okay Buy who had phones, they've gone after each and every phone number *issued* that day. But somehow, the way you and Sabine orchestrated it, the phone wasn't purchased through normal means, nor was it registered in a normal way. So I checked the employees and their phone numbers and narrowed it down to yours, and that's how I'm talking to you. Now."

"Okay, makes sense. I'll be getting rid of this phone then."

"It's not just the phone they're going to get you with; it's the emails you send from your laptop. That's how they found you in Stamford. If you didn't know, the FCG has a private corporation that pays for location-based data from GoogleFace. It's expensive, and they have to pay each time they access it, but we're talking about unlimited funds here – funds given to them by the American taxpayer."

"Your minute is drawing to a close," I said as I looked at Grace. She was crouched in front of me now, same as Veronique, both of them listening intently to what Dr. Ken Kim had to say.

Grace's brow was furrowed, a look of concern in her blue eyes.

The phone cut out for a second and he continued. "What I'm trying to say is that every time you send an email, they're able to track you. If you stop sending emails or send them through an encryption app, you're fine. But as of right now, they know where you are and are coming. Shit. They're coming *now*, Gideon – you need to go!"

I was panicked at that point. I'd just used my laptop not too long ago to email some readers. I was so screwed.

"We've got to go," I whispered to Grace and Veronique. They quickly stood and went to our room to begin packing.

"I want to help you," Ken said. "Please let me help you. I don't know how much longer they're going to let me live, but I want to help you. They'll come after me, just like they came after Bobby. I ... I fucking know they will. I'm surprised they haven't already; I was there when Sabine escaped. One more thing. To prove my intent, I want to give you a code you can put into their systems that will improve their abilities."

"A code?"

"That's right, another code," said Ken. "As you likely understand by now, you can modify their abilities to some degree. They don't level up, per se, but there are ways to unlock abilities that were previously hidden. One of them is by entering codes into their drives. We didn't give them all these abilities at once – not that they couldn't have figured them out on their own."

"So they are arranged codes?"

"Yeah, something like that. But I have one for you. Do you have a pen?"

Grace, I thought.

Yes?

I'm going to tell you a code in a second, can you write it down for me in there?

"Okay, I'm ready," I told Ken.

He rattled off a string of letters and numbers. "XFLT16689L147DDFBERV."

I repeated it back to him, thinking each number and letter as I said it aloud.

Got it, Grace said inside my head.

"Scroll to the bottom of the list of available options, and you'll see an input section. Put this code there. And yes, the same code works for both of them. Like I said, they could figure these abilities out on their own – they may have already done so – but this will speed up the process. We'll be in touch."

"Thanks for the information." I hung up the phone and turned it off. I disconnected the battery, removed the SIM card, and once again – just like I'd seen people do in movies – threw the phone over the balcony. I bent and twisted the SIM card and flicked it onto another balcony.

My laptop would be next.

Everything was saved in the cloud anyway, but it still pained the writer in me to smash it to pieces.

Luckily, by the time I got into the room, Veronique had already done that for me.

My laptop looked like it had been dissected by an alien, and all of its metal pieces lay in a circle around its square body.

"Keep the balcony door open," Veronique said as the metal pieces lifted into the air. Just like with the man's fillings back at the biker bar, she turned the pieces of my laptop into projectiles. The bits of metal flew out the window and down to the Tennessee River.

"Ready?" Grace asked me.

"Yeah, let's get out of Chattanooga. And maybe something to eat along the way."

A smile spread across her concerned face. "Pizza?"

"I was thinking barbecue."

She thought about that for a moment. "Barbeque pizza?"

I chuckled as I looped my duffel bag over my shoulder. "Sure, barbeque pizza."

Chapter Three: I Want an Ice Cream Truck in My Back Yard

We drove south toward Jackson, Mississippi, a barbeque chicken pizza on the seat between Grace and me. Veronique sat in the back of our big truck, and every now and then, I would catch a glimpse of her through the rearview mirror, her skin porcelain, her blonde hair sharply framing her face, her dark eyes fixated on me.

"Are you sure you don't want a piece?" Grace asked Veronique. She took one last bite up to the crust and threw the rest out the window.

"I'm fine," Veronique said.

"What's with the crust?" I asked Grace. "I thought you like the crust."

"We saw on TV that the crust has more carbs," she replied. "So you could enjoy the pizza, but if you throw out the crust, you cut like twenty-five percent of the carbs."

I laughed. "You can't believe everything you see on TV. But I guess that makes some sense. Not diet-wise, but just in the sense that you're throwing away a portion of the pizza, so you're definitely going to cut some carbs."

"I think barbeque pizza is very good," Grace said. Lights from the cars flashed across her soft skin. She was in her normal form, Scandinavian on fleek, and she wore my sweater and pants.

I don't know why she always reverted back to this form, but there was something kind of cute about it.

"It doesn't smell so great," Veronique said. "It reminds me of a bathroom."

"I guess …" I glanced at her through the rearview mirror. "I guess a lot of meats kind of smell like a bathroom if you think about the smell in that way. I mean, there are similarities. Anyway, enough bathroom talk."

"It's too bad we had to leave the hotel," Grace said. "We really like that show."

"Which show is that?" I asked.

They were constantly watching some show about tearing down houses and rebuilding them. Or maybe it was remodeling crappy places, or possibly it was a real estate show.

I had no idea. I was usually busy on my laptop when they were watching TV.

As nice as it would have been to hop onto the bed and rest between them, a beautiful woman on either side – a harem in the making – writing a book took time. It took a lot of time, and that was why so many writers I admired were a little bit on the chubby side.

Writing is a sitting sport.

What better way to describe the act of sitting for hours and hours to bleed onto an empty page with the hope that someone will read what you have to say? It's hell, but you're in charge, and for a good many writers, their calculated words are the one thing they control in their hectic lives.

As my mind wandered, skipping over books I'd read and lessons I should have learned from them, Grace and Veronique told me their favorite program was about a pair of brothers who fixed houses and sold them for a profit. Their second favorite show was about a married gay couple who did the same thing, and their third favorite show was about a group of teenagers who did pretty much the same thing.

"We're going to take this place down, make it right, and sell it at a good price!" Grace said, now in the form of one of the brothers.

Veronique laughed, a long and harsh laugh that seemed fake, the way I envisioned how rich people laughed while vacationing in the Hamptons.

"Do more," she said as she clapped her hands together.

Grace's form morphed into a young girl with orange hair in a side braid. "Sure, we're just kids, but that doesn't mean we can't flip this house! So we're going to start in the bedroom, knock the bedroom walls out, expand the bathroom so it's a master bathroom, not the little bathroom that it was before. And it's a kid's house, so we're going to put a jungle gym in there. Why not, right? And the backyard? Basketball court, a pond, and an ice cream truck. Because who doesn't want an ice cream truck in their backyard?"

Veronique laughed again. "I want an ice cream truck in my backyard."

They continued talking about the houses they had seen flipped, how they would flip them, and at some point, I returned my focus to the road and Dr. Ken Kim.

Who was he really trying to help? He had given us a code, but for all I knew, it would *activate* the GPS system in the two women.

There was no way of telling, and curiosity wasn't going to get this cat, or writer, or the Cherry Blossom Girls (the name I had started to call them in my head).

Their abilities were fine; they were where they needed to be. At least until I could fool around with Veronique's a bit more.

I looked in the rearview mirror and caught a glimpse of myself, bearded and now with a badass looking scar. I couldn't believe I'd made such an amateur mistake of not encrypting my emails.

Seemed about right, though; even though I'd been at this for about a week now, I still had no idea what I was doing.

And if it was Ken who put all the information on their drives, I should have asked him about my photo and why it was there.

The mystery continued.

Chapter Four: Dorian Gray and the T-Rex Made of Energy

We stopped at a gas station at a quarter after midnight, and I figured now would be a good time to switch vehicles. We found a man in a station wagon, gave him the keys to our truck, and transferred our things to the back of his car.

"This one is not as nice," Veronique said as she got in the back.

I waved her concerns away as I went inside the convenience store to get a cup of coffee. I nodded at the attendant behind the counter and glanced around in search of liquid crack.

A punk rock looking woman with jet-black hair and deep red lipstick stood nearby, staring at me. She wore a leather jacket, tight black jean shorts over a pair of fishnet stockings, and black military boots. Her midriff was exposed below the short tank top she wore under her jacket, and I could see the swell of her breasts above the top.

I nodded at her, looked away awkwardly as I normally did when I saw hot women, and made a beeline for the coffee station.

There weren't many options, and the coffee looked like it had been brewed two days ago. But what could I do? I filled up a twenty-ounce cup, added a bit of hazelnut creamer just to give it some flavor, and took a sip of the lukewarm beverage.

I sighed. It tasted like yesterday's McStarbucks warmed for fifteen seconds in the microwave.

I glanced back at the woman and noticed she was now holding a paintbrush. She was also staring at me in a strange way.

She lifted the paintbrush to her lips, placing it in her mouth and holding it there for a moment before taking it back out.

As if she were conducting an invisible orchestra, the punk rock super began tracing an image in the air. Purple magic took shape as she moved her brush.

The door swung open and Grace entered, surprise spreading across her face as she saw the woman.

Gideon, get down!

The woman lowered her paintbrush and a human-shaped form appeared, its body made of blistering purple energy. It charged at me with fists on fire. An invisible force moved me to safety just in time to miss its first strike, my coffee flying out of my hand in what felt like slow-motion.

As if they were on wheels, the aisle shelves thundered toward the woman with the paintbrush, the result of Grace's omnikinesis.

Just before the shelves reached the woman, she disappeared in a flash.

The gas station attendant stood up from his hiding spot behind the register, a shotgun in his hand. "I want you both to get the fuck –"

The human made of purple energy slammed into the counter, exploding anything its body came into contact with. It continued forward, pressing *through* the counter, and even as the attendant fired his shotgun, it reached the man's body and exploded that too, spraying gobs of red goo everywhere.

I nearly lost my barbeque pizza as a clump of human landed on my shoulder.

I stumbled backward, where I was met by Grace. By this point I was crouched down, my ears ringing from the weapon's report, my fingers covered in the man's blood, which I tried to wipe off on my shoulder.

Veronique stepped into the gas station, her hands lifting into the air as screws and bolts from the shelving became projectile weapons.

She was breathing heavily, hyper-aware as she scanned the area.

"What the hell is going on?" I whispered to Grace, who stood next to me, her hand on my shoulder.

"It's Dorian Gray."

I shook my head.

I'd read Oscar Wilde's book of the same name, so that was the first thing that came to me. Then my thoughts jumped from that to the clump of body matter on my shoulder, the body matter scattered all around me, the fact that we were in a gas station in the middle of nowhere, and we'd been attacked by a human shape made entirely of *flaming purple energy.*

My brain was running wild again.

"We have to find her," Veronique said. She looked like a southern badass in her cowgirl get-up, her hands red with energy, screws and bolts buzzing around her like wasps.

"What are her abilities exactly? How do you know about her?" I asked Grace, still catching my breath.

"Later," she assured me as she looked around, ready for another attack.

"Come out, Dorian, and paint me a picture," Veronique shouted, her hands clenching into fists.

"Can she paint anything into existence?" I asked, connecting the dots.

My answer came in the form of a T-Rex that chomped into the corner of the building, tearing a portion of the ceiling out, and exploding all the lights and electric outlets.

The charged T-Rex ripped more of the ceiling away, using a kick from its clawed leg to smash a wall.

I wish I could say this was your normal T-Rex with the little bitch arms, but no. This one had been customized to bring death to the three of us, and since that was the case, it had two huge weapons instead of arms, each with muzzles the size of beach volleyballs.

And they could shoot.

A searing blast tore over my head and went straight into the beer cooler nearby.

The explosion that followed sent shards of glass into the air, accompanied by the sweet sick stench of adult beverages.

I was running by this point toward the back exit, trying to get my ass out of there before the T-Rex fired off another shot.

"Grace, Veronique!" I cried.

I'm here, Writer Gideon! Grace wasn't far from me, covering her head as she ran.

I turned just in time to see Veronique press her hands in front of her as if she were moving chi. Half the metal in the store scissored toward the T-Rex.

Since our attacker was made of energy, the only thing those random chunks of metal could do was cause mini-explosions all over its body as the projectiles attempted to pass through. But that was better than nothing, and the T-Rex expended more and more energy as hunks of metal struck its form.

Eventually, like the person made of energy, the Cretaceous abomination began to dissipate, no longer able to cause damage.

Veronique was still in a battle-ready pose, more metal fluttering around her just in case she needed to use it quickly.

"Where did she go?" I asked as I surveyed the damage.

The energy Dorian created had done some pretty strange things, either exploding or melting everything it came into contact with. *Did she really conjure this stuff with a paintbrush? Was it activated by her saliva or was it just her schtick?*

I moved through what was left of the convenience store, my nose twitching at the smell of burning plastic, food wrappers, flesh, and anything else flammable.

Veronique smiled grimly as I approached her, and a few bits of metal fell out of the air.

"Thank you," I said in earnest. "Both of you." I turned to Grace. "I was just getting my coffee. She would have blasted me if you hadn't done something."

"They've started sending others for us," Veronique said, as more metal fell.

"Fuck, so they still know where we are. Shit." I glanced at Grace, who was still looking through the damage, one hand poised at the ready just in case she needed to act. She could use her abilities with her mind alone, but similar to Veronique, it seemed that physical movement had some psychological effect that possibly strengthened the attack.

I mean, if I were superpowered, I'd be making poses too.

That's a strange thing to be thinking about, I told myself. But then again, we'd just been attacked by a woman with a paintbrush who conjured up a goddamn dinosaur. And a guy's body had exploded, leaving my shoulder a mess.

"We should move," I told Veronique as I cautiously stepped over to a rack of clothing that had been partially burnt to a crisp. There were still a couple of shirts, so I took one that had the American flag on it just to have something change into.

"Nothing?" Veronique asked her counterpart.

"I don't sense her at all," Grace said. "It's like she's completely vanished."

"You should have used your powers to take over her mind."

"You know that doesn't work as well on some of us," Grace reminded her as she moved to the door. "Normals, yes, but not us."

Normals. I recalled Angel using a similar term. I guess everyone needed a name for someone unlike them.

"You took over *my* mind," Veronique reminded her.

"I did, and I'm surprised I was able to. But like I've promised, I won't do it again. Believe me. I tried with Dorian, but she resisted, so I

37

sent the shelves after her. I was only able to get a flash of who she was and the powers she had. The charging power. That's all I could discover."

"I already knew that about her. I don't know how she got away so fast, though."

I heard sirens in the distance.

The rest of the metal around Veronique fell. As we made our way over to what was left of the entrance, I glanced at the convenience store's office.

The cameras.

"Destroy everything in that room."

Veronique turned to the office. The walls rippled and the metal inside zipped around. Then the ceiling caved in. I juxtaposed this with the time I had tried to destroy the surveillance data at the hotel in East Haven.

Veronique's method was much easier.

We were back on the highway just a minute or so later.

The station wagon we'd acquired before Dorian showed up smelled musty on the inside. The owner was a cigarette smoker, something I should have looked out for in the beginning. Ash was everywhere, scratch-off lottery tickets littered the floor, and there were burn marks on the plastic door handle.

As soon as we were far enough away for me to think we hadn't been followed, I eased up a bit on the speed and started in on the questioning.

"Tell me everything," I said, looking from Veronique through the rearview mirror over to where Grace sat beside me. She was still in her base form, but now she wore a tight black turtleneck sweater and black jean shorts over a pair of fishnet black leggings. It seemed she frequented three forms: the Asian one inspired by the geisha on the wall of my basement apartment; her Scandinavian supermodel shape that may or may not be what she actually looked like; and her ponytailed brunette in yoga pants.

All were equally hot.

"Did you get your current clothing idea from Dorian?" I asked, noticing the fishnet tights under her shorts.

I recalled the buxom woman with jet black hair and crimson lips. An image of her placing her paintbrush between her lips flashed in my mind's eye, followed by an image of the gas station attendant exploding.

And all I had wanted was a fucking cup of coffee.

"I thought you'd like the outfit," Grace said, her hair darkening and the color of her lips deepening.

39

Stop reading my thoughts.

Sorry, bad habit! She said in my skull.

"To answer your request," Veronique said, "Dorian Gray was stationed at our facility from 2025 to 2028. I trained with her. You didn't see it, and it no longer exists, but one of the stops of the hyperloop pod beneath the Rose-Lyle facility was an above-ground training space outside of Hamden."

"Ah, you trained with her; that's how you knew."

Veronique nodded. "And I've taken down one of her energy dinosaurs before. The things she creates can be stopped – either by time, by reaching their target, or by tossing as many solid objects at them as you can."

"And they could have killed you if they touched you?"

"That's right."

I shook my head. "I can't believe they trained you like that. They probably spent millions of dollars to create you, then they trained you in a way that could have ended your life prematurely if you'd made just one mistake."

"Is there a better way to train?" Veronique asked. "Knowing one's life is on the line changes the way they fight."

Two faster vehicles appeared behind me, and once I passed an eighteen-wheeler, I transitioned to the slow lane and let them go around, not interested in a dick-measuring contest, especially in a station wagon.

"You two know who Dorian Gray is, right?"

"Yes, that woman," Veronique said.

"Oh, she's named after a book," Grace said before I could explain.

"That's right, um, *The Picture of Dorian Gray* is about this guy who wishes a portrait of himself would age rather than his physical body. As time passes and Dorian becomes more and more evil, the picture becomes hideous. There's a lot of philosophical undertones, or whatever."

"Interesting," Grace said. "I'd love to read one of your books. *How Heavy This Axe?* That looks intriguing."

I grinned. She was patronizing me; in an instant, Grace would know the ending of *How Heavy This Axe?* and how it was about a transgender dwarf abandoned by his people and how, rather than run away, the dwarf killed them all and ended up alone, until a dragon showed up and they became friends with benefits who lived happily ever after.

Who doesn't love a happy ending?

"I can't figure out how Dorian found us," I said, back to the subject at hand. "I mean, of all the gas stations. How did she know to go to that one? How is that even possible? And how did she get away so fast?"

Veronique thought for a moment, the lights of the highway cutting horizontal arcs across her face as I observed her through the rearview mirror. I yawned. Adrenaline and drowsiness were a strange combo; I was alert but tired, ready to sleep as much as I was ready to run.

"She never moved that fast before," Veronique finally said. "I don't know how she left. Maybe she thought I would kill her. It wouldn't be hard to do so; I almost did before."

"We shouldn't kill her," Grace said, *clearly* reading my thoughts. "Not if we can help it."

Veronique sat back and pulled her knees to her chest. She wasn't wearing her seatbelt. "You're suggesting we make friends with her and ask her to join us?"

I took over from there. "We'll figure that out later. First, we need to come to grips with how she found our location so quickly. If she can do that, so can the rest of the people who are after us."

"So, we're supposed to kidnap and ask her?" Veronique laughed. "You two share a delusion. An inspiring delusion but a delusion nonetheless."

"We've already agreed that we are going across the country to destroy these facilities," I replied. "What if there are more like you two who want to join us? What if more want to be part of our movement?"

"If we could weaken her," Grace said, "I could wipe her mind. Then she'd be our slave."

42

I gulped.

I'd never heard Grace refer to the people whose minds she took over as 'slaves.' I recalled Chip Parker, the guy who helped us back in New Haven. The taxi driver too. And a host of others who played a smaller role in our narrative. I hesitated to call them 'slaves' because of the negative connotation of the word, but that's really what they were.

I decided to let the comment pass.

"And what's with the paintbrush? Did she use that when you two trained together?"

Veronique nodded. "It's what she uses to activate her ability. It's kind of like the ... What do wizards use again?"

"Wands?" I asked.

"It's like her wand; her power is activated by her spit."

"I noticed that. It would definitely make it hard for her to kiss someone."

Grace laughed. "You're thinking of kissing her?"

"Is that what my mind says?"

Her eyes flashed white. "No, you're just being geeky as always."

"I believe the word is cheeky."

"From what I remember, any of her bodily fluids carry this ability. Her blood too. So, doing other things with her would also be a bad idea," Veronique said.

Other things with her? Time to change the subject.

"Charged spit or not, it looks like we need to always be on high alert. We can't even get gas in the middle of nowhere without getting assaulted. And if *she* was able to find us …"

I kept expecting to see a helicopter appear in the rearview mirror, its spotlight trained on us. This triggered the memory of our escape from Stamford and the multiple helicopters that Veronique brought down.

Talk about a rough afternoon.

"Let's trade cars soon," Grace said suddenly. "This car has too many memories."

"Yeah, and it's stuffy back here," Veronique added.

"We can roll down the windows," I suggested.

"No," Veronique said. "It'd be smarter to change vehicles, just in case Dorian saw what we drove away in."

Chapter Five: Mother is Watching

One more gas station later, somewhere near Tuscaloosa, Alabama, and we had a new ride. We'd planned to be quick at this one, simply pulling up to the nearest car, trading out, and hitting the highway.

"Much better, huh?" I said as I started up a fairly new Toyota Camry.

It had a lot of room inside, and a ton of bells and whistles. I turned it to auto drive almost immediately, not feeling like navigating the eighteen-wheelers on the road.

"Definitely," Veronique said as she got comfortable in the back.

"Grace?"

"Memories still," she said, touching the glove box. "But not as bad. Nice. Comfortable. It's fine, Writer Gideon."

We arrived in Jackson, Mississippi, a few hours later; I was surprised I'd made it through without coffee. Veronique was asleep in the back, and Grace was even dozing off.

"Not yet," I told her, as I pulled into a hotel parking spot. "I need your help."

We had a ton of cash on us, but I still needed her to stop the front desk clerk from taking our information.

She yawned and got out of the car, morphing into her brunette form, this time with her hair braided over to one side. The car door opening startled Veronique awake, and she jolted up, ready to fight.

"Relax," I told her, "we're just checking into a hotel."

The clerk, a middle-aged woman with glasses and odd warts along her neck, was reading a book about the Bible when we entered. She had just managed to give us a dirty look when Grace took over her mind.

We were getting better at this now. I no longer even needed to speak to the hotel receptionists; we simply entered, and Grace did the rest.

With her eyes focused on the computer screen, the woman typed some information, probably something about Edward and Jill King and Cherry Blossom Girls, Inc., which Grace had instructed her to delete later.

We were given a room, and as if we'd never existed, the woman turned her attention back to her Bible book.

This wasn't as nice as what we were used to staying in; it was a typical roadside motel, and we were lucky to get two double beds.

Veronique claimed one, Grace and I claimed the other.

46

There was an unspoken thing about Grace and me sleeping together, and I got the hint that she didn't care where I slept. Something at the back of my mind told me this, but I didn't act on it. Not yet anyway.

I would have time to act on my feelings for her in the future.

And as it would turn out, that future came even sooner than I expected.

As soon as Grace went to take a quick shower, Veronique called me over to her bed.

"Would you prefer to sleep here?" she asked in a robotic, yet playful way. She'd lightened up some, but there was always a harshness about her.

I was tired, but not tired enough to say no to a request like that.

"We really should have gotten a room with three beds," I said half-jokingly.

She sat down on her bed. "Or just a room with one."

Damn, if Veronique didn't know how to shut me up with one simple statement. It could mean anything, but I was a man – a man who had grown up in the twenty-first century and had seen a lot of porn – so I got the feeling it meant something else.

But it could have been innocent.

Her statement could have also meant that she'd kill us both and get a room alone.

"You know what, sure, I'll sleep over there tonight. I slept in Grace's bed the last two nights."

"Three nights, four nights, you always sleep in her bed."

I changed into my American flag shirt and got into Veronique's bed.

She was still in the country clothes we'd gotten from WalMacy's, a pearl snap collar shirt and tight jeans. She unbuttoned her shirt and let it drop.

Just as she was about to unhook her bra, the shower flicked off in the other room, the pipes in the walls creaking as the water pressure let up.

I swallowed hard as her hand fell onto my stomach and then moved to the space just below my belly button. My insides were melting, and it wasn't because she was using her power on me. No, it only took a light touch from her to turn me on, and as much as I wanted to resist, I felt like it was impossible.

But I didn't want to piss off a telepath, at least not tonight, especially after what we'd been through.

"I think I'll just sleep over there tonight."

A glint of anger flashed in her eyes. I felt the energy suddenly leave my body. Her hand was still on me, and I knew she was draining my life force.

"Stop it," I whispered. More energy left my body, and I pushed my ass out of her bed, hit the floor and nearly cracked my head on the nightstand. I scrambled into Grace's bed.

Veronique laughed. "I'll be here whenever you're ready."

Oddly enough, Veronique zapping a little of my energy made it easier for me to sleep.

I'd been having pretty terrible nightmares over the last few nights, anxiety-driven dreams in which I was being choked by Angel, or shot by the MercSecure men, or worse, watching Grace die and Veronique get split in half by some unseen force.

I didn't want to lose them.

Hell, I still hardly *knew* them, but these two women had fundamentally changed my outlook on life and my perception of reality. I needed them, and I hoped to prove myself useful enough for them to feel the same about me one day.

But as I said, that night at the hotel in Jackson, Mississippi, was different.

I slept like a baby, or like a super baby, hardly remembering the moment between lying down and actually going to sleep. I knew Grace was next to me, and I sensed her whispering something in my head, but even then, I didn't know what she was saying.

Six hours of sleep isn't a lot, but six hours of solid sleep is worth its weight in tooth fairies.

"Anyone going to breakfast with me?" I asked the next morning.

The writing itch had come on strong, but I had nothing to write with aside from pen and paper, which meant we would need to visit an electronics store today.

Not surprisingly, Grace came with me to breakfast, and we shared two paper plates stacked with stale bread, plastic eggs, yesterday's sausage, and coffee that tasted like goblin ass.

"We'll get better food later too," I said as we went back to our room, where I found Veronique sitting on the bed with her legs crossed.

Having no smartphone meant I had to do things the old-fashioned way, so I called up to the front desk and asked them where the nearest Okay Buy was located.

The lady at the front desk was pretty shocked I would ask such a dumb question, especially since everyone had a smartphone or access to the internet, but I explained my phone was broken, and I had no idea how to get there.

With the directions in hand, we left and got there at just about the time the store opened.

After I picked up several items – a laptop, three prepaid phones, and another smartphone – we were set.

Grace worked her magic, and while we got the phones activated (all of them registered to the sales guy), Veronique checked out the VR video game section. A company known as Proxima had come out of nowhere recently with some of the most innovative VR gaming ever created.

I'd tried it. It made me dizzy, but that didn't stop me from wanting to get a piece of the VR pie.

GoogleFace maps fed me deets on my newly-activated smartphone, and I calculated that we could get to Austin today, but it would be late.

I preferred to get some rest and have a little more dialogue with this David Butler character before we arrived, and to do so, I'd need to get my emails encrypted.

I was so distracted by these thoughts that I didn't see the words that had been burned into the front hood of our Camry.

"Gideon," Grace said, grabbing my arm. My eyes dropped to the still smoldering phrase: *Mother is watching.*

I gasped.

Grace's immediate reaction was to take over the minds of others who were leaving Okay Buy. She had them fan out, searching the parking lot for anyone who could have done this.

Veronique also scanned the perimeter, standing in front of me as we moved to the vehicle.

"Do you think they put a bomb on the car?" I asked. It was a stupid question, but the way the two were acting had me on pins and needles.

"Stay close, Gideon," said Veronique as we reached the Camry. I took another look at the phrase, *Mother is watching*, and noticed it had started to blacken around the edges. "Get your bag, and we'll find a new car."

"Got it." I popped the trunk and grabbed my duffle bag, our backpack, and what was left of our snacks.

A black Ford Explorer pulled up, and the driver's eyes turned white almost immediately. He got out of the vehicle, helped me load the stuff in the back, then switched keys with me while Veronique and Grace stood guard.

Ten minutes later, and a dozen miles or so down the highway, my hands were still shaking.

I tried to focus on the road; found it impossible. I turned on the Explorer's auto drive feature, finally taking a deep breath to calm my nerves.

"Shit, this is intense," I whispered.

52

"It was clearly Dorian." Grace was still in the form she'd taken before we went to Okay Buy: a redhead with freckles and a tight plaid shirt. As I glanced at her, she kept the clothing but morphed back into her base form, the front of her plaid shirt pressing forward as her breasts grew.

"Definitely, Dorian," said Veronique from the back seat. "She likes to fuck with people."

"But how is she tracking us?" I asked. "How is it even possible? Do you think Dr. Kim would know?"

Grace considered that for a moment. "He may know more."

"I'll send him an email on the smartphone after I've installed encryption software," I told them. "He can call me on one of the prepaid lines, and we'll get rid of it right after. I think that should cover all our bases. Can you get the phones out, Veronique?"

Veronique reached over the back seat and got the Okay Buy bag. She fished out the phones and handed them to Grace, who placed them neatly on her lap.

Thank god for auto drive.

I took me a few minutes to get the device set up with my email information and the encryption software installed. Once that was done, I fired off an email to Ken with one of the prepaid phone numbers.

My inbox had about fifteen other messages related to my book, but I ignored those for now. *Mutants in the Making* seemed so far away, so distant compared to my current dilemma. I would have to get back into it later … if we survived this.

After a few minutes, the phone rang.

"Glad to hear from you," Ken said instead of hello.

"Let's make this quick: who is Dorian Gray and how is she tracking us?"

A note of concern was evident in Ken's voice as he asked, "They sent Dorian?" I heard the sound of rapid typing on the other line.

"She attacked us last night, *right after* I spoke to you. Well, not right after, but within a few hours."

"I had nothing to do with that," he said.

A Volkswagen blazed by on my left, the driver busy talking on the phone as she drove.

"I'm hanging up if you don't tell me what you know," I said.

"Hey! I'll tell you all I know, just ask. Let me see if there's anything in her file. Please, relax."

Grace glanced over at me, apprehension on her face. I smiled briskly at her, letting her know I was in control.

"She just tagged our car as well," I said.

"Tagged your car?" Dr. Kim asked.

"She used her power to burn 'Mother is watching' on the hood of our vehicle."

"Damn. Okay, I'll tell you what I know. First, what did Veronique already tell you?"

"That she trained with Dorian."

"I see, and that was a few years back. So, Dorian has learned a couple of new powers since then. They're remarkable, really."

"Like? Time is of the essence here, Ken."

And no, time wasn't of the essence, but I wanted him to speak quickly so he didn't have time to consider what he was telling me.

"She can teleport. That's one thing Veronique probably didn't know."

I activated the Bluetooth and put Ken on speakerphone. "Say that again."

"She can teleport."

I watched in the rearview mirror as realization flared in Veronique's eyes.

"Okay, that explains some things. How is she finding us?"

"It's the craziest thing," Ken said. "She developed this unique ability of premonition that's tied to her art skills."

"What are you saying?" I asked.

"She can draw primitive pictures of another location, focus on it, and *teleport* to that location. She only has to get a few of the details right for it to work. Look, you'd be stupid to think MercSecure and the FCG aren't tracking your every move. They know," Ken whispered. "And they know about your vehicle switching. But they can't ever catch you in time. That's clear. So, congrats there."

"Thanks. But that still doesn't explain how she was so precise."

"I'll get to that in a moment. Whoever you are, Gideon Caldwell, you've managed to avoid detection in an era when most data is readily available. I mean, like I said, you've made mistakes, but the fact that you're constantly on the move has made it hard to track you. It's remarkable, really, but they *are* following your trail, always about a day behind."

"Cut to the chase," I told him as the Ford slowed on its own to change lanes. "How did she find us?"

"Dorian has been tasked with finding you."

"I fucking know that, Ken. Wait, who tasked her? Mother? Fuck, I need to understand the hierarchy of what's going on here; the ladies haven't been so forthcoming … Dammit, Ken, I'm hanging up," I said, panicking again.

"Don't hang up! To answer your question, I don't have much to say about the person you call Mother. But if it helps you to understand, yes, she's been tasked to get you by Mother. Dorian knows your general location, and she's able to sketch where she thinks you might be."

"So she could attack us anytime?"

"Yes."

"Thanks, Ken," I said. I rolled down the window and tossed the phone out. Then I asked Grace for my smartphone and immediately rerouted us a different way. "No hotels tonight," I told them.

"Where are we going to stay?" Grace looked over her shoulder. "There's room in this car, but maybe it isn't large enough."

"Let's call it a makeshift Airbnb. Dorian is expecting us to stay in a hotel, and she's tracking us somehow. Shit. I shouldn't have tossed the phone out the window."

Veronique laughed.

"Yeah, sorry, that was stupid. We'll talk to Ken later. Anyway, sorry, thinking out loud here. Maybe she has a Cerebro type of thing."

"A what?" Veronique asked.

Grace nodded as she quickly sifted through my thoughts.

"Never mind. And sorry for relating everything to X-Men. I'm just used to thinking of superheroes and mutants through that medium."

"We aren't mutants," Veronique said.

"Technically, we are," Grace said. "Our powers are from exploited mutations."

"Either way, we have to do things that Dorian isn't anticipating," I said. "She expects us to stay at a hotel. Once these points line up, she'll find us. So now we do things a little more unexpected, and we keep on high alert. Dorian could appear at any time."

"We should change cars again," Grace said, "just in case she saw us get into this vehicle."

"Good call. We'll get something at the next rest stop I see. We have to keep her guessing."

Chapter Six: Writing, Crawfish, and a Visit to the Local Strip Club

We switched our cars somewhere near Vicksburg, Mississippi.

We now had a Nissan Altima with black leather seats and a sunroof. Or was it a moonroof? There was no telling, but it was a nice day outside, so I decided to open it. Grace had eased up some but Veronique seemed like she was still on high alert.

I put the car into auto drive and finally called Luke on GoogleFace.

"You there?"

"Hey!" He was sitting in front of his computer; I could tell because of the glare on his glasses. He stood, and a cat jumped off his lap. "Where have you been?" he asked, concern and kindness in his eyes. "Haven't heard from you in a day or so."

"It's been a pretty crazy twenty-four hours."

"Tell me about it," he said as he moved to a chair by a window. I saw him lock eyes with Veronique in the back seat and wave.

"Hi," was all she said before shifting to the other side so she wouldn't be in the video.

What came out of my mouth next was word salad, but Luke was able to parse through it and get an understanding of what had happened.

"Are you serious? There's another one, and she's after you now too?"

"Everyone is after me."

"I'm so glad I'm in Canada."

I laughed. "What? You think they can't get you in Canada?"

"If they ever asked, I'd say I was a fan who offers good advice. I'm not worried about them coming up here. If I were in a different country, yeah, maybe, but the American government plays nice with Canada."

"You're kind of like our cute little brother."

"You're kind of like our bully bigger brother."

We both laughed.

"Okay, the gamer in me has to ask: Have you had a chance to play with their stats any?"

"Not as much as I'd like, although …"

I hesitated to tell Luke about Ken Kim but figured I should put all my cards on the table, especially since he had given me good advice before.

So I gave him another 'long story short' version of Ken Kim and David Butler in Austin.

Worry creased his brow as he frowned. "I don't know if I'd trust anyone if I were you, aside from any writer friends you may have in Canada."

"I probably should have just come up to Canada."

"We'd love to have you! And it'd harder for them to get you."

"To further answer your question about playing with their stats: Ken gave me a code that he says will upgrade their abilities. He didn't say which abilities, and I'm afraid to put the code in. I don't know if we're being tracked, and to tell you the truth, just thinking about it gets me biting my nails and looking over my shoulder. It's not healthy."

"I can't imagine what I would do if I felt my government and a private security company were after me. And this new one – Dorian Gray, huh? She paints energy into existence, and it solidifies and can attack you? What in the actual hell? And she can teleport and has a premonition ability too?"

"Stranger than fiction, right?"

He shrugged. "I don't know what to make of it. I mean, I'd love to tell some of our mutual friends. But this story …"

"No, don't tell anyone. They can read my book if they want to know the truth. I'm already paranoid as hell. I don't want to be dealing with a bunch of people asking me questions, nor do I want to defend myself to other authors."

"There are hungry wolves watching, always," Luke said in a low voice. "I wouldn't be surprised if someone published a book like *Mutants* in the next few weeks. People see the sales rankings, an open market, and they dive in. Considering that your book is the only one in the creative non-fiction gamer sci-fi genre and that combining sci-fi with creative nonfiction is a big seller, I'd bet good money someone will try to tap your market. Soon too."

"Let them try," I said, thinking of the second installment. "The second book will be out shortly, and it turns *everything* up a notch."

"I'll bet. Send me a copy ASAP and good luck!"

It took us about another hour and a half to get to Shreveport, Louisiana. The only thing I could recall from the drive was a shitton of billboards using retired sports celebrities to advertise casinos.

The roads here were terrible, crumbled, filled with potholes, and faded by the sun.

Because of the fact I was surrounded by superpowered females, it didn't matter if we stayed in the good or bad part of town, but since we were living the high life, we drove around until we found a pretty nice neighborhood and a large, two-story home.

It had a modern touch, with a wall of windows that faced to the east, protected from the neighbors' prying eyes by a willow tree. There was a touch of old in the house as well, from the swing set out front to the stones that were used to make the walkway.

It would be a nice place to stay, at least for a night.

As we got out of the car, and I went to the back to get our bags, Veronique touched me on the arm. I spun to her, a little too quickly, the fear at the back of my mind that she wanted to feed always present.

"What's up?" I asked, regaining my composure.

"I need to feed tonight."

I was about to say, 'You just fed yesterday,' but decided not to push those buttons. Besides, she was the only thing that may save us from Dorian if we were attacked by the killer artist anytime soon.

Veronique needed to be well-fed.

I rubbed my hands together. "Fine, but we'll need to decide on a place."

The idea of a strip club came to me, and I was just about to toss it aside when Grace told me it was a good idea.

I smirked at her. "Do you really know every single thought I have?"

"Who says you're the one having the thoughts? I've never visited a strip club," she said as she moved toward the house.

There were two cars parked in the driveway so we figured someone was home.

Now back in her brunette-in-athletic-gear look, Grace knocked on the door, and after about a minute, a middle-aged woman greeted us.

She wore a low-cut top, jeans with decorative sparkles, and her gray and brown hair was pulled into a loose ponytail. She may have been younger than she looked, but her skin had been severely violated by the southern sun, so it was hard to tell.

As Grace's eyes flashed white, I instructed the woman to take her family, wherever they happened to be, and go to a casino in Lake Charles for the night.

I gave her three grand and told her to have a great time.

She let us in, packed a bag, and left the house to us. It was a nice place inside, too – spacious, with plenty of furniture, nicely carved wooden decorations, and several rooms upstairs.

Even if we figured out what to do with Dorian and stopped her from predicting where we would go, staying in nice homes was definitely the way of the future.

Grace and Veronique seemed to like it as well.

They walked around the place, commenting on what they would do if they owned it and ended up hanging out for the rest of the afternoon while I worked. At some point, Grace made lemonade, or possibly, the lemonade was already made, and the two chilled in the backyard by a pool, sipping from ice cold glasses.

Luckies.

It was strange to think this was probably the most they'd ever relaxed in their lives. I mean, sure, Grace could 'relax' in her solitary confinement back at the Rose-Lyle facility, but I wouldn't exactly call that relaxing, even if she had picked up meditation or yoga, or some other spiritual practice.

I was glad to see them at ease, and I would have joined them if I didn't have some work to do.

Alas, the work of a writer never ends, because no writer ever feels as if they're done. Also, no writer should use the word 'alas' and take themselves seriously. Regardless of my verbiage, I could finish a million-word manuscript and be itching to start the next one, even though I had no idea what I was going to write about.

There's something almost painful about an empty page, something that makes a writer want to fill it. And even a page full of words won't appease all readers. As Stephen King once said, "You can't please all the readers all the time; you can't please even some of the readers all the time, but you really ought to please at least some of the readers some of the time. I think William Shakespeare said that."

Or Bob Dylan.

Even now, looking back at all this, and having written everything that I could about the experiments, I still feel there's more to say. I still feel that I can uncover the truth, however small the truth nugget may be. Digging a little deeper and filling an empty page hardly satiates, but it does scratch that itch.

Besides, any writer will tell you that what they do is a sickness. Writing is an incredible malaise that sweeps over you, a flaming carrot on a stick, a tree falling in a forest that no one hears but your demented ass. Hopefully, whatever your sickness is becomes contagious.

Of course, I didn't write any of this while sitting in the study of our nice Airbnb; I was focused on trying to add as many words as I could to *Mutants in the Making* part two, beefing up the manuscript as best I could. There was a lot to cover, from what happened at the Rose-Lyle facility to Dorian's appearance.

Since it was creative nonfiction with a sci-fi gamer twist, I didn't need to have the buildups and foreshadowing that I would have put in a fictional title. As fun and harrowing as it was to relive all the shit I'd been through, a writer's work can be boring, and it took me four hours to get down about seven thousand words.

There were a few bathroom breaks in between, an occasional jaunt over to the window to check on Grace and Veronique by the pool, a glass of lemonade, and a ten-minute stretch in which I questioned my writing ability. I also had to clean my glasses a few times. Damn things kept fogging up.

As one does when they are experiencing success, I checked my sales numbers frequently. They were looking good – damn good, actually – and the time to get the second installment out was hot. The reviews weren't too shabby either. Most were four or five stars, an occasional three stars, and one percent were one star.

Again, not bad. And fuck the haters.

"Anyone hungry?" I asked as I opened the sliding glass door to the backyard.

Veronique, who was relaxed on a lounge chair, slowly raised her hand.

"We'll feed you later. Sorry, that came out weird."

She shrugged. "No, makes sense."

"I'd eat something, Writer Gideon."

Grace approached me in a tight, two-piece bathing suit. It was something straight out of the *Sports Illustrated Swimsuit Edition*, with just a small amount of fabric stretched across her breasts and a nearly nonexistent bikini bottom.

"Too much?" she asked, her face turning red.

I laughed. "To eat Cajun food? Yes. To go to a strip club later so Veronique can feed? No."

She morphed into a jean jacket, a low-cut blouse, and tight jeans. The final touch was a pair of cowboy boots embroidered with *Día de Los Muertos* skulls.

"Where did you hear about cowboy boots?"

"I didn't hear; I saw. We looked in the owner's closet. She has some very cool stuff. Very fashionable."

Veronique nodded. "I will get a pair in the future."

"What is it about cowboy boots that you like, exactly?" I asked, trying not to grin like an idiot at the two. They were adorable, and at least one of them knew it.

Grace shrugged as she tried out the pair, walking toward me, stopping just as she reached me, then turning away and looking at me over her shoulder. "They're sexy, right?"

I ran my hand through my beard. "Sure."

I took my smartphone out, GoogleFaced 'good Cajun places' and found one about three miles away. It was a quick drive, and as we pulled into the parking lot, I figured now would be as good a time as any to get another vehicle.

Goodbye Altima, hello Nissan Rogue.

It was the newest one too, the plate still a paper tag. The guy driving it, a man in a ball cap with a fishing hook on the bill, waved at us as he drove away in the Altima.

The people in the South were definitely friendly.

"Describe this Cajun food to me," Grace said as we entered the restaurant. It was small and smoky inside, the tables made of wood, a stuffed alligator hanging on the wall. "It smells very spicy and fishy in here."

"That is an accurate description. Let's have an interesting dinner. Just trust me on this."

"Welcome!" cried a red-faced woman with a waist like Santa. She sat on a stool, and rather than take us to our seat, she pointed a Vienna sausage finger at the booths in the back. "You and yo' pretty friends can sit right back thure."

"Thanks," I said. We went in the direction she'd indicated and found a clean table with a roll of paper towels on it.

Veronique squeezed in next to me, and Grace sat across from us.

The menus came and our waiter, a light-skinned black man with hazel eyes and freckles, complimented Grace on her jean jacket before leaving to bring us water.

"Let's see …" I found the po'boys on the menu and placed an order for two, as well as three pounds of crawfish.

Veronique lightly sipped from her water as I explained to Grace how the states in America were different, very different, and how Louisiana was pretty much nothing like Connecticut, yet we were all united under the guidelines set forth by the FCG, the Federal

Corporate Government, which had a rotating cast of yearly sponsors that were allowed to showcase their logos on government documents.

A win for everyone.

"They talk different," Grace said, starting to morph into our waiter. Her skin folded from the center point in her face, and I was just barely able to remind her of one of our cardinal rules: no shifting in public.

"Sorry," she said as her form flickered back into place.

I glanced around; no one had seen her transform.

The food came, and the girls watched me curiously as I showed them how to eat a crawfish, which began with pulling its head off, squeezing the meat out, and working my ass off to get just a little sliver of protein.

Grace wasn't buying it, so she stuck to the greasy po'boy and the simmering potatoes, sausage, and spice-covered corn that came with the crawfish.

"I didn't know a human could fill themselves up on water bugs," Grace said as I attempted to eat my weight in crawfish.

"It's very unattractive," Veronique added.

"It tastes better than it looks," I said and bit into the corn.

Strip clubs. I'd only been about three times, all when I was in college at Southern Connecticut State. I had a roommate who was into making it rain – I didn't know this was a thing, but apparently it was – and he loved cashing out a hundred-dollar bill into ones and tossing the money at the woman dancing on the pole.

I guess that's what happens when rap videos raise our youth.

While I was definitely in a position to make it rain, our goal at the titty bar was to let Veronique feed.

We purposefully chose the shadiest looking one I could find with the lowest reviews on Yelp. I wanted something sketchy, dark, and a place where people wouldn't go asking questions. Full Exposure fit that bill, especially with the review that read, "I was stabbed here 2x. The fact that I came back after the 1st stabbing tells you just how badass this place be. #threestrikesandyouout #Humble 🙏"

I put on my bulletproof vest after reading that, just in case things got out of hand.

The doorman came under Grace's spell as we approached. He was a big Mexican guy with two tear tattoos – I still needed to get me one of those … kidding! – and in a matter of seconds, his eyes flashed white.

Hell, he even let us in without taking the door tax, saving me thirty bucks. Not bad!

Like most strip clubs, Full Exposure was shadowy and cavernous, the poles and stages set up like little beacons of light to call in the creatures of the dark. A circular bar took up the center of the space, and the walls were lined with sofas for lap dances.

There were a few VIP sections, and I figured it would be best if we went there first, just to get our bearings and separate us from the masses.

The music was loud, the bass rattling my bones, and there were five or six dancers working.

The stripper on the center stage, a pale white woman with tattoos all over her thighs and ass, was bent in front of the shiny metal pole, her rear to the audience. Another, on a stage not far away, was twerking while a couple of black dudes made it rain, each of them with a stack of bills.

Twerking was awesome to watch; it stirred something primitive in me. I was distracted for a moment as the woman did her thing, dollar bills slapping against her back.

Veronique touched my arm and I glanced back at the two of them.

"Ahem, VIP," I told Grace, which she relayed to the first waitress who approached us.

The waitress wore a New Orleans Saints T-shirt tied at the front and boy shorts. The dimples on her ass bounced as she led us to one of the VIP areas, which was demarcated by a red rope.

If you're thinking I've never had VIP service before, you're right.

I felt like a million bucks, like a Trump heir holding court over the masses below. As soon as we took our seats, a man in a black suit stepped in front of our VIP area and crossed his hands behind his back. Our protection. Shit, I almost wanted someone to try something just to see him in action.

Still, we needed to be in complete control.

"Take his mind just in case," I whispered to Grace.

She nodded, approached the man, and placed her hand on his arm.

That was all it took.

We now had our very own beefy, shaved-head security guard.

Not two minutes later, the waitress returned with a bottle of vodka, courtesy of a man sitting alone in another VIP area.

"Is he drunk?" I asked Grace as she looked over at him. He wore a leather vest, a leather hat with silver buckles on it, and had an unlit cigar in his mouth.

"No, but there is something else wrong with him."

"Something else?"

The flashing lights, darkness, and abundance of naked women only reminded me of just how odd a strip club was. *What would it be like with the lights up? What would it be like without the music?*

Grace nodded. "He is another kind of drunk."

"Drugs."

Veronique didn't quite lick her lips, but she did look around with hunger in her eyes. "When can I begin?"

"We have to make sure the person isn't drunk, which is a mistake on my part, because it's a damn strip club and everyone's drunk." I thought for a moment as Grace opened the bottle of vodka.

"You're not going to like that," I told her.

"It's for you," she said with a smile as she poured a glass.

She handed it to me, and out of courtesy, I cheersed the man who'd bought us the bottle. *Please don't come over, please don't come over,* I thought as I returned my attention to Veronique.

She wasn't at all fazed by the strip club. Grace, on the other hand, looked around with excitement and curiosity on her face.

Remember, no shifting, I thought to her.

I know, Writer Gideon, I'm getting ideas for later.

"Later?" I mouthed as she locked eyes with me.

Need I exaggerate?

If ever there was a time to take a shot, it was to that last statement. I finished the shot, wincing as it burned its way down my throat.

A strip club was a bad idea.

I knew it after Grace couldn't locate anyone who wasn't intoxicated in some way. I knew it when the cigar man who bought us the bottle invited himself over to our table.

"We'll have better luck just walking around outside," I told Veronique, who eyed the drugged out man with malicious intent. As he spoke, his words tumbling out of his mouth and quickly being consumed by the loud bass, Veronique moved closer to him.

"Grace," I started to say, but the shifter was watching a pregnant lady dance on the center stage.

Did not expect to see that, I thought.

"We need to go," I said, getting to my feet. The last thing I needed was Veronique on whatever that guy was on.

She had already placed her hand on his arm but quickly let go. "Fine," she said and stood as well.

"You can feed soon," I told her. "Let's just look for something outside."

Chapter Seven: Surprise Visit

"Have everyone return to their food and drinks," I told Grace as we entered the McStarbucks near our borrowed abode. It was the first thought that came to mind, and yes, it was devious, but Veronique needed to feed, and what better place than America's favorite restaurant coffee peddler to find people? "I don't want anyone to know we were here."

I glanced at the ceiling and found a few small, spherical cameras. "Veronique?"

She followed my gaze, and the metal inside each camera was stripped from its socket, disabling any chance for us to be on film.

Aside from when we entered …

The vodka definitely had me feeling a little more daring than normal.

I told Grace to find five people who weren't intoxicated and tell them to sit against the wall. Five people stood, walked to the wall, and sat, the expressions on their faces completely blank.

"Thank you," Veronique said as she approached.

She didn't kill them, but similar to someone donating too much blood, the people didn't look very good after she finished. Their skin had shriveled up and tightened, their eyes had sunk into their faces, and veins had appeared on their arms and legs.

The last person Veronique stepped in front of twitched, her throat tightening convulsively. For a brief second, I thought the woman knew, but the look of realization was gone in a flash.

Innocent bystanders, I told myself.

Veronique needs to feed, Grace reminded me. *They'll be okay.*

I shook my head as the rest of the people in the restaurant sat or stood without moving a muscle, almost as if Grace had frozen time.

Focus on the good things, a voice said in my head. Grace's thoughts or mine? Who knew?

So I did what anyone in a depraved situation should do. I waited until we were out of the McStarbucks and switched my thought pattern.

Manually.

Think of something else.

I was expecting to get a good night's sleep, after a little one-on-one time with Grace. She'd already hinted at that. At least there was something to look forward to, something to wash the gruesome McStarbucks scene out of my head.

When in doubt, think about sex.

I settled into my seat, started up the car, and drove away, confident that I could get us home despite being a little drunk.

Something flashed in the rearview mirror.

Dorian Gray was sitting in the back seat next to Veronique.

"Shit!" I said as Dorian quickly drew a small sphere of purple energy and disappeared.

The sphere exploded. I swerved into a street lamp, the airbag deploying instantly.

My world became a series of red flashes and traumatic vignettes of my own death. My face was powdered by the airbag. I touched the back of my head; it was sticky with blood from the minor explosion.

What the ...

The Nissan's lights were flashing, the horn was blaring, an exclamation point on the dash was blinking and doing somersaults.

I sucked in a breath of air.

Grace's hands were pressed around my face.

"Gideon!" She yelled, or better, *she mouthed,* as my ears were still ringing from the explosion. Once she saw I wasn't responding, she kicked open her door and came around to my side to help me out.

"Where ...?" I started to ask.

78

I saw the blood in Grace's hair and choked up.

I'm fine, stay with me!

The door opened, and I stumbled to the ground, nearly cracking my head on the pavement. I pushed myself up to find Grace standing near me on high alert.

"Where's Veronique?" I said, dizzy as I looked left and right.

I heard metal tear from the Nissan and knew Veronique wasn't far away.

The metal surrounded us, forming a protective barrier comprised of bolts, lug nuts, and other assorted tidbits stripped from the vicinity, including the panels of a mailbox and a couple of aluminum cans.

Dorian stood on top of a nearby parked car, her paintbrush moving from her mouth to the open air as she drew an eight-foot-tall muscled man with gun arms. She was in similar clothing to what she had on yesterday, almost gothic attire with fishnet stockings and a pair of converse this time.

As soon as her creation was set, the man began firing spherical bolts of purple energy at Veronique, who dodged to avoid them and came back with a sea of metal to prevent the next blast. She then tore the roof off the car that Dorian stood on, but Dorian was long gone by that point.

"Come on," Grace said, pulling me to the sidewalk. We were in a residential district, only a few blocks from our makeshift home. There must have been people watching, but I was too focused on where Dorian would appear next to notice them.

"Hide," Grace hissed.

"But …"

"You're injured."

"So are you …" I said, moving my fingers through her matted hair.

We locked eyes, and I obeyed her immediately.

I won't let pain come to you, she whispered in my head.

Dorian reappeared across the street.

Veronique hurled as much metal as she could, but Dorian was already gone again. The metal hit a car, broke its windows, blew out its tires, and set off its alarm, adding to the cacophony of noise already blaring around us.

We would draw attention soon if we weren't already, but it was impossible for me to act; Grace had control over my mind and my body, and all I could do was watch as the psychic quietly approached the center of the conflict.

And by the center of the conflict, I meant the middle of the street, where Veronique stood. Grace was poised, ready to use her powers at a moment's notice, her chest heaving as she sucked in air.

Veronique kept turning, looking for Dorian, red energy moving up and down her fingertips.

Suddenly, a ghost-like energy creation ballooned into existence and charged at Grace. Taking a play from Veronique's book, Grace used her power to pull the doors off our broken car and fling them at the energy creature. Mini explosions erupted, and metal melted with fiery hisses. I was still trying to make sense of it all.

With the flick of her wrist, Veronique pulled more paneling from a vehicle on the side of the street and threw it in the direction of the creature. The mixture of iron, aluminum, copper, and steel hit the energy being in the side, pieces of the metal passing through it as they sparked, disintegrated, and exploded.

Grace let go of her hold over my psyche as she moved to toss something else at the being.

Dorian appeared right next to me, her form fizzling into existence.

My reaction was instant.

I pulled my fist back and punched her in the face, throwing her sideways as her paintbrush fell to the sidewalk.

I hit a girl.

Not my style, nothing I'd ever done before, and even though she was trying to kill us, I felt guilty as hell. I'd hit her good too, knocking her out with my fist, a fist that now pulsed with pain, a fist that had never struck another human being until now.

I shook my sore hand out as Veronique walked over to me, a sly grin on her face as if my balls had finally dropped and I could now join the hunt. She knelt and placed her hand on Dorian's forehead, her fingers flashing red as she drained the woman's energy.

"I can't believe …"

"You saved us a lot of bullshit," Veronique said, looking up at me. She seemed neither impressed nor disappointed.

"Are you okay?" Grace asked, moving to my side.

"I … It's not like me to do something like that, I just reacted. I … I'm …" I rubbed my knuckles.

She smirked as she read my thoughts. "Stop panicking; you did what you had to do to help us."

"Don't kill her," I told Veronique.

"Are you suggesting we take her with us?" She removed her hand from Dorian's forehead. The punk rock diva's skin had already started to dry, and even in the meager light of the streetlamps, I could tell that her eyes were beginning to sink into her skull.

"We have to try to do something for her. She was only following orders. Maybe we can even find out more if we don't kill her." I exchanged glances with Grace. "But we need to go, *now*."

"As you wish," Veronique said and stood up. "But I'm not going to make the same mistake I did with Grace. I will feed from Dorian every couple of hours until we're ready to sort the situation out."

I bent down, placing my fingers on Dorian's neck to find a pulse. Her skin was hot to the touch, almost as if she was overheating. *She's still alive,* I thought as my hand instinctively went to her neck port.

"Let's find a vehicle," I told them. "We'll go back to the house, get our things, and get out of here – just in case there are others around as well."

"Don't forget her paintbrush," Grace said as I lifted Dorian into my arms.

Not able to get a firm grip on the unconscious woman because her body kept slipping down, I eventually flung her over my shoulder and carried her that way. "Is it a good idea to give that to her?" I grunted.

"I wasn't going to give it to her; I was going to see what we could discover about it."

"Got it, do that. But let's keep it away from her. I don't know what her powers are without that thing, but I don't want her to wake up and be able to use it."

Chapter Eight: Put Her in the Trunk and Drive to Texas

We took the first car we could find, which was some type of Kia four-door sedan with a pretty large trunk. It was a weird off-purple color, maybe light plum, and the interior reeked of coconut lotion. But it would do.

I was still slightly delirious, the back of my head still wet with blood. Once we got back to our hideout, Grace checked it out and told me it was just an abrasion.

Fuck, was I glad to hear that.

As the ladies packed our bags and checked to make sure we hadn't left anything behind, I got cleaned up in the bathroom and applied some rubbing alcohol to the wound.

It stung, but it was a good, healing sting that woke my ass up. I was still a little jumpy, but I was better than I had been just fifteen minutes ago.

Back outside, I found the two women moving Dorian to the trunk, her hands and feet bound tightly with coat hangers. We wouldn't be able to keep her in there forever, but that was where she was going until we got to Texas.

I was just turning back to the house for a final check when I got a message from Luke.

Luke: Update me.

Me: Let's talk about the Main Character in the story I'm writing.

Luke: LOL. Yeah, let's.

Me: The MC went to a strip club so the vampiric one could feed. Then they were attacked by the teleporter who could conjure kinetic energy. Now the teleporter is in the trunk of their car.

Luke: The MC has someone in the trunk of their car? Hold up, let me do a quick search to see if that's a great way to suffocate someone or not. Okay, I stand corrected. She won't suffocate in there. But they've started installing glow-in-the-dark handles so a person in a trunk can open it from the inside, FYI. I can't believe we're having this conversation.

Me: I can't either. But we're getting out of here.

Luke: I'm not going to ask where you're at or where you're going, but don't drive for too long – it's getting late.

Me: We won't. G2G.

Luke: All right, well it's off to bed for me and the misses. Good luck!

"Your friend seems like a nice guy," Grace said as she passed by me with the backpack we'd picked up in New Haven over her shoulder. She tossed it in the trunk with Dorian, then we climbed into the vehicle. I started it up and drove away.

I was suddenly tired, my body coming down from the adrenaline surge.

There was still a voice in the back of my head that was upset with me for punching a woman, but I told that voice to shut the fuck up.

There was a good chance Dorian would have killed me if I hadn't reacted the way I did. Like Veronique, she had training, and she was probably used to having the upper hand.

Don't beat yourself up, Writer Gideon, said Grace as I pulled onto the highway, immediately zooming up past the speed limit. *You saved us. I'm proud of what you did; you acted quickly, and your action changed the course of that fight. It was amazing.*

Hardly, I thought back to her.

We are now in control of Dorian. If you hadn't done that, she may have hurt you or one of us.

You're right. It just goes against my nature.

Everything you've done over the last week goes against your nature.

She had me there.

So I kept driving, yawning, blinking away the troubling memories, and once I felt like we were far enough away that I could put the vehicle into auto drive, I did so.

The Kia handled pretty well, and I had a brief thought that I had now test-driven more cars than most people would drive in their lifetime.

Well, not quite yet, but if we kept switching out cars …

Just relax, do what Grace said, a voice whispered in my head.

"You are ridiculous," I told the shifter, smiling over at her.

"It's *Writer Gideon's Life*," she said in Ira Glass's voice. "Each week we take a look at Gideon Caldwell and the trouble he's gotten himself into. This week, *Dorian and Her Magic Paintbrush*. Stay tuned; it's going to be a hell of a story."

"Do one of the property guys," Veronique suddenly requested from the back seat.

Grace morphed into the property guy – a fucking tool if I'd ever seen one – and gave a quick spiel about the house's foundation and how they were planning to gut it, much to Veronique's delight.

As they continued to role-play, I found myself more and more interested in the type of humor they liked. I didn't think they'd enjoy the typical comedy we had nowadays, which seemed to be mostly about dicks, balls, sex, getting drunk, wives, and kids.

The Cherry Blossom Girls enjoyed a simpler humor, and Grace's ability only made this work even better. There was almost something childlike in the way Veronique would request for her to morph into and speak as someone else.

But that wasn't the only thing on my mind as I drove – or, as the Kia drove itself. I was also thinking about the woman in the trunk. *Can she be turned? And what would happen if she woke up in the trunk? Is this really a smart idea?*

I was definitely interested to see what was on her drive.

That would be the first thing I did when we arrived at our next destination. I figured we could stay in a hotel now because we didn't have to worry about her premonition ability affecting us, especially if we kept her passed out.

At some point in our journey, I began wondering more about her strategy, and if it had been part of her plan to be captured by us. It was a long shot, and there was no way she could have known I would have reacted the way I did, but Grace and Veronique may have been able to take her.

Grace was much stronger than she let on, and while she didn't have as much sway over superpowered individuals, she could have used her ability to broadside Dorian with something while Veronique distracted her from the front.

I need to know more about Dorian's abilities.

That much was clear. Everything else was speculation. But as soon as we got to our next destination, I was plugging in. I didn't care if I had to brew coffee all night – I was going to discover *something*.

We would be in Texas within the hour. I searched on my smartphone and found several hotels in Longview.

I located the most expensive one and put a flag on it.

Might as well do this shit in style. After all, as John Milton said in *Paradise Lost*, "Better to reign in hell than serve in heaven."

Chapter Nine: Playing with Stats

If you guessed the Marriott again, you would be correct.

Everything is bigger in Texas, or so I'd heard, and even though I'd only been driving in the state for an hour, I could confirm that this was definitely a thing. Including the hotel. What they don't tell you about Texas is that everything is horizontally – not always vertically – bigger, so everything is essentially fatter.

A grower, not a shower? Actually, that little line my ex used to describe my penis didn't really apply, yet it was the first thing that came to my mind as I pulled our borrowed Kia into the Marriott's parking lot shortly before midnight.

"What's the plan?" Grace asked as we got out.

Of course, she knew the plan; the plan when checking into hotels hadn't changed. We were Edward and Jill King, CBG, Inc., and we already had a reservation that was paid for by our company.

"Should we get two rooms?" Veronique asked as I popped the trunk.

"We'll get whatever suite they have. Hopefully it's got two separate rooms so we can keep Dorian somewhere else."

Veronique stepped over to the trunk. "Let's just see what they have. And don't worry about Dorian; I'll take care of her this time."

Nope, don't like the way she said that, I thought as we grabbed our bags and walked into the hotel.

Rather than have me carry her, Veronique used her metal-wielding ability to drag Dorian along behind us, using the metal on the teleporter's jacket, belt, and jean shorts. She dragged her roughly too, Dorian's heels scraping against the pavement as she pulled her over the curb.

I had forgotten I was wearing body armor, and after taking a few steps toward the hotel's entrance, I definitely felt it. The armor was heavy, starting to chafe some, but I'd need to keep it on for a little longer.

The sliding glass door opened, and we were greeted by a large painting of a cowboy riding a bull, which was pinned to the wall above a stuffed deer. We moved around this grand display of southern power, still towing Dorian behind us.

Due to the late hour, the lobby was empty. The receptionist, an Indian man who reeked of cigarettes and looked like he hadn't slept in weeks, was looking at his phone when we came in.

The moment Grace saw him, he belonged to her. He began typing away on his computer, his eyes suddenly white.

"Okay, room 206," he said in accented English as he gave me the key card. "Check out time is at eleven."

I hesitated for a moment.

It was already late, and I really needed to do some work on my manuscript, especially before we got into whatever we would get into in Austin.

David Butler could wait a day.

Sensing my thoughts, Grace immediately corrected the receptionist. "Actually, we'll be here until the day after tomorrow, so two nights."

"Ah, I see that here," the man said as he wagged his head left and right. "Okay, enjoy your stay in Longview. Continental breakfast is from seven to ten."

Still under Grace's spell, the man merely looked at Dorian as she was dragged away.

"Thanks for adjusting the dates," I told Grace when we took the elevator to our second-floor room. "I need time to finish up this manuscript. I'm sorry the hotel isn't more interesting. I wish there was more to do around here."

"That's okay," said Veronique. "We can watch our shows."

I keyed everyone into the room, and Grace took over with Dorian's body. Her eyes flashing white, she lifted the woman into the air and placed her body on the sofa chair near the window.

No balconies here.

This place was way too corporate to have a balcony with a view, and besides that, there really wasn't a view anyway, as the hotel overlooked a four-way intersection.

The clothes hangers burst out of the closet, startling me.

They flew toward Dorian, and as the hangers that had already chained her wrists unwrapped, the new ones strapped her arms and legs tightly to the chair.

"Don't kill her," I reminded Veronique as I set my bag down.

"As you wish."

It was a spacious suite, with two large rooms and a rectangular bathroom joining them. I opened my duffle bag and got the mini USB cable out. Grace took my bag to the second room, leaving Veronique and me in the first.

"I guess that's where you're sleeping," Veronique said under her breath.

Rather than answer – and really, what was I supposed to say? – I ignored her.

I had no idea how this would play out when I plugged into Dorian's neck, and as I approached her, Veronique skidded across the bed and stopped me. She pressed her palm against my chest, fingers glowing red.

"Hey …" I started to protest. But she turned away from me to Dorian and placed her hand on the teleporting artist's head, draining even more of her energy.

"Not too much," I whispered.

"We can't have her waking up," Veronique said as she topped off.

Her skin more radiant than it had been a couple of hours ago, Veronique lay down on the bed and found the home improvement channel on the TV. Grace returned from our room in my clothes – a statement if there ever was one – and sat on the bed next to Veronique.

Don't worry, we'll get along. And if you have tension, release it.

I gave Grace a funny look.

Your idea of a relationship is different than ours, Writer Gideon.

"Okay," I said, just to clear Grace's voice out of my head. I plugged into Dorian's neck and a prompt asked me for the password.

1QAZ2WSX3EFV4321QWEASD.

Thanks, I thought to Grace.

94

The password worked. I logged in easily and was presented with a shadow box. Not a lot here, nothing like what was on Grace and Veronique's systems, which gave more credibility to Dr. Ken Kim's statement that he had put that stuff on them to be discovered.

Of course, this begged a whole series of other questions, like: *How did he know someone would try to access them unless he was planning to free them?*

After a little poking around, I found Dorian Gray's base stats.

Build: 7.543

Base height: 170 Centimeters

Base weight: 49 kilos

Strength: 2

Intelligence: 6

Constitution: 7

Wisdom: 3

Dexterity: 6

Charisma: 8

Well, at least she had charisma and constitution going for her, which surely counted for something.

I cycled back to a different menu to find out more about her abilities. As it turned out, most of her energy abilities were set at low levels. I kept them that way for now.

Main: Ergokinesis

Overcharge: 2

Charge Capacity: 4

Charge Integrity: 3

I scrolled to the space below the dials to get an explanation of what these three things were, even though they were pretty self-explanatory. From what I could decipher, setting Overcharge as low as possible kept her creations from becoming volatile too early through the overuse of her abilities.

Charge Capacity referred to the size of the items she could create out of thin air. Increasing this would allow her to charge even larger things. Like Veronique had said, Dorian's charge ability came from her saliva and other bodily fluids.

It was a weird ability, but then again, so were Toad's abilities as well as an assortment of other mutants from my favorite reference. You'd think I'd have a Professor X quote in *Mutants in the Making* by now.

Not a bad idea, actually ...

Charge Integrity dealt with how long the charged item she created actually lasted. By increasing this, it would take longer for her creations fizzle out.

I backed out of that folder and went to her Main Second folder, which spawned another shadowbox of dials.

Main Second: Teleportation

Tele-Sphere Radius: 2

Conscious Spatial Awareness: 10

Recharge Speed: 6

Restoration Speed: 6

There were a few other options, but akin to when I saw Veronique's abilities, they were blurred out.

I briefly messed with the dials and found that adjusting the Tele-Sphere Radius up reduced the Recharge Speed and Restoration Speed. So, the larger the objects she teleports, the slower they were teleported and restored.

I wasn't able to adjust the Conscious Spatial Awareness dial, and once I checked the description, I realized why. This prevented Dorian from teleporting directly into an object and killing herself.

Useful.

But how does the teleportation work?

I started checking folders on her drive for answers. I wasn't going to be able to parse through an explanation on quantum teleportation, but at least I could get a sense of what was going on.

The only problem was, her drive was pretty much empty. No videos, no PDFs of various facilities, no extra notes about her abilities or the project, no nothing.

I had the notion of going back into her teleportation ability and adjusting the speed down, but I figured that even being able to teleport at a speed of one would allow her to move away faster than we could do anything about.

And what if she was teleporting when Veronique touched her and both of them disappeared? That would be monstrously shitty.

So I left things as they were.

It was late. I was no longer drunk, but I was a little loopy, and I really wanted to get some work done the following day. Ha. Even after all this, I was planning to write the next day.

You see what I mean when I say writing is a sickness?

Rather than debate the voice in my head, or scold myself for not hitting my word count, or get out my new laptop and check my book stats, I decided to wash my sins away.

I took a brief shower, washed my writer bits, and thankfully, no one joined me this time. Once I toweled off and was feeling fresh to death, I popped my head into the first room, announcing to the two women that I was going to sleep.

My phone buzzed, just as I got into the bed.

> *Where the fuck are you? I'm giving you some real data here and you still aren't here? Ever heard of an airplane? Don't be a dumbass. This is happening now, happening fast, and they may start moving people if you don't hurry up and get here, so whatever you're doing, stop doing it.*
>
> *Get your ass to Texas.*
>
> *-David Butler*

Dumbass? Is this dude drunk?

I wasn't about to call off the trip just yet, especially due to the fact that Grace had seen Mother in the picture taken in Austin, but I was glad to be visiting David with Veronique and Grace at my side. The guy may or may not be stable, and if he wasn't stable, it'd be helpful to have some muscle around.

Speaking of muscle, I was just about to nod off when Grace entered the room and flicked off all but one of the lights.

Chapter Ten: Pornographic Insight

"Come to the edge of the bed," Grace said as she changed her form. The change started from the center point of her body and worked its way out, a ripple of color and skin and clothing immediately settling into place.

She now wore a neon yellow fishnet halter top with matching bikini bottoms and a pair of high heels – also yellow – with six-inch stilettos.

The strip club, I thought as she approached the bed, hips swaying.

No noobs in the room this time.

I moved to the corner of the bed and sat up, erect in two ways.

Once she reached me, Grace swept her long hair over her shoulder and turned her back to me. She sat down on my lap, just as she had seen the strippers do in the club, and as she gyrated her hips, my mood changed from sleepy and concerned to happy-go-lucky – or better, happy to get lucky.

"How do you want me?" she asked as her skin began to darken.

Her hair thickened, braids formed, and her hip size increased. A black woman now, Grace twisted around and kissed me. As we kissed, her form began to morph again, this time changing into a light-skinned Asian woman with bleached blonde hair and a Monroe piercing.

She stood, bent before me so I could get a good peachy view, and touched the tops of her high heels, swaying her ass back and forth.

The color of her thong and Neon halter-top went from yellow to purple as her skin turned caramel, her hair long and flowing, her features that of someone from Latin America.

She turned to face me, her hands covering her nipples as she moved her shoulders up and down.

I licked my lips, thanked Jeebus, promised to curb my wicked ways, and finally, reached my hand out.

She slapped it away. "No touching," she purred as she turned her back to me and lowered herself onto my lap again. She resumed gyrating her hips against me. "They'll kick you out of the club."

"Yes, ma'am."

It was amazing how much the promise of sex shattered the millions of thoughts racing through my skull.

That's one of the things I like most about getting lucky; it's an ultimate form of escapism requiring physical effort that's rewarded with a nearly indescribable, but amazing, full-body sensation.

And sure, better writers than I had put in their due diligence to describe exactly what an orgasm feels like, but if someone who had never experienced an orgasm read about it, could they really understand what it felt like?

Could you say having an orgasm was like having the rug swept out from beneath you and falling into a galaxy of vibrating dandelions?

"Quiet, Writer Gideon," Grace said as she thrust against me even harder. "And you aren't tipping me."

I glanced at the duffel bag that contained all the cash and then back to her. "Are you serious?"

She raised an eyebrow at me, and as she did, her facial features began to morph, settling on a hot Latina with braided hair. She bent forward, kissed me, and bit at my lip as she pulled away.

I cleared my throat. "If you want to get tipped, you're going to have to get off my lap so I can get the cash."

"Stay where you are."

She stood and went to retrieve the cash for me, making sure I was thoroughly focused on her movement as she left the bedside. She returned with the duffle and dropped it at my feet. I quickly reached down and got a stack of hundreds.

Grace morphed back into her base form, her long blonde hair, blue eyes, soft skin, incredible body. "What do you want me to wear?"

"Is 'nothing' an answer?"

"You can't tip me if I don't wear anything."

She stuck with the outfit she'd been wearing the entire time: a fishnet halter top and a thong. She turned, looked at me over her shoulder, and as she did, I put my first hundred in the side string of her thong.

"Is this a good fantasy?" she asked as she raised her hands and placed them behind her head.

"I, yeah, sure, it's ... unexpected."

Her form rippled slightly, her back still facing me, which I took to mean that she'd changed her appearance, but hadn't adjusted her body size very much.

"Your mind is too busy," she said, looking over her shoulder again before turning to face me once more.

I silently toasted HBO as she climbed back into my lap, her knees at my sides. She thrust her hips forward, grinding against my hard-on.

"You like it?" she asked.

Daenerys Targaryen, or better, the actress who played her, bent forward to kiss me. She pressed away just as her form morphed into a sexy cosplay version of Mystique.

"This is who I'm like, correct?" she asked, her skin blue and covered with ridges, her orange hair slicked back.

"No, I mean, yeah. But different." Rather than fumble on any more words, I slipped another hundred-dollar bill into her panties. As she changed back to her base form, she started unzipping my pants.

"Ooo, I know who I can be," she said, and her features morphed into Natalie Johansson's. "Can I?" she asked as she got to her knees.

"Please do."

A couple things need to be addressed: No, I never thought my writing career would involve penning a passage about a blowjob. I also was unaware – and quickly became hyper-aware – of just how much porn I had consumed and how it affected Grace's understanding of sex.

She'd only seen sex in movies before meeting me, and then she was able to tap into my mind and its deep vault of porn. By 2030, watching porn had become as American as apple pie, if apple pie was something consumed in secret – more so by men than women, but still by a good majority of the population.

You could blame a change in morality over the last thirty years, or you could blame the real culprit: the internet. Either way, it was a common thing in many people's lives.

If someone wanted to watch porn before the internet, they had to go to an adult store, rent or purchase a video, and either use one of those sticky-ass private rooms to watch it, or take it home and figure out a time to watch it when their spouse, roommates, and/or kids weren't around.

Of course, some people were more progressive and watched it with their significant other, but my point remains: it was a little bit more difficult to get it at that time.

Then, the internet.

And I was Generation Z, the post-internet generation.

Porn has been around me in some shape or form for my entire life, whether it be a classmate at school showing me something on his smartphone, the presidential pee tapes, subscription movie services increasingly pushing the boundaries, or the Two Girls One Cup reboot of 2025.

All this to say, Grace started by giving me a pretty sloppy, hardcore BJ, all thanks to the porn I'd seen.

And my reaction wasn't what I would have expected or fantasized. My first reaction was to push her away. I had created a monster. She took that to mean I wanted her to go harder, which was not the case!

"You can't ..."

"I can't what?" she asked, looking up at me. "I thought you wanted this." Confusion swept across her face as she tuned into my thoughts.

"Do you see what I'm thinking here?"

She nodded.

"I guess I'm trying to say … you shouldn't look in my mind and believe the things I've seen are normal. Because they're not normal. Then again, maybe nothing is normal. Well, maybe they're normal to some people, but no, don't look in my mind for those types of things."

"So no blow job?"

I nearly slapped myself. "Of course, blow job, but just take it easy. No reason to get … um … too hardcore."

She wiped her mouth and shrugged. "You seem to have watched a lot of that."

"It's become a norm in pornography."

"Why's that?"

Oh shit. I went with the first explanation that came to my lips. "My guess is that the more men lose control over the world, the more they look to entertainment that shows them a side of masculinity they assumed they once had. It's all a false representation though. Shit, I'm not trying to ruin the moment here."

"You aren't," she told me. "Your wild mind is interesting. It has seen so much but experienced so little. It's hard to separate the differences sometimes because I don't quite understand the memory."

"That's why you shouldn't be reading my mind. Look, Grace, just be yourself, and forget what you see in here." I tapped my temple. "Because I am a product of my generation."

Shut up, Gideon! You're ruining the moment. A voice inside my head hissed. This was definitely my voice – well, that or the voice of my penis.

"Just, yeah … sorry. Take it easy. Don't read my mind. I thought that was a rule."

"Don't read your mind, don't turn into Veronique, don't shift in public, don't turn into your mom, and don't give you sloppy hardcore blow jobs." Grace laughed and climbed back onto my lap. She pressed the fabric covering her crotch aside so that my quickly hardening penis was now pressed against her wet mound. "Any more rules?"

I chuckled. "Let's keep these rules to ourselves, how's that? Especially that last one."

"I like you, Writer Gideon," Grace said as I slipped inside her.

"I like you too," I told her. "A lot."

Chapter Eleven: Veronique's Stats

Get your head in the game, was my first thought when I awoke the next morning. There were a ton of things I needed to handle, and I had no idea how I would compartmentalize them.

So rather than relive the slightly awkward yet badass bit of lovemaking I'd been privy to the previous night, I decided to make a list of current issues that needed to be addressed.

I sat up in bed, grabbed the pen and paper on the nightstand, and started jotting things down.

1) Find out why my picture was on Grace's drive. To shorten this note I wrote: *Picture Grace Drive.*

I knew I didn't have superpowers, even if I felt that way when Grace was next to me controlling someone, and I was simply giving commands. Regardless, there was more to this story, and I didn't want it to become an unfinished plotline.

2) Decide if you will use the code Ken Kim gave you to supposedly upgrade Grace and Veronique's abilities, written as: *Upgrade, yes/no?*

It could be an attempt to track us.

I wasn't certain where I stood on the Ken Kim front. After all, Dorian did show up within hours of our first conversation. For all I knew, his interest in our situation was a ruse meant to get close to me. I decided to forego using the code for now.

3) Figure out what to do with Dorian, or as I wrote it: *Dorian.*

If we let her heal up, was there any possibility she would join us? Or would she be like Angel, dedicated to her role even if she'd eventually be decommissioned? Since her abilities allowed her to instantly move away from us if given the chance, freeing Dorian, even briefly, could be a terrible decision on our part.

4) Come up with a plan to handle the Austin situation became simply: *Austin.*

We would definitely need to meet David Butler in a public place. I was starting to second guess meeting him at all, but getting to the bottom of the Mother situation would help me better tell the story of the secret program that created Grace and Veronique. Which lead me to my next point:

5) Mother, aka: *Mother*

If she really was as powerful as Veronique claimed, then getting to her wouldn't be easy. And this begged the question: What would we do after we got to her? What was our endgame?

Our endgame is stopping these experiments and uniting the subjects that care to be united, Grace said in my head.

Ah, so you're up.

I am.

"I'm going to play devil's advocate for a moment," I said aloud. Grace still had the blanket up to her neck, and her eyes were closed, which made talking to her in this way even stranger. "What good will destroying the facilities do?"

It will prevent them from torturing people like me.

"I get that reasoning, but what happens if they just build more facilities?"

That's why we have to go after Mother too and anyone who decides to work with her. Doing so will prevent them from creating more of us. You are over-analyzing this, Writer Gideon. We find, we destroy.

"You're sounding more and more like Veronique."

With her eyes still closed, Grace's face began to morph into Veronique's.

Maybe it is better to be a warrior than a thinker.

"Point taken."

She reverted back in an instant, clearly toying with me.

Go get cleaned up. It's time to write. Will you finish your next novella today?

"I don't know. I'm inspired, but I still need to write at least ten thousand more words."

Then do it and get inspired. Look at your sales. People are enjoying this book. You probably have more emails too. And the cover is also nice.

"Got it." I slipped out of bed and went into the long bathroom connecting our two rooms to find Veronique sitting on the counter completely nude, her nipples erect and a devious look on her face. "Sorry," I said as I started to turn back.

"I was waiting for you." The door shut behind me and locked.

"This is not a great time ..."

She got down and took two steps closer to me. "I need new clothes," she said once she was about a foot away from me.

"Okay ..."

"I don't like the country clothes."

"That's fine; we can get you new clothes."

"Why are you so nervous around me?" she asked, placing a hand on my chest.

"I think you know why."

"When you're ready." With that, Veronique moved away, glanced at me one last time, and stepped out.

"Damn," I muttered when I caught a glimpse of her ass as the door shut.

Veronique would be the death of me.

A quick shower, a visit to the breakfast buffet with Grace, and two cups of coffee later, I was ready to write. Books are all about pacing and keeping the reader reading. This is the exact opposite of what it would be like to describe writing.

So, I'm going to gloss over it a little.

Rather than tell you about how I got off to a late start because I couldn't figure out how I wanted a certain passage, or how I confused what happened in chapter ten with what should have happened in chapter nine, or how it took me at least fifteen minutes to install updates on my new laptop, I'll just report back that I was able to get about four thousand words written.

I had headphones on at that point, listening to a YouTube super intelligent brainwave frequency track for focus.

I'd hit a roadblock.

There was a section I needed to fill in regarding Veronique's abilities, but since she hadn't let me check her drive, I was still missing that section.

I could hear her and Grace in the other room, watching yet another home improvement show, and I figured she could spare a moment.

For the sake of literature?

That line might not work on her, but then again, it wasn't very long ago that she was threatening to kill me if I didn't write a book in two days.

So, I tried it.

"Hey, Veronique," I said as I went into the other room.

I glanced from the two women on the bed to Dorian, who still sat in the chair with her eyes closed. It was a weird visual, and I tried not to look at her too much because it was like staring at a corpse.

"Can I help you?" she asked, without looking away from the TV.

"I know we've been putting it off, but I need to go through your stats and abilities again. It's for the book. I should be finishing today, and I'd like this stuff to be in its own section. It's important. It's for the sake of literature."

She shrugged. "Okay. Tell me what happens," she said to Grace as she got up and joined me in the other room.

I had to laugh. "I've been asking you about doing this for days, and now you just say 'okay' and come in? We could have done this way earlier."

"I don't know how I feel about you plugging into me, but you said it was for the sake of literature, so we'll see what happens." She narrowed her eyes at me.

113

"I promise not to mess with anything, I just wanted to examine the grayed-out sections of your abilities menu."

"Grayed out?" she asked as she lay down on the bed.

"Last I checked, portions of your abilities were grayed out and I couldn't adjust them."

She shrugged. "I don't really want you adjusting them."

"That's fine, but I need to know what you're capable of and I might be able to make you stronger by seeing them. I won't change anything without your permission, how's that?"

"Okay."

The air conditioner clicked on and I glanced at it.

"Did it scare you?"

"No, just not used to always hearing that thing turn on and off by itself."

Once I plugged in, I went straight to Veronique's abilities.

"This will only take a minute," I reminded her, "so relax."

Interesting, I thought when I saw that the grayed-out options were now visible.

As it turned out, Veronique only had one overarching superpower, and to my surprise, her vampire-like ability was actually an extension of that power.

Main: Metal Absorption and Modification

Wielding Capacity: 5

Adaption Speed: 6

Alloy Integrity: 4

Blood Metal Conversion: 6

Blood Metal Conversion? I read the description again, impressed.

Veronique wasn't draining a person's life per se; she was *absorbing* any and all of the metals in their body, which eventually killed them because it increased the toxicity of these metals as they moved out of their bodies.

"And it's also what you feed on," I said, looking up at her. "You convert this metal into sustenance – or more specifically, your body does."

"So now you know. Happy?"

"If you want me to play around with adjusting any of these abilities, let me know. For example, increasing your Alloy Integrity might make the structures you create stronger and better. Not that they aren't already good. The thing is, your abilities are all around the mid-level, ranked from four to six. Wielding Capacity, Adaption Speed, Alloy Integrity, Blood Metal Conversion. They're all mid-level."

She thought about that for a moment, still staring up at the ceiling to avoid messing with the cord sticking out of her neck. "And Wielding Capacity would allow me to modify larger objects, right?"

"I believe so."

"See what happens if you turn that one up."

Turning the Wielding Capacity dial up increased Alloy Integrity, but doing so brought Adaptation Speed down.

I played around with the settings for a moment until I leveled them out somewhat. Now they looked like this:

Main: Metal Absorption and Modification

Wielding Capacity: 7

Adaption Speed: 5

Alloy Integrity: 5

Blood Metal Conversion: 6

"I think we've done enough for today," Veronique said. She unplugged the cable herself and sat up.

"Yeah, no problem," I said. "I mean, it's up to you, but I hope we can do more later. I know you're sensitive about your drive, but there's a lot I'd love to play with."

"I know you want to play with my drive," she said, holding my gaze. "And maybe you'll be able to soon."

116

She got off the bed and left the room, leaving me to my laptop.

Chapter Twelve: A Day in the Life of a Fugitive

I reread the newest message from David Butler.

> *Where the hell are you? I thought you'd be in Austin by now. I have important details to show you and I'm waiting for you to get your ass here.*
>
> *Update me -- DB.*

"What's with this guy?" I thought as I typed out a quick reply: *We'll be in Austin tomorrow. Let's meet in a public place.*

I hit send and received a reply back within seconds.

> *No, we will meet at my place.*

He gave me the address and I quickly found it on GoogleFace maps.

It was in the western part of Austin, not far from Bee Caves Road. Judging by the size of the houses in the area, I could see that he lived in the rich part of the city.

About twenty minutes and a ton of GoogleFace inquiries later, I found that my initial assumption was most definitely true and that it only got richer the farther west you traveled.

Interesting. I'd heard Austin was an appealing place to live, its only drawbacks being the housing prices and its terribly hot summers.

Most Americans knew Texans and their pride. I'd already seen it coming into the state: the big flags in front of people's houses, the sticker flags on the backs of their trucks, the 'Don't Mess with Texas' road signs. It was the exact opposite of what I was used to in New England, which focused more on patriotism as a whole – something that was shared, rather than hoarded and shielded.

The thoroughfares were set up differently here too. Cities in the other states we'd driven through were set away from the traffic, usually hidden from view by trees. Everything in Texas was built right along the road; you could literally have the entrance to your home jutting off the highway.

From what I could tell, this was the way Longview had been built; a city sprouting around the highway, cushioning it like a hotdog bun.

"Barbeque or Mexican food?" I asked Grace as we prepared to leave the hotel.

She chose barbecue, and after Veronique drained just a little more energy from Dorian, we hit the streets.

Coleslaw, baked beans, cornbread; potato salad, ribs, pulled pork, grilled chicken, brisket – Grace and I ate like Southern royalty. Veronique ate a little, mostly the brisket, and once we finished, we took a quick trip to the mall to get her more clothing.

I would have preferred to stay at our hotel while they shopped, but I was worried about them going out alone. If they were captured, or if something happened to them, I would be completely screwed. Aside from the fact that I'd be stuck in a hotel room with Dorian, who would eventually wake up, I would be without a purpose and without the two women who were the reason for my crusade.

A crusade? A sci-fi writer going up against the FCG and MercSecure could be considered one of two things: a suicide or a crusade. I was banking on the latter.

The other reason I wished they could have gone alone is that I hate malls. There's nothing scarier to me than a mall full of people. From shootings to terrorist attacks, malls had become hotbeds for public violence.

To the generation following mine, malls would be nostalgic. To my generation, they were slightly toxic.

But I couldn't let the two go in alone.

"Let's make this quick," I said under my breath as we left our vehicle. We would get a new one when we came back; another chance to test-drive a different model.

Grace and Veronique were also not feeling the crowd at the mall, even if it was relatively small. There were just too many people around, so we tried to make it as quick as possible.

Aside from purchasing a Houston Texans jersey – mostly because it seemed a little lighter than my New England clothing – I stood outside the stores, taking notes on my smartphone about what I wanted to write later that day and keeping an eye on the crowd.

I was getting close to completing the second *Mutants in the Making*, and if I worked hard at it, I could have it done by tonight.

We were only four hours away from Austin. Rather than stay where we were another day, I figured we'd leave later that night so we could get a feel for our situation once we arrived.

For once, everything went smoothly while we were on our shopping excursion.

Veronique was disappointed that the mall didn't have any mil-spec outfits, which was kind of funny. I suggested we go to an outdoor store, but I figured most of the stuff in Texas wouldn't be what she was looking for. There would be plenty of camo and bright orange jumpsuits, but there wouldn't be form-fitting black bodysuits.

So she got the next best thing.

With Grace as her shopping assistant and 'funding' all the purchases, they found a few outfits Veronique liked, as well as a jacket

– although, it was already ninety-something degrees outside, so definitely *not* jacket weather.

She also bought a lot of undergarments from Victor and Victoria's Secret, a store that used to be just for women but had changed by 2030 due to gender binarism debates.

We got back to the hotel, and Veronique drained more from Dorian. I started writing my ass off, and right around the time I'd gotten to the end point, I ordered a pizza.

Everything was going according to plan.

Sound the trumpets and bring out the booze! I had finished my manuscript, AI had edited the chapters, and I was ready to birth my creation onto the masses. Other writers be damned – make room for Gideon Caldwell at the top!

With a fresh manuscript in its appropriate folder on my computer, I pulled up the EBAYmazon dashboard, uploaded the cover, fleshed out the product description (damn, did I hate doing that), and uploaded the final file.

It's missing something ... I thought as I reopened the file. I went through the collection of book quotes I keep and picked one by Ralph Waldo Emerson: "We, as we read, must become Greeks, Romans, Turks, priest and king, martyr and executioner; must fasten these images to some reality in our secret experience, or we shall learn nothing rightly."

I went for the $0.99 price point, only because I didn't need money any longer, and I was going for that big Andy Weir launch part deux.

After checking everything for a final time, I put the book up for sale, which meant it would take ten to twelve hours to be approved.

I closed the laptop and exhaled audibly.

Grace and Veronique were back on their home improvement show, this one about fixer-upper homes in Britain, and there I was in the other room feeling like a million bucks.

Actually, finishing a book doesn't quite feel like a million bucks. It feels more like a burden has been removed from your shoulders, only to have another one ready to drop – aka the next book. But it did feel good at the time, and even a brief interlude of not having the book on my shoulders was worth its weight in gold.

With nothing better to do, aside from pat myself on the back, I went into the other room to wait for the pizza.

"Room for me on that bed?" I asked, half joking.

"Yep," Veronique said, moving aside so I could crawl between them.

How I kept living every fanboy's dream, I had no idea, but I wasn't complaining. With Grace on my left and Veronique on my right, I tried to keep my focus on the television. Once this failed, I turned to my phone and saw that Luke was active.

Me: Bruh. What's going on?

Luke: I'm revamping the cover for the first Star Defacer book. What do you think?

Me: Definitely cool. I liked the first one too. It had a vibe.

Luke: I know, but now that the series is selling, I want to do a little rebranding and upgrading.

Me: Nothing wrong with that. I like the little skull in the middle, with the spiky head. Looks killer.

Luke: Hell yeah, people love skulls. I don't know why.

Me: Me neither. Maybe it's because humans have a weird fascination with their own mortality and the skull represents a watered-down version of this.

Luke: 💀 💀 *Publishing a philosophy book next?*

Me: Hardly. Just trying to make it to Austin in one piece and get my ass some 🍕 🍕

Luke: I feel that. Damn, Gid, I got about three hundred questions for you. But I'll start at the top. Did you hit pub on Mutants in the Making 2?

Me: It's like you're reading my mind or something. I just did, like ten minutes ago. So, it'll be up by tomorrow for sure, but maybe even by tonight if the EBAYmazon gods process it quickly.

Luke: Last I checked, you're holding your ranking, which means people are digging it. I hope the second book grabs even more readers.

Me: It should. The second book gets into details of the assault, and Angel, and Dorian Gray. But just the start of that story, because I don't know how that's going to play out.

Luke: LOL. Yeah, she's there now.

Me: Did I already tell you that? Sorry, I'm in a bit of a daze. I somehow managed to write ten thousand words today – six thousand in a frenzied afternoon sprint. My hands are killing me. I'm just glad to be inside with the A/C and some pizza coming.

Luke: A/C. Oh that's right, you're down south.

Me: Hot as balls.

Luke: Did you go with the pink cover for MM2?

Me: Yeah, I think it'll look good, especially on reading devices. You want to see some of my throwaway covers?

Luke: Hold on, let me go to the bathroom, take my pants off, and sit, just in case I feel the urge to shit myself.

Me: Ha! They're not that bad. Okay, I made this one three days ago. I was a little delirious at the time. Terrible, I know. But speaking of skulls ...

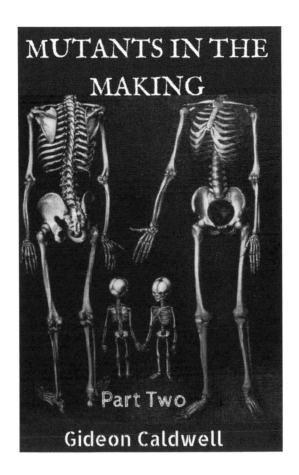

MUTANTS IN THE MAKING

Part Two

Gideon Caldwell

Luke: *The two big skeletons had sex, and those are their children.*
Also, the adult skeletons are headless.

Me: *I definitely wasn't at my best when I made that. I also made*
this one. Warning: I don't know what I was smoking when I thought
this would be a good cover. Sometimes I have to make a bunch of
crappy covers before I can really hit my stride and make one that
looks good.

Book II

Mutants in the Making

Gideon Caldwell

Luke: Brutal, and by brutal I mean brutally bad.

Me: Yeah, definitely not good.

Luke: Were you trying to cover her nipples with font? Because you failed. LOL. Also, are those supposed to be little explosions behind her?

Me: They're flowers.

Luke: Well, I can say that I like the font.

Me: I also made this one:

Luke: What's she supposed to be looking at? Looks like something from a Poltergeist remake.

Me: A light, a beacon of truth.

Luke: Okay. I see it now. How is it that you make such terrible covers and then make one that just hits?

Me: No idea, but luckily, fourth time was a charm.

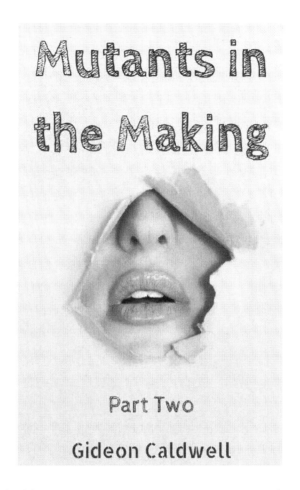

Mutants in the Making

Part Two

Gideon Caldwell

Luke: Looks like a winner to me. Hey, got a question for you. You said you're planning to meet this guy in Austin. You going prepared?

Me: I believe I'm going prepared. I have two human weapons with me, and I was able to modify Veronique a little bit.

Luke: Great, what were you able to do?

Me: Well, the readers that like stats and modifying abilities will love the fact that I was finally able to dig down a little deeper into

Veronique's situation and figure out more about her power. Turns out, she's not a vampire.

Luke: LOL.

Me: She actually drains the metal from people's bodies. Sounds weird, but you know there's a lot of different metals floating around in our bodies and bloodstreams. I'm not claiming to be a scientist here, obviously, but that's what she does. Hell, she's done it to me, and it feels really strange.

Luke: Wait a minute. Her ability allows her to modify the atomic structure of the metal and pull it through someone's skin? If I were reading this in a book, I would call BS.

Me: I wouldn't call BS, only because I'm not so hot on the 'science' part of science fiction. I'll leave that to Neal Stephenson and some of the military sci-fi guys who can roast me any way they want over this shit because the fact of the matter is, it's true.

Luke: What you are experiencing and writing about isn't fiction, so that's why it's kind of funny I'd call BS on it.

Me: What can I say? Even my own life has some plot holes. I'm sure there's more to the science part, but I'll let someone else explain that.

Someone knocked at the door. Pizza had arrived.

Me: Shit just got real.

Luke: What do you mean?

Me: Pizza's here. Got to eat and run.

Luke: Enjoy, and good luck!

As Grace got up from the bed and moved to the door, she morphed into a Texan she'd seen earlier. Her hair was frizzy and big, and she wore a pinkish-red button-up shirt, a bolo tie, a pair of tight Wranglers hugging her ass, and some elaborate cowboy boots. No cowboy hat though, which made me wonder if she couldn't morph a hat. But she did get the accent down.

"Howdy," she said when she opened the door.

"Two Hawaiian pizzas, one with chicken instead of Canadian bacon?" the delivery driver asked.

"I do believe that's what we ordered – ain't that right, Kenny?"

I looked at Veronique. "Am I supposed to be Kenny?"

"That's right, Grace," Veronique said, trying for her best, deep-voiced country accent and failing miserably. Luckily, the delivery guy couldn't see us.

"Great," the guy said and handed Grace the pizza.

"Now, Gerald, you gonna get on over here and get these here pizzas or what? Can't ya'll get your butts off the bed?"

"I'm Gerald and you're Kenny, right?" I asked Veronique.

She nodded, a genuine smile spreading across her face. I then tried to imagine what the delivery driver was thinking when he saw a hot country girl open the door and say there were two men in the room with her, both on the bed. Good thing we were going to wipe his mind.

"Can I feed too, Gideon?" Veronique asked me, her hand falling on my arm as I slipped off the bed.

"Later," I said. She shrugged and turned back to the TV. I took a deep breath and approached the door. Grace gave me the pizzas. Damn if they didn't smell good.

"Yep, that's right," Grace told the driver, "I already done paid ya'll."

"Oh," the man said as he looked at the receipt he still held. "I see that now."

"No, we can pay." I put the pizzas down on a table near the door and grabbed my wallet, pulling out two twenties. I gave the driver forty bucks, told Grace to make sure he didn't remember any of this, and we bid him farewell.

"I love pizza, I love, *love* pizza," Grace said, morphing back into her base form.

I opened the box and frowned at the greasy mess dotted with pineapples. "Don't get your hopes up."

The pizza wasn't so great, but at least it was cheesy. I guess that's the thing about most pizza – it has cheese. But this pizza was definitely not the best I'd had; hell, it wasn't even the best I'd had from Wendy's Hut.

Still, it hit the spot.

After we finished eating, we packed up and headed to our car, Veronique using her powers again to drag Dorian behind us.

Chapter Thirteen: Endgame Dreams

We headed west on I-20 and eventually reached the outskirts of Dallas. The farther we got away from the eastern part of Texas, the drier it became. It was still hot outside – our Subaru's temperature said it was eighty-eight degrees – and the cityscape quickly morphed from 'gone country' to 'urban cowboy' as we zipped by Dallas.

"It's so big," Grace said as she looked out the window.

We weren't cutting through downtown Dallas as much as we were skirting around it. The highways all made circles around the city, reminding me of a spider web. We only touched the lower right-hand quadrant of Dallas as we transferred to I-35, but we did get to see the city, the lights at night, and the new buildings under construction.

As she normally did, Veronique sat in the back seat with Dorian next to her.

Every time I glanced in the rearview mirror, I either caught a glimpse of Veronique looking directly at me – which was kinda creepy – or Dorian sitting there with her eyes glued shut – also creepy.

We have to figure out what to do about her, I thought as I drove around a slow-moving Ford Escort.

We will.

I smirked. *You aren't supposed to be reading my thoughts.*

There's nothing else to read.

You can read my phone.

Reading while riding gives me a headache.

Then find something different to listen to, I told her. For the last twenty minutes, we'd been listening to a local Tejano station, which was kind of cool, but which was also starting to drive me mad with its up-tempo beats.

"Would you like to listen to NPR?" she asked in Ira Glass's voice. "I'm Ira Glass, and each week, we take an adventure across America in search of secret government facilities."

"Man, Ira would *love* to get his hands on this story," I said. I took over the wheel from the auto drive function; I felt like being in control at the moment.

"Yes or no?" she asked, still using his voice.

"No, for now. Let's get some music going, something dancy."

Grace flipped through the stations until she found one playing disco hits from the 70s.

I tightened my grip on the steering wheel. "Disco works for me."

So, after going through Waco, Round Rock, and a slew of other smaller cities, we drove into Austin jamming disco. I wouldn't recommend three hours of straight disco to anyone; that said, it did make the drive faster.

"Who's ready to stay in a mansion tonight?" I asked as we took the 183 exit, heading toward MoPac and Westlake Hills.

MoPac passed over Lady Bird Lake, and Veronique pointed at some of the mansions that lined the water.

"Stay at a mansion in Austin? Let's do it."

We took the Westlake Hills exit. To get to the lakeside mansions, we'd need to take the loop around and then hit one of the roads that cut through Zilker Park. I wanted to find one that wasn't gated in. Not that we couldn't get in a gate with Veronique and Grace's abilities.

After driving around for a few minutes, we found a gateless home the size of a grocery store. The entrance sloped down to a five-car garage. To the right of the garage was a door that a giant could get through, and, I shit you not, a bridge from the parking area to the front door.

We'd need to get rid of our current vehicle, but that would be easy once we found a family member.

We left Dorian in the car as we approached the front door, where Veronique worked her magic to let us in.

The first person to greet us was a kid, a boy about ten years old, who was walking across the living room to get something from the kitchen. Grace immediately took over his mind and told him to introduce her to everyone in the house.

She followed him, and soon, Grace also had the husband, the wife, and a teenage daughter in the living room and under her spell.

"The first thing I want to happen is for you to get rid of our vehicle," I told the husband, "and come back here with an UberLyft."

The husband was a fit guy, someone who worked out regularly, with a sprinkling of white in his beard and large eyebrows. He simply nodded at me and left.

The other three stood before us, completely transfixed.

The wife had had a lot of work done on her face and body; Botox and a boob job – those were just things I noticed off the bat. There was nothing that really stood out about the boy, aside from the darkness of his hair. And the teenage daughter looked pretty much like the boy, only taller, with zits on her chin and wearing designer pajamas.

"Shall I get Dorian?" Veronique asked me. "Also, I'm a little hungry."

"Yeah, bring her in the living room."

I didn't know if the place we were standing in was a living room or something else entirely. I would later find out that the house had *two* living rooms, and this room – which featured a piano and a floor-to-ceiling view of the lake outside the window – was simply the foyer.

Or something like that.

Like I said, I'm not great with architecture.

Veronique returned, dragging Dorian behind her. The family ignored Veronique as she placed Dorian on one of the sofa chairs and made sure she was properly drained of her energy.

Grace yawned. "I'm getting tired, Gideon," she said and went to sit next to Dorian, which was a bit strange considering the circumstances and the fact the family still stood there, waiting for orders.

"We need to handle the family before you can go to bed. Have them all to go to one of the bedrooms upstairs – the son's bedroom, that's fine. Whatever. Does he have a bathroom in there?"

The boy nodded.

"Great, tell them to turn off their phones and stay there for the next twenty-four hours. Eventually, they'll snap out of it and wonder what the hell's going on, but we'll be long gone by then."

She yawned. "And can I go to bed after that?"

"Sure, just stay up long enough for the husband to get back."

While Grace sat in the living room waiting for the husband's return, the rest of the family went upstairs to the boy's bedroom. That was the last I'd see of them. Meanwhile, Veronique and I took a tour of the place.

It had seven bedrooms, six bathrooms, two living rooms, an enormous workout room, two offices, and a very nice, but small backyard that overlooked Town Lake with access to the water via a dock.

"Let's see what vehicles we're working with," I said.

We entered the garage through the kitchen to find a Cadillac Escalade and two Porsches – one an SUV and the other a sports car. The teenage daughter had a Volkswagen, and there was also a completely restored 1955 Thunderbird in the carport farthest from the kitchen.

I don't know what they did to get all that money, but it didn't involve publishing $0.99 ebooks.

I pressed the button to open the garage door just as lights flashed in the driveway – the husband returning in an UberLyft.

He hardly made eye contact with me as he went back into the house and, I assumed, straight up to his son's bedroom.

Before going back inside, Veronique and I stood on the bridge that led from the garage to the front door. It was a warm night, and mosquitoes buzzed in the air. It was also humid, and I was glad I didn't grow up with this type of climate. Sure, the cold and the snow could get old, but this heat …

Rather than think about how I was from New England and wasn't used to the South, I went inside to find Dorian still sitting on the couch in the foyer.

"Let's just make sure she sleeps for the night," Veronique said as she approached the teleporting rocker. She placed her hand on Dorian's head, and a red aura formed around her fingers.

I looked around for Grace and found her asleep in one of the living rooms. Figuring it'd be nice to get a good night's sleep as well, I found one of the guest bedrooms and lay down on the bed.

Dammit. I should have bought something aside from this ironic Houston Texans jersey I got at the mall.

I took off the jersey and tossed my pants and socks to the floor. Most of my clothes were for colder weather, not this heat. I figured I would check the guy's closet for things to wear tomorrow, but I had a feeling he and I didn't share a style. Still, maybe he had some collared shirts.

As I lay there on the bed, I heard the door handle twist open.

Even though my glasses were off, I knew who it was just by the sound of the door. It didn't sound like a door being opened normally; I'd heard Veronique use her power enough times to notice the subtle difference between something natural and her ability to command metal.

Or maybe I just intuited it was her.

"How are things?" she asked, almost deadpan.

It was then I remembered that her charisma was quite low; maybe she didn't mean to be as stiff as she came across.

"Things are okay. I'm a little nervous about tomorrow."

"Why?" she asked and sat on the bed beside me.

"I just have a feeling we're going into something kind of strange. We need to be ready. I don't want you two to kill anyone if you don't have to, nor do I want to do something that'll get us in even more trouble than we're already in. This guy may actually have information that could help us."

"And if he doesn't?"

I placed my hands behind my head. I could feel that my hair was already starting to grow out, and if I was truly going for the shaved-head look, I'd need to get a haircut in the next week or so.

This got me thinking about when I'd decided to shave my head at the black barbershop in New Haven. It was right after I received the scar on my face – a scar I had since grown used to. It was still healing, actually, still a little pink. Once the skin hardened, I'd look like a fucking mercenary. So that was something to look forward to.

"Why are you smiling?"

"Just getting high on my own supply, sorry."

She lay down next to me and I felt tension increase between us. We looked at each other for a moment. My mouth opened, and words spilled out. "So, like I was saying, I'm a little worried about tomorrow. Yep, definitely worried. Damn tomorrow. Today was nice though. But tomorrow, who knows what could happen?"

"I'm not worried."

"Of course you aren't. You can pretty much do anything with your abilities."

Veronique moved just a little closer to me. She now lay on her side, strands of blonde hair in her face. "You place too much confidence in what we can do."

I reached out and brushed the hair from her face.

"Damn right I do. All I can do is drive, write, and try to put the pieces together so maybe we can actually complete this puzzle. I mean, not that it's a big puzzle. We're talking about a government experiment, super soldiers ... that sort of thing. Nothing deeper than that, I'm afraid. I get it. Sorry, I'm talking out loud. I just worry sometimes about the endgame."

"Endgame?"

Her hand landed on my cheek and I swallowed hard.

"Yeah, endgame. Let's say we do this – we destroy the facilities and take care of Mother, unite the people with superpowers and play that whole thing out. What next?" I asked, my voice softening.

It was strange to be this close to Veronique, especially knowing she could drain my energy in a heartbeat. Even as I stared into her dark eyes, I knew she could turn the tables very quickly.

But would she?

That was the thing about her; even though she'd shown me no sign she would double-cross us, or that she would turn on me, I still remembered the Veronique who burst into our room back in East Haven and later took me hostage.

It was still hard to separate the two; the trained soldier and the Veronique I had come to know.

"Why are you so worried about our endgame?" she finally asked. "This ends when it ends, and there's little we can do to stop it from ending at that time. We don't know the future, we only know what happened in the past. And for Grace and me, what we are doing now is far better than what was happening to us in our past. So, was that our endgame? What happens after an endgame?"

I smirked at her. "I don't think you understand the term 'endgame,' at least in the same way I do."

"Oh?" she moved her hand from my cheek to the side of my neck.

"And I'm not trying to mansplain here, but the whole idea of 'endgame' is that it is the end of the game – hence, 'endgame.'"

"I see. In that case, we will win, and Grace and I will design a very nice home for all of us to live in. Somewhere secluded. But with access to a city."

"And by 'we,' do you mean me too?" I asked, a slight hesitation in my voice.

"I suppose. I suppose you can live with us. I'm sure Grace would like that. Maybe I would like that too. But you're going to have to write more books because that is your superpower. Your superpower is writing books. So, if you live with us in this beautiful house we're going to customize and remodel, you have to write books. You can have a writing room and a nook, I believe it is called."

I laughed. "That is a great fantasy right there."

"Maybe we can get a dog and have some kids."

I gulped. "Have kids?"

"We can start a family, I don't know. Just dreams, endgame dreams."

The door opened, and Grace walked in, wearing a robe. She yawned, saw that Veronique was on the bed, and stopped.

"We were just talking about our dream home," Veronique said, getting up from the bed and leaving the room. "The one you and I discussed."

Holy shit, does Grace have Veronique in check?

Yes, I do.

I froze as I heard Grace's voice in my head.

But if you'd like her to stay in here for tonight, that's fine by me.

Veronique was gone before I could respond.

Grace got into the bed, yawned, and turned to me as if nothing had just happened. "I'm very tired tonight," she said, her eyes going from slightly white to iceberg blue. "Too much shopping, disco, pizza, and barbeque."

"Goodnight, Grace."

Try as I might to fall asleep, I lay awake for thirty more minutes, thinking about all that had happened.

I didn't know where I stood on polyamory, having more than one love interest at a time. And I didn't want to figure that out right now. I wanted to be prepared for tomorrow, but I had no idea what to prepare for. For all I knew, we would just meet this guy and he would give us some information and things would go fine.

But they could go the opposite way as well.

Chapter Fourteen: Dorian Wakes

I was up earlier than anyone else in the house. I knew that because it was just a little after five a.m., a time when no one in their right mind should be awake. My email inbox was full; my new book had been published.

I looked at my smartphone for a moment longer just to confirm this. I could check my sales and ranking later. It was actually the last thing on my mind as I moved out of the bedroom and into the hallway to get something to drink.

We were on the upper floor, and I was thirsty.

Rather than drink from the faucet, I headed downstairs and was greeted by a beautiful sunrise underscored by a zigzag of pink on the surface of the lake.

It was weird to see Dorian just sitting there in the sofa chair, perfectly still, her eyes closed. Eerie didn't begin to describe it.

I got some expensive juice from the fridge and filled a glass.

"I don't know what we're going to do with you," I said as I returned to Dorian and sat across from her. Her black hair, her punk rock accouterments, her petite body – she looked the exact opposite of Grace and Veronique.

But then again, who knew what Grace actually looked like? I hadn't forgotten the time she showed me a thin, dark-haired woman with acne when I asked her to show me her true form. She hadn't shown me that form since, and for all I knew, she was just messing with me.

There was a lot I'd never understand about shapeshifters. And I always had this feeling she was hiding something from me. Whereas Veronique wore her personality on her sleeve; I understood who she was, and I usually understood her intent.

But Grace, not so much.

They'd make great fictional characters, though. One, almost a girl next door but with a secret. The second one, dangerous, but soft at the core. Maybe after all this was finished, I would get to writing fiction again, and I could let those characters play out in my mind.

My rambling, author-centric thoughts came to a sudden halt when Dorian's eyes opened.

I gasped as her black eyes locked onto me. I could feel the blood draining from my face.

"Uh …" was the only sound my throat could make.

I felt as if I'd woken a sleeping lion, that I had come face-to-face with a carnivore.

"Thirsty …" she whispered, her throat quivering.

"You're thirsty?"

We both glanced at my juice.

Oddly enough, I'd had this feeling of complete and utter apprehension before. And it was with Veronique, when she assaulted Grace in the hotel at Stamford and had come for me.

One thing I'd learned about these types of encounters was that you could either stare the beast down and figure out what it wanted – which could result in your death – or, you could run.

As I had before, I chose to make peace with the predator.

Not saying a word, I took my glass of juice to her. She tilted her head back slightly and I brought it to her parched lips. She quickly finished the juice.

"Do you want more?" I asked, my nerves tingling.

She nodded. I looked toward the kitchen, which now felt like it was miles away.

For all I knew, she could teleport away by the time I returned. Or she could create a person made of kinetic energy to kill me. It didn't have to be a person … could be anything, really.

But my name is Gideon Caldwell, and I am an idiot.

So I went to the kitchen and got her some more juice, and she was halfway through the next glass when Grace and Veronique appeared.

Veronique practically launched herself at Dorian. Her hand fell on Dorian's head, and as it glowed red, the teleporter's eyes rolled back. Veronique narrowed her eyes at me. "You are an idiot, Gideon."

"I was just thinking that."

"I'm just glad I heard you leave the room," Grace said.

"Wait, were you able to see what I was doing up here?" I touched my face. *No way she's that powerful.*

Grace nodded. "But you already knew I was."

It was true; I'd already sensed this. But it was early, and I was still a little bit delirious.

Veronique continued to drain Dorian.

"Lighten up a bit," I told her. "She could have done something, but she didn't. We're going to have to deal with her at some point. What if we can turn her?"

Grace placed a hand on my shoulder. "You can't trust everyone, Writer Gideon."

"I trusted you," I said to her. I looked at Veronique. "And I trust you, even though you once basically tried to kill her and imprisoned me."

"People change," was all she finally said.

"Exactly, which is why I think Dorian could change." Confidence returned to my voice. "It's just a hunch right now, but we're going to have to work with her if we want her to join us and see our side. We can't kill her – or at least we shouldn't – and her abilities would be monstrously helpful to our cause."

"Maybe you're right," Veronique said, "But for now, we keep her sedated."

"I'm fine with that."

"Who's hungry?" Grace asked, trying to lighten the mood.

"It's five in the morning," I reminded her.

"Almost half past five now."

"Actually, that's a great idea."

Once again, Grace had implanted a thought in my brain.

Magnolia Cafe on Lake Austin Boulevard was open twenty-four hours.

From the reviews I'd read, it looked like it had pretty damn good food. But there was also the Omelettry, another GoogleFace recommendation, and they had amazing pancakes, apparently.

It was a tough call, but I had to go with the pancakes.

We found the Omelettry and got there about twenty minutes after they'd opened. It was a well-lit place, with a drawing of anthropomorphized eggs on the walls.

Our waitress came, a tattooed and pierced Austin hipster with short hair on one side and long hair on the other. Cool.

The coffee was poured and even Veronique had a cup.

I ordered 'The Economical' with buttermilk pancakes, and Grace had a yogurt parfait with gingerbread pancakes. I got a couple looks from the guys who came in, especially when they saw me sitting with Veronique, a hot blonde with strikingly sharp features, and Grace, who had gone with her brunette in yoga pants yet again.

I had never been the envy of other guys, never been a bro'd out guy's guy for that matter, and it was still strange to see people look between me and the two women with me, trying to figure out how I had pulled it off.

"No shifting in public," I reminded Grace as her hair began to change to match our waitress's. I finished my coffee. The waitress spotted it and went for a fresh pot.

"Okay," she whined.

The food came, and we dug in.

I started with the pancakes, spreading out the big lump of butter on top and smothering it in syrup. From there, I moved to the sausage, the eggs, and another cup of coffee to boot.

Grace started with the pancakes as well and finished her parfait off relatively quickly. She shared one of the pancakes with Veronique, who ate it, but didn't seem to enjoy it very much.

"It's too sweet," she said.

"It's good for you," I assured her.

"Why do I feel like you're lying to me?"

"I'd never do that."

"Grace?" she asked.

"He's lying."

My knife started to bend backward, and as I put it down, Veronique dropped her hand onto mine. "Careful," she reminded me, to Grace's laughter.

"Please bend my knife back."

After we finished eating, we headed back to MoPac, and from there, I let GoogleFace Maps route us to Butler's house.

The estates in West Austin rivaled some of the mansions I'd seen in Greenwich, Connecticut. No, they didn't have an Oceanfront view, but they did have helipads, pools, hundreds of private acres, and amazing views of downtown Austin.

Even better, most of them didn't have gates. You could seriously just drive up to these million-dollar homes and park.

We were in the Porsche SUV – the first time I'd driven in a Porsche, actually. I would have driven our host's neon green Porsche 911 GT3, but it only fit two people. Still, the SUV handled like a beauty, and it could get going pretty quickly on the highway.

"Anybody want to check it out again?" I asked as we passed Butler's house. It was tucked away, I'd give it that. And down the winding driveway looked to be another guest house, only adding to the spread of the estate.

The girls didn't say anything. I glanced at Grace next to me and saw that she was the fullest I'd ever seen her. Her hands on her stomach, she had already switched to the waitress's haircut, and her eyes were closed as she dealt with her food baby.

I started to laugh. "You doing all right over there?"

Grace yawned. "You woke us up pretty early."

"My mistake," I said.

We passed the place again. There weren't any turrets, and I didn't see anything in place to protect it from superpowered individuals, so we continued on.

154

We arrived back at our current mansion at half past seven. Dorian was just where we left her, and I even checked on the family upstairs.

I can't emphasize enough how creepy Grace's ability can be. I knocked on the door of the son's bedroom and was told I could enter. Once I opened the door, I found all four of them sitting on the edge of the bed next to each other, staring at the wall, their eyes white.

It only took me about two seconds to have seen enough of that, so I shut the door and went back downstairs.

Since we had time to kill, I figured I would check on my book's deets. While Grace and Veronique napped – this time in the same room as Dorian – I pulled out my laptop.

I logged on and saw I was moving books like crack in the 1980s.

Since the release of the second book, I was averaging close to a hundred thousand page reads a day, which for two novellas, was hella good. I almost baited myself into checking reviews, but like I had done in the past, I shied away from doing that.

Better that way.

I started the absolutely terrible task of going through my emails, trying to figure out which ones I should respond to, which ones were spam, and which ones were worse. A good two dozen readers had contacted me about my story, a few wanting photo evidence.

There was another message from David Butler, reminding me that our meeting was at noon. There was also a message from Ken Kim, asking me for an update.

I ignored them.

I still had two throwaway phones, so maybe I'd give Ken a call at some point. Or he would call me because that was what happened last time, and I was still highly suspicious about it.

With several hours to kill, I did what anyone with access to a computer and some free time did.

Nope, not porn.

Rather, I surfed the web aimlessly, watching cat videos, catching up on some of the subreddits I followed, and reading about new video games that were coming out.

Had I known what was going to happen next, I would have at least gotten halfway prepared. I was a fool, and the fact that I didn't have a plan was about to come back and bite me in the ass.

Chapter Fifteen: Snack Attack

The only thing we needed to do before we left our borrowed mansion was make sure the owners didn't come looking for their Porsche SUV.

Easy peasy: I had Grace convince the family they never owned the vehicle. We'd be way out of Austin with a new vehicle by the time they unraveled those pieces; it was easier that way.

With Dorian laid out sideways in the cargo area of the Porsche, we headed to Butler's place.

It was already in the 80s outside, so we would need to park in the shade. I didn't plan to be there very long, at least for this visit. And I planned to keep the SUV running while we were inside, which was easy to do because there was an option on the keyless entry to cool the vehicle.

We drove around Butler's neighborhood first, looking for any suspicious vehicles. There weren't any; everything was hunky-dory. The only person even around was an extra fit white lady jogging up a hill, her skin glistening in the sun.

I wore my bulletproof vest under my Houston Texans jersey, which was heavy and made me look like I'd gained a couple pounds, but I was playing it safe.

After one more check through the hood, we pulled into Butler's driveway.

Veronique was the first to get out of the SUV.

She surveyed the area, and once she gave us the hand signal, Grace and I got out. The two formed a security perimeter around me as we made our way to the front door, Grace on my right, Veronique on my left.

I'd long since turned in any semblance of masculinity I hoped to gain as part of this trio. It wasn't like I'd be worth a damn if someone started shooting at us or we were attacked by another super.

I was fine with that; I didn't mind being the weakest link.

The intercom came on just as we reached the front door.

"Welcome, Gideon Caldwell. Please enter and enjoy the snacks in the kitchen. David Butler will arrive shortly. Estimated time of arrival is three minutes and fifteen seconds."

It was a very AI voice – Alexis and Siri's bastard. I exchanged glances with the two superpowereds, got confirmation, and we entered.

After Grace and Veronique checked the foyer, we walked on a nicely polished wooden floor to an open-concept space kitchen that included a dining and living room area separated from the front door by a single wall.

On the bar were some cookies and other, healthier snacks like carrots and ranch dressing. I received an email from David almost immediately, reminding me that he was running a bit late because of a prior meeting and that he'd be here in a couple of minutes.

Hell yes, I was suspicious.

I began looking around, lifting up any flower pot, trinket, or decoration I could get my hands on to see if we were being recorded. I checked behind the 120-inch flat screen TV and moved each book on the bookshelf, just in case it opened to a secret room. Speaking of books, my fuck was this guy into sci-fi harems. Every book he had featured two women and a man on the book cover.

What a played-out trope.

Butler was also definitely a fan of space opera movies, and there was really only one space opera movie big enough to have posters that could cover all his walls. So, I checked the posters too.

"There has to be something," I said to Veronique.

At that moment, a few of the picture frames and silverware from the kitchen began to rattle.

My heart skipped a beat. I glanced over at Veronique to see that she just was preparing ammunition and exhaled audibly with relief.

The pictures fell out as their metal frames lifted into the air and joined the silverware, all of which hovered around her.

"Good call, but don't kill him until we know for certain he's trying to kill us."

Yeah, that sentence sounded strange, but as Jay-Z once said, "This isn't the life I chose; rather, it's the life that chose me."

I always liked that quote.

I moved to the kitchen, still not able to discover anything. Damn, was I paranoid. I had a feeling this was a bad idea to come here. I tried to suppress the feeling, but it kept boiling to the surface.

As she had done before, Grace spoke to me in my head.

Relax, Writer Gideon, we are prepared if anything happens.

I know, I thought back to her, *but this is just really freaky. Maybe we should have met the guy somewhere else. I don't know why we agreed to his demand to meet him here. It's his turf ...*

The lock on the back door clicked and we all turned to it, Veronique's makeshift weapons facing the back door as well.

"Is he locking us in?" I asked.

Still in control of her weapons, Veronique used her powers to unlock the door. We stood there for a minute, all of us poised and ready for something to happen.

Grace was the first to fall.

She was standing near a vent, and as she surveyed the room, she simply … fell.

I glanced at her just as Veronique fell, followed by her projectile weapons, which plinked against the floor as they landed around her body. I then realized I was growing delirious, that everything was starting to blur, that I could *taste* something in the air.

The television flickered on as I too fell to the floor.

I saw the outline of a man on the screen, speaking to us in a syrupy voice as I lost consciousness.

Chapter Sixteen: Botched Interrogation

I didn't know where I was. The walls were all black, and there was nowhere to sit but on the ground. My mouth was dry, there wasn't a smell I could discern in the air, and I felt a migraine taking shape.

I was the only one awake; Grace and Veronique were both passed out next to me.

Taking a deep breath in, I glanced around, trying to get my bearings. My eyes were still slightly blurred. It was a large room, about the size of my garden apartment back in New Haven, but it was very spare.

Are we in some type of workshop? I thought as I looked up at the halogen lamps shining down on me.

My ankles and hands were cuffed together, and as I studied the cuffs I saw they were connected to a long metal chain that went behind my back.

The realization came to me like a knife in the gut: David Butler tricked us, poisoned us. Whoever this guy was, he *definitely* wasn't on our side. And I should have seen it coming.

"Grace, wake up," I said with a scratchy voice. "Please …" I looked down at her lifeless face. "Please, Grace … Please, one of you."

They looked like they were asleep, both also chained to the wall but lying on their sides. I noticed that Veronique's chains were made of plastic, but there was still metal in the vicinity. All she had to do was use my cuffs. Poor planning on Butler's part.

"Let us out of here!" I screamed, going with the panicked victim act.

"Shut the fuck up," came a voice from outside. The door opened and a large man with a long gray ponytail and a white beard entered.

He had the body of someone who kept relatively healthy, and his white beard almost reminded me of the Dos Equis guy. He was in a button-up shirt and a pair of striped black slacks. The only thing off-putting about his outfit was his black leather boots, big steel-toed numbers with enough grip on the soles to scale a wall.

"David? David Butler?"

"In the flesh," he said. "Now relax, and don't say anything until I'm done talking. By the way, it took you damn long enough to get here. No one likes waiting, but I'm glad you finally came."

His accent wasn't Texan, but it was definitely American. Maybe he was from the West Coast. I couldn't tell, and it really didn't matter, so

I cast the random thought aside. My head was still spinning, and seeing the guy filled me with a toxic combo of fear and fury.

Even though I was scared shitless, something came over me; the same sudden boost of confidence that had filled me when I first went toe-to-toe with Angel.

"You're fucking dead," I growled. "Once these two are up … I can't … man, I don't know what they're going to do to you. Fucking … dead."

"Is that so?" He opened up a small, metal case and withdrew a syringe.

"What the hell is that?" I tried to pull my arms away.

"It's to make sure they don't wake up," he said with a laugh. "You three are going to make me a lot of money."

I had to stall him. I didn't know how long Grace and Veronique would be out, but I had to try to keep Butler from knocking them out even longer.

"Why are you doing this?" I asked, changing my tone. "What purpose does it serve you to turn us in? That's what you're planning to do, right?"

"No, I'm planning to keep you for myself." He moved to stand before me. "Joking. I know, I know, it's not a great time to be teasing you. And no, I'm not the type of guy who would hold three people hostage. So, since I'm going to turn you over to them I might as well be honest: this really is for the money. Plain and simple. You see this house?"

House? I glanced at the four corners of the room and made the assumption that we were in his attached guest house.

"It's not cheap to live here; the property taxes in Austin alone could buy a home in the Midwest. My last discovery is what bought this place. Maintaining it has taken its toll on my bank account."

Delay him, Writer Gideon.

Grace? I thought.

Please ...

But as it turned out, he was so eager to share his story that I didn't have to encourage much rambling on his part.

"You see, I was one of the software engineers who helped design the systems in their necks. Surely you've plugged in?"

I nodded.

"Now," he said as he waved the syringe, "there's probably some things you don't know about a government contract. One of those things is that everyone – and I mean *everyone* – works on a different piece, so no one knows what happens when all the pieces fit together. I was just working on the database stuff – we'll call it that because my guess is you aren't really up-to-date on different types of database software."

"What makes you think that?"

"I've done my research on you, Gideon Caldwell. Self-published writer who worked at a Yale gift shop, huh? A degree from Southern Connecticut? From Rhode Island? All those things check out?"

I nodded. I was experiencing a weird mixture of anger and fear. If I were writing a novel about this, which I technically was, I would find it hard to describe what was going through my mind at that time.

I wanted to lash out at him, but I also realized we were trapped, and that if I wasn't able to delay him from injecting Grace and Veronique …

"So, you're selling us back to them?" I blurted out, hoping to keep him talking.

He smirked. "I'm selling *them* back to the researchers, not you. You're going to be charged with … hmmm, I don't know, how many federal crimes? But that's not really my concern. In fact, I might just let you go. If you beg for it. Yeah, I've never seen someone beg, I think that would be kind of interesting. Then again, I might just keep you until they get here."

I swallowed hard.

I knew there would be no justice for someone like me, and as I considered this – of all fucking times – a quote from Hunter S. Thompson came to me. "Justice is not cheap in this country, and people who insist on it are usually either desperate or possessed by some private determination bordering on monomania."

Nope, there'd be no justice for my ass if the FCG got me.

"Have you told them yet?" I finally asked.

"Not yet. I have to make sure I have leverage first. I mean, clearly I do, but who's to say they won't send more superpowered individuals after me when I tell him I captured these two? I have to play this smart."

"How did you find out about us? Did you really read my book?"

He laughed. "You've got to be more careful next time. Did you honestly think publishing a book about all this would make a fucking difference? I just stumbled upon it, honest to God, which is what makes this even better."

"What do you know about Mother?"

"Mother?" He considered that for a moment. "Haven't heard of her. Why?"

"Never mind."

"Why are you asking me about Mother? Who is that? What am I missing here?"

I hadn't written about Mother yet. I wanted more details before I did that, and since I had only seen a picture and pieced together very limited details about her from what Grace and Veronique had told me, I wasn't ready to talk about her in my series.

"I said, never mind."

"Never mind, my ass," he said and grabbed Grace's arm. "Do you know how long this is going to put her out? Could be days."

"Don't do it."

"Yeah, I'm going to do it, and after I get to the other bitch, you're next."

A powerful sense of anger welled up inside me. "You're going to regret this," I snarled.

"Oh, I doubt that."

And almost as if on cue, Dorian Gray stepped into the room.

Chapter Seventeen: She's with Us

David Butler went from tough to about to shit his pants in a matter of seconds. He stumbled backward, the syringe in his hand his only weapon.

Dorian observed him for a moment, an indecipherable look on her face. Her hair was a mess, and she looked a little wobbly, but she also looked pissed as hell.

Damn, did she look pissed.

The punk rocker placed a finger in her mouth, took it out, and traced a long line in the air. Boiling purple energy formed at her fingertip as she continued the line.

Once it was complete, she brought her hand back and *flung* it at David Butler.

The line of energy sliced right through his neck, cutting his head clean off and cauterizing the wound at the same time. Her blast slammed into the back wall, fizzing and sparking, his head bouncing away somewhere to the left.

I was going to be sick.

I had seen dead bodies before … hell, I'd help to move a few, but seeing a head bounce, roll, and then stop so it was looking right at me, mouth agape, was too much to handle.

I gagged and was just barely able to stop from vomiting. The smell of singed flesh was terrible, nauseating.

"Holy shit …" With a deep breath in, I steeled myself, fully aware that I was next.

Dorian approached me, and as she did, she placed her finger in her mouth again.

I turned away from her so that the chain holding me to the wall was now visible. I wasn't whimpering or begging for my life; I knew this was it, and there was nothing I could do.

Dorian Gray was going to kill me.

A small explosion beside me produced a wave of heat against my exposed hands. I felt my chain fall away and glanced around to see that she'd saved me instead.

"Stand up," Dorian said, her voice hoarse.

I did as I was told. My legs and wrists were still bound, but I could at least move.

Fight back? The thought, my own, was one of the dumbest I'd had in a while. I didn't need to look at the severed head across the room to be reminded of that.

"I want answers," she said.

"Answers?" I tilted my head as I took her in. I was still shaky, and whatever noxious gas Butler had used against us had my head doing somersaults.

Grace, I thought, *please, if you can hear me ...*

Just a little longer. Stall her.

"What answers do you want?"

Dorian took a step closer, sizing me up. The heels of her boots brought her to about the same height as me.

"Why did you take them?"

"Them?" I asked, looking at Grace and Veronique. "I didn't take them, they ... well, they took me. Kind of strange to say it like that, but it's the truth. Grace showed up on my doorstep. Veronique tried to capture us and later joined us once she found out what we were doing."

"What *are* you doing?"

"We're putting an end to the experiments that created people like you and people like them," I told her, my confidence wavering.

It was odd to tell someone that you were trying to stop their species from flourishing. I decided on a different approach.

"Let me rephrase. Creating superpowered individuals in a lab to serve the Federal Corporate Government is an abomination."

Her brow furrowed. "How do you know we serve them?"

But I was so impassioned by what I was saying that I missed her question. "It's against the agreed-upon social norms of humanity. Just think about it: Grace was kept in solitary confinement most of her life; Veronique and you were both trained to be killers, but they'll retire you once they develop a better version. Can't you see what is going on here and how it's wrong?"

"My original question was: How do you know we serve the FCG?"

"I don't, but they funded your creation and …" I looked at her unsteadily. "Who do you serve?"

"We serve Mother."

There's that name again, I thought, taking in her blank expression.

"And Mother must serve someone. I'm not saying you're delusional, but there's no way Mother is getting funding from the FCG and protection by one of America's elite security companies *without* catering to a higher force."

She didn't say anything, and for a moment, we just stared at each other.

"You seem like a nice enough person," I finally said, *clearly* talking out of my ass. "And I think you get what we're trying to do here. We're trying to expose these experiments and put an end to them. I'm a writer, and I've already written two books about these experiments – well, they're novellas, but still."

"How can you care about something you know nothing of?" she asked.

"I know plenty about it. Grace … you know what her ability is, right? She put *everything* into my mind. She gave me the ability to see and feel what she went through."

"Grace?"

"You call her Sabine. Her new name is Grace."

"Okay," Dorian said. "I did not know new names were possible. How can you trust her?"

"I trust her because she trusts me. Same with Veronique. Not a week ago, she was trying to kill me. Now … now, I fucking love having her around. Bygones be bygones. What I'm saying here is …"

"Yes?"

I raised my chin slightly, trying to look as leaderlike as possible. "Join us. Let's bring an end to this together. Or go off on your own, *leave Mother*."

"Join you?" Dorian paced back and forth for a moment. She glanced from Veronique to Grace and back to me.

"What happened to your face?" she finally asked me.

"My face?" I touched the scar on my cheek. "That would be Angel. Know him?"

She raised an eyebrow. "You survived an encounter with Angel?"

"I survived two," I said.

"How do I know they won't kill me when they wake up?"

"Because they listen to me. I listen to them too. We listen to each other."

She stared at me skeptically.

"Look, this isn't some situation where I'm the alpha male and these two obey me. Fanboy fantasies aside, I'm kind of the driver of the group. I write the books and do the driving. If anyone is the alpha, it's Veronique. Lateral leadership. That's what I'm trying to say. We work together. We live together. We do everything together."

"You're like a family."

"I … yeah … we are. Hell, I basically abandoned my real family when I took off with them." My throat tightened. That was something I wasn't proud of, something I'd never be able to rectify. I didn't want the FCG going after them; the less they knew the better.

Still, I needed to call my mom at some point. But the longer I put it off, the easier it became.

"And why are we here at this house?" Dorian asked.

"The guy you decapitated claimed to have information for us. He may still have information, somewhere on his computers, but what he was really trying to do was sell us back to the FCG."

"To Mother? Why would she spare this guy's life?"

"I don't know. Maybe she doesn't know about him. He didn't seem to know about her. Anyway, he said something about being out of money and needing more. He read my book. Yep. I fucked up by not coming into this situation the right way. I should have been much more careful."

She smirked. "You talk a lot."

"Sorry, you could seriously kill me in a matter of seconds, so I'm a little nervous. Also, I'm sorry I punched you back in Louisiana. My mistake."

"I'm not going to kill you, and that's fine. It was a natural reaction."

"If you aren't going to kill us, what are you going to do? Are you going to … turn us in?"

Dorian looked down at her hands, nodding slightly to herself as she considered her options. Finally, she locked eyes with me and offered a thin smile. "No, I'm going to join you."

Chapter Eighteen: Pizza and Gruesome Jokes

I shit you not, that was exactly how our conversation went down. Dorian Gray promised she wouldn't kill me and said she was going to join us.

Then she came over to me, licked her finger, and placed it on my handcuffs. The first one fizzled and snapped, followed by the second. She then went for the cuffs on my ankles.

"Damn, your ability really is activated by your saliva," I said, still not believing she'd flipped so easily. I was naive, sure, but I wasn't naive enough to think that someone who had tried to kill us just a few days ago could switch sides so easily.

Then again, that's exactly what happened with Veronique. So I relaxed my guard some. Not that I could have done anything.

"If it's tied to your saliva, how do you kiss someone?"

Dorian shook her head. "Are you serious?"

"It's an honest question," I said as she removed the final cuff. Damn, it felt good to be using my arms and legs again.

"I don't normally kiss people, but I can tell you that I don't explode the fork or melt the glass if I eat or drink, so it has to be intentional. Does that answer your question?"

"I … yeah, that does. Sorry. I'm an idiot."

She cocked her head. "I thought you said you were a writer."

"Same difference?"

Dorian didn't laugh at my joke, but she should have.

Writers are a weird breed of human. If you give them any amount of power, it goes straight to their head, something I've seen in the indie writer community since I became part of it. Suddenly, they're giving out writing advice, or lecturing people on what constitutes good writing, or writing books on writing, or trying to keep up with the famous drinkers of the past.

Shit, even I had let the little bit of fame I got from releasing *How Heavy This Axe?* go to my head, and that was just after fifty sales over a three-week period.

One of the drunker authors I know celebrated after just ten sells in a five-week stretch. The dude got so schwasted he ended up on some country road outside Kansas City riding an ATV with his shirt off screaming about how he was the new William Gibson, until local law enforcement caught up to him.

And don't get me started on writing and drinking. That never ends well. While it has resulted in some of the best books ever written, the lives of those who write them usually pale in comparison to their books.

Me? I'll stick to banging superheroes.

That's one way to put it, Writer Gideon.

Grace? Are you ready to stop pretending to be dead?

I'm still passed out. This is the part of myself I've imprinted on you.

You're kidding me.

"Why are you looking at me like that?" Dorian asked.

"Sorry, voices in my head."

Grace, we need to talk about that. How much longer until you wake up?

I can't predict these types of things.

You did in Stamford ...

Sooner than later. Also, regarding Dorian, I will take a solid look at her and see if her intentions are true. If not, Veronique will kill her.

Hey!

"Should we take a look around the place?" Dorian asked. "That is why you came here, right?"

"Right, but I don't know how we're going to get into Butler's computer if it has a password. I literally know nothing about him."

I took another gander at the headless body. Shouldn't have done that. I started to dry heave and had to go outside to throw up what was left of breakfast.

Just as I had predicted, we'd been in Butler's guest house. Most of it had been gutted and the bottom converted into a workshop, which was where he would have kept us if Dorian hadn't saved our asses.

Dorian led me along the winding path that took us to the back door. We slid the door open, and after making sure there was no toxic gas in the living room and kitchen area – and by no means was this a scientific study; I simply sniffed the air and opened some windows – we headed to the fridge.

"I figured you were thirsty," I told her as I pulled out two ginger ales.

She took a sip and her eyes went wide. "This is really good."

"Definitely some good stuff." I started searching the kitchen for food. I was hungry, and I eventually found some snack bars in a walk-in pantry. I wolfed down two of them, figuring it was good to eat something, especially after what I'd just been through.

We continued upstairs and found that Butler had an entire room dedicated to virtual gaming. He also had a pair of guestrooms, and his master bedroom had been recently cleaned, evident by how perfectly the sheets and blankets were pressed.

Did he have the place cleaned before we came?

Butler really was a weird guy, but he had crossed the wrong people.

I wished I could have learned more from him about this experiment, and how he came to figure it out. It would have been great for *Mutants in the Making 3,* but his sudden death put a damper on that idea. Dorian had killed him the way someone swats a fly; it was almost sad how quickly he died.

I guess it would be better to go that way, having your head cut off – better than getting tortured, shot a couple times, burned to death, or boiled in acid. Personally, if someone gave me a choice of how to die, I would choose to freeze to death.

"What are you thinking about?" Dorian asked.

"Weird ways to die and which I'd pick if given a choice. Sorry, my mind is still, um, spinning a little from what happened back there. Hope you understand. I'm not always this crazy. Scratch that. Yes, I'm usually this crazy, but it comes with the territory."

"And what territory is that?"

"The territory of being a writer? I don't know."

She shrugged. "You sure blame a lot on being a writer."

"It's a sickness for which there is no cure but death."

We checked out the bathroom, which was super nice, and another little study he had adjacent to one of the upstairs bedrooms.

Jackpot.

I couldn't believe my luck. Like my cross-dressing uncle, David Butler liked to print everything out – from email correspondence to GoogleFace maps to just about anything he could find online.

And I meant *anything*. Dude had even printed out porn, as well as some tasteful hentai prints, most notably some *Ladies vs. Butlers!* and *R-15* pics.

"All the info we need is in this room," I told her with a grin.

"You think so?"

"We should just stay here tonight. I'll go through all this and see what I can uncover. We can get on the road tomorrow. I don't know how long we should stay here, but considering that there's a dead body in the guesthouse, I'd like for it to not be very long. In fact, once Grace is well again, I'll probably send her to the neighbors to mindwipe everybody."

"Mindwipe?"

"I don't know how much experience you have on the outside, but I'm guessing you're kind of like Veronique. You live in the facility and if they need you, they send you out. Is that assumption accurate?"

She nodded.

"Well, as you'll probably come to realize, you can't just go around showing off your superpowers out in the real world. People take notice, and as much as I want to expose what's happening, I'd like to not have it done in a twenty-first-century media frenzy kind of way."

Dorian looked at me funny. She really was cute, her black hair framing her face and her 'I'll put a boot in your ass' style. I didn't have much experience with women who looked like her. There weren't many punk rockers in Connecticut.

"What?" I asked after she didn't say anything.

"You're publishing books about this, but you don't want there to be any media attention? How are you going to get more people to know about it? How are you going to get the *right* people to know about it?"

"Those are all valid points, and I'm probably going about this the wrong way," I said.

We took the stairs to the bottom floor where we found Grace and Veronique in the living room, watching us suspiciously. The metal on the floor started to twitch as it lifted into the air.

"She's with us," I told Veronique.

"Grace already explained that to me."

The tension in the room was palpable; I held up my palms. "Let's just keep it cool here. I know you two have fought each other before – "

"Writer Gideon, I think we should order some pizza for Dorian. That would probably make her happy."

All of us looked at Grace in time to see her morphing into David Butler and speaking in his voice. "I sure would like some pizza, but I can't eat any because I can't digest food any longer."

I looked in horror from Grace to the other two superpowereds. Veronique and Dorian both started laughing as Grace did her spot-on impression again.

If all it took was pizza and gruesome jokes to make them happy, then we weren't as bad off as I thought.

Chapter Nineteen: Broken Bird's Nest

"Are there cherry blossoms in Texas?" Grace asked me as we set the pizza on the table. We'd ordered two pies actually, this time from a local place that specialized in Chicago style pizza. I wasn't a big deep-dish man, but I wanted to give them a taste of Chicago.

"I think it's too hot for cherry blossoms," I told her, handing Dorian a plate.

Veronique had already eaten, which was creepy to say considering that her meal consisted of draining Butler's decapitated body. But I suppose a meal is a meal. She'd also had a slice of the deep-dish pizza, which she didn't seem to enjoy.

Grace and Dorian, on the other hand, pretty much finished one whole pie themselves.

There wasn't a lot of banter between them yet, but I figured this would change after Grace and Veronique introduced Dorian to their favorite TV shows. Or vice versa. There was really no telling how Dorian's personality would affect the other two.

One thing we did finally get around to talking about was her teleportation ability. When asked how far she could teleport, her only response had been, "Far."

It was true, she could sketch something and teleport there, but it was difficult, and it had to be an exact replica. This was why she had a smartphone. She would look at pictures on GoogleFace and use them to make her sketches.

Speaking of sketches, Grace had given Dorian's paintbrush back, much to her delight. She explained that using the paintbrush just felt better to her, even though she could technically perform her ability just by licking her finger.

Or licking anything for that matter.

While we'd been waiting for the pizza, she showed us how her saliva could ignite a piece of paper. It was one of the weirdest abilities I'd ever heard of.

Things cooled off the rest of the night. The three watched TV downstairs while I went through Butler's papers. Remembering that Grace could touch objects and know something about their history, I called her up to the room after an hour of going through things, and she started helping me.

"How are you doing?" I asked her. She was in my clothing again, her hair braided over to one side.

"I'm good," she said as she looked through a stack of papers. "We were watching a show about a home in Santa Fe. I really want to visit there."

Pictures of Santa Fe appeared in my head and I immediately recognized them as being transplanted. They were just too fresh for me to have seen or generated them on my own.

"Cool, we'll try to stop there then," I told her.

"Thanks. Maybe there will be cherry blossoms."

"Probably not, but there will be cacti."

Grace approached me and placed a hand on my cheek. "Your beard is getting too crazy," she said sweetly.

"I'll see what I can do about that," I told her with a chuckle. "But writers and beards go hand in hand."

"It looks like a broken bird's nest."

"I guess that's one way to describe it."

She touched the computer table and her eyes flashed white. "I think we'll find something if we keep looking. I have a very good feeling about that."

I sighed as I took her in, admiring her Scandinavian model form, and the way my pants and low-cut top clung to her curves. "You are so interesting to me."

"I think you're interesting too," she said and turned to me, wrapping her arms around my shoulders and leaning in to kiss me. "Want to do it right now?"

"Shit yes I do, but …" I took a deep breath. "We've got to keep searching."

"Fine." As if she'd never initiated the offer in the first place, she returned to her papers. "Have you checked your sales for today?"

"Not yet. Well, I mean this morning I did, but not since. I've been a little preoccupied. I'd also like to talk to Luke and catch him up on what's happened." I'd put my phone on silent and hadn't looked at it in a while.

It took us at least another thirty minutes of going through piles of paper and flirting with each other whenever we got close, but we eventually found something beneath a removable floorboard in the closet: a suitcase sealed with a chain.

"That's an archaic way to seal something, especially for someone who uses databases."

But maybe he was on to something, I thought as I brought the case downstairs to Veronique.

"Think you can open this?"

The chains fell off and I thanked her. Veronique and Dorian were still watching something about rebuilding a home in Santa Fe. Dorian sat with her hand covering her mouth as she awaited the final reveal with rapt attention.

I couldn't help but probe.

"You actually like this, Dorian?"

"What's not to like?" she said without taking her eyes off the television. "I would love to build a house and have the room that I want and everything my way."

"Yes," Veronique said, nodding, "everything your way. Everything everyone's way. That's what all this is about. The only people who won't get their way when we're finished are *them*."

Dorian nodded in agreement. "Gideon told me everything. I still need to think about some things, but I know what you guys are doing is … It's the right thing to do. I remember the others."

"I remember the others too," Veronique said in a low voice.

"Great," I said and headed back upstairs. I secretly wanted them to bond, especially for Veronique's sake, so rather than butt in, I felt it best to leave them alone and go see what Butler was hiding.

Today was proof that things could change very fast if we got sloppy. And there might not be a Dorian in the car next time. Hell, if there hadn't been a Dorian this time, our little narrative would have ended.

I couldn't forget that; I really needed to keep my head down and not do any more stupid shit.

Famous last words.

As soon as I got back to the study, I set the suitcase on the table and opened it to find a single manila envelope that read, 'Facilities.' Inside the envelope were several folders, a treasure trove of information.

There were five main locations, each with their own folder, including the one we had destroyed in New Haven. There was another in New Mexico, two in California, and one in Washington state. Each folder had a series of schematics of the facility, known contractors and food vendors, documents with the acronym AEFL stamped on them, as well as other details such as estimated staff numbers.

"Can you look through all these and save their images to your memory?" I asked Grace.

"Definitely," she said as I handed her the papers.

"We'll go to New Mexico tomorrow – to Santa Fe – and plan our next assault from there. Now that there are three of you, this will be a lot easier."

Boy, did I turn out to be wrong about that.

Of course, there were some sexcapades that night.

Grace and I had to celebrate the fact that we were still alive, and what started out as a cuddle session quickly morphed into both of us pleasuring each other and then going at it, Grace switching her forms as we changed positions.

At one point, we were doing it doggy style and black lines began to stretch across her skin.

"Zebra stripes?" I asked, breathless and losing steam fast.

"Is it okay?" she asked, looking over her shoulder at me. Her face now belonged to that of a famous pop musician.

"It's ... different," I said as I slid in and out of her, watching the zebra pattern on her ass change color.

She got back on top and morphed into Halle Lawrence, considered one of the hottest actresses around. Even odder, she had been in some of the newest X-Men movies playing Jubilee.

I didn't know if Grace had pulled this from my psyche, but I was definitely into it.

"You like that?" she asked, her voice now that of the famous actress. "You want it harder?"

"Sure?"

She started gyrating vigorously, like she was trying to screw in a giant bolt with her hips.

No pun intended.

My proof of writerdom was by no means giant – hell, it was average at best – but the way she was grinding into me made me feel like it was larger, like I was the Dirk Diggler instead of the John Hodgman of sci-fi writers.

Once I finished, I rolled to my side, breathing heavily.

She placed her hand on my chest and curled up next to me. It was a proper ending to a potentially horrendous day.

I was suddenly thirsty, so I put on my shorts and went to the kitchen to get some juice.

Veronique and Dorian were still watching television, the light from the screen casting blue arcs over their faces. They both stared at me as I entered the living room.

"He's thinner than I thought," Dorian finally said, as if I wasn't there at all.

"His clothing is a little bulky. I think he used to be a bit heavier but lost some weight and still has the same clothing from before." Veronique offered me a rare smirk. "You have time for more?"

"More what?" I asked, assuming she couldn't possibly mean what I thought she meant.

Veronique returned her focus to the television, acting as if she hadn't said anything. Dorian simply laughed as she waved me away.

Chapter Twenty: The First Grenade

I decided to cook breakfast the next morning. Butler had plenty of food, so I was able to make a pretty good spread of eggs, bacon, toast, English muffins, and grilled potatoes. I was no Chef Boyardee, but it didn't take much to whip up a decent breakfast, and judging by Grace and Dorian's response, they liked it too.

Veronique, as usual, didn't eat anything. She did, however, enjoy her coffee.

We all sat around the kitchen table, and I showed them my sales for the previous day. Damn, did I like seeing that sales dashboard. I also discovered I'd been selling other books as well, most notably *How Heavy This Axe?* which gave me the impression it may experience a comeback.

By the mercy of the gods, fuck yeah!

Naturally, having an open laptop led to us watching some funny TwitchTubeRed videos that involved cats.

"It would be so nice to own a cat," Grace said. "I would train it to speak."

"Train it to speak?" Dorian considered that for a moment. "I mean, I suppose you could do something like that."

"I never tried communicating with an animal," the telepath said, "but I believe it is possible. Maybe we can walk around the neighborhood later and find an animal. I would love to try this."

"Sounds like that would be a pretty funny trip to go on," I said. "What about you, Veronique, you into it?"

Veronique reached for a single piece of bacon, examined it, and took a bite. Her eyebrows rose, and she nodded. "It would be nice to get out," she said and reached for a second piece.

I went to the kitchen and brought back more grilled potatoes, dishing them out on their plates, listening as Grace played a video of a baby pug getting tickled.

The window shattered as a grenade sailed into the living room, spewing smoke as it bounced off the sofa.

A trained soldier, Veronique's first response was to strip every bit of metal she could from any object in the room and fling it toward the back windows, blasting out a ton of glass and letting in more air from outside.

Then I heard the helicopter.

"Get Gideon!" Veronique shouted to Grace as she focused on the attack point, waiting for whoever had struck to make their next move.

The next move came in a wave of bullets, all of which were stopped in midair.

"Now!" she yelled.

I was just starting to duck when Grace grabbed my hand and pushed me toward the garage. One glance over my shoulder and I saw Dorian teleport away just as more bullets cut into the living room.

"We can't leave Veronique," I said stupidly to Grace, my voice partially muffled by the noise around us. Just as she had done at the hotel in Stamford, Veronique turned the floating bullets back toward the helicopter, but she didn't release them yet.

More smoke grenades soared into the living room and were quickly tossed out by Veronique. She had the look of a mad conductor on her face, waiting for the helicopter to get into position so she could unleash her metal orchestra.

And release it she did. As the bird finally got into view, she hurled all the waiting bullets – hundreds of them – at its windows. They plinked ineffectively off the glass, doing nothing to stop the chopper.

A determined look on her face, Veronique pulled the railings off the windows and spun them toward the helicopter blades. Upon impact, the machine tilted sideways. The pilot tried to right it, which only tilted it in the other direction before it finally spun down.

Just as the helicopter crashed into the back yard, the front door of the home exploded open.

"Gideon, listen to me, you have to get down and get away!" Grace grabbed the sides of my head and looked me in the eye. "Do not make me take over your mind! Just take cover, and let us try to handle this," she said, speaking fast. Her grip around my skull tightened, her thumbs digging into my temples. "I'll be here, always."

"Got it, got it, got it," I said as she led me down the hallway and into the garage, where I found a place to hide. I could hear Veronique tearing metal off walls and ripping apart anything else that had metal in it in an effort to stop the onslaught. This was followed by the sound of more bullets.

The garage was large, and there were a couple motorcycles in the right carport. As Grace left me, two men in black body armor burst inside, their guns trained on her.

And then they became our men.

Their eyes flashed white, and they returned to the melee, now fighting on our side.

Flip as many as you can, I thought to Grace.

I felt like a coward for hiding in the garage; this seemed to be the perennial problem for me regarding our little association. I had no powers, aside from the fact I could write quickly, which was anything but a power.

Can you imagine a superhero whose power it was to write quickly? That one wouldn't even have made it to the desk of Stan Lee's assistant's assistant.

So, like a coward, or possibly like anyone with no combat training and no weapon skills who was fully aware they were in the middle of an assault lead by people with *real* abilities, I hid behind the goddamn recycling container.

Whatever was going on outside sounded like an Iraq war movie. I was shocked that MercSecure and the FCG had brought this much firepower to a west Austin neighborhood.

Another helicopter announced itself and I heard more weapons being fired, the creak and crunch of metal, men yelling as their own team shot back at them.

The garage door caved in and I almost jumped out of my skin.

I tried to get as low as I could, and I even entertained the idea of putting the recycling container over my head, which was stupid in retrospect but seemed totally viable in the moment, but it worked in *Metal Gear Solid!*

As I peeked around the side of my hiding spot, I caught a glimpse of who had punched in the garage door.

Angel.

He looked nearly the same as before: well-built, brown hair tangled in his face, lantern jaw, and dark eyes. But there was something different about him too.

His skin looked bad, which I attributed to the explosion on the rooftop of the Rose-Lyle facility. He had survived it, he'd healed, but it had still left its mark.

Angel took a menacing step in my direction, his hands at his sides like he was going to wring my neck. And that was when one of the motorcycles lifted into the air and cracked him in the side of the head.

I looked back at the garage door to see Grace standing there, her eyes blazing white, almost as if they were on fire with white-hot energy. I'd never seen her look that way before, her power curling in wispy tendrils of energy off her face. It was eerie.

Angel pushed himself off the ground, turned to Grace, and flew at her like a torpedo.

"Grace!" I cried as they collided and tore through a wall.

Seconds later, Angel was tossed back into the room.

I'd had enough. As stupid as it was, I got to my feet, dusted my pants off, and turned to Angel, ready for anything. I wanted nothing more than to bash his face in for attacking Grace.

Of course, Angel was already standing by the time I reached him.

"So, we meet again, Gideon," he said, his dark eyes locked on me.

197

"That's right, motherfucker." I realized cursing had no effect on him, but it did make me feel tougher. "Yeah, we meet again."

My voice was shaky. I could barely feel my hands even though they were clenched into fists, and there was a weird sensation happening in my chest and stomach.

But I wasn't going to let true fear stand in my way.

"Do I need to ask this?" Angel pushed his hair out of his face. "Do you really think a normal like you has any chance of stopping someone like me? Do you *really* think that? Because the way you're standing, it seems like you've actually bought into that myth."

Rather than answer, I ran toward him with my fist drawn, aiming for his chin.

A jolt of energy swept me to the side, and I turned just in time to see Grace standing behind the wall that had been blown away, her body framed by bits of pink insulation and wooden framework.

"No!" I shouted as Angel flew at her again. This time he didn't tackle her; instead, he grabbed her and they both rocketed through the ceiling.

Oblivious to the action around me – and the fact that there were loads of security vehicles, two helicopters, men with guns, you name it – I ran out the garage door, my focus on Angel and Grace as they sailed higher into the sky.

Like an airplane petering out, Grace would use her power to toss Angel off his trajectory, but he'd regain it and continue upward until they were hardly a spark on the horizon … until they disappeared completely.

I fell to my knees, and just as I did, three armed men approached me with their weapons drawn.

"Get on the ground! On the ground! Hands behind your head! We *will* engage! Get on the ground, now!"

I put my hands behind my head like the men told me to. Any courage or confidence I had was up in the sky right now, going god only knew how high.

I watched with utter anguish as Grace and Angel spiraled back down. Angel made a crater as he hit the ground, Grace slung over his shoulder. I didn't know what he'd done to her up there, but she was completely out.

Looking left, I saw Dorian standing with her paintbrush in her mouth, blood streaked across her forehead and cheeks, Veronique at her feet. Dorian lifted Veronique by the hair to show me her blood-smeared face, eyes rolled into the back of her head.

"You fucking bitch!" I scrambled back to my feet. "You double-crossing dirty … fuck! Fuck!" I cried out as a black bag was placed over my head. My hands and legs were zip-tied and I was roughly pushed back down. Still in shock, I stumbled forward and tried to run.

Nope. A hand grabbed me and tossed me down again. I felt the muzzle of a gun press into the back of my neck.

"Stay still," a man growled as the weapon dug into my flesh.

I was completely distraught. I felt like sobbing, I felt like raging, I felt like screaming and trying to wake from this terrible nightmare. I could barely stand when they pulled me up.

My knees buckled, but the men holding me made sure I could walk.

I had been so focused on my own shock and rage that I hadn't even heard the helicopter land. Sure, I felt the wind beating against the black bag over my face, but I was hardly cognizant of the fact that the chopper was there until I was shoved inside it.

It would be my first helicopter ride, and it was taken completely blindfolded.

Chapter Twenty-One: Mother

Grace! I screamed inside my head as the helicopter lifted into the air. My chest constricted and I felt sobs welling up in my throat, but I suppressed them. Dorian had betrayed us; she'd led them straight to us and we had fallen into their trap, the second trap we'd fallen into over the last two days.

I should have known better ... Please, Grace, say something to me, tell me you can hear me. Please.

Nothing, dammit. Nothing.

The helicopter landed about ten minutes later and I was led away from the beating chopper blades. From what I could tell – which was hard to process considering my delirium – I was scanned into one room, then scanned into a second, handed off to another person, and finally led down a long hallway.

"Welcome home," a man said as he removed the black fabric covering my head.

He was a grizzly mercenary in chiseled body armor with gray lettering that read 'MercSecure' across the chest. Bald, with a neatly trimmed mustache, and sharp green eyes. A paid killer.

There was another man with him who wore a balaclava, not unlike a Mexican DEA agent. He held a cattle prod, just in case I got out of hand.

"Where am I?" I managed to ask, my eyes adjusting to the light.

"Move to the right so I can take off your zip cuffs." I did as instructed, and he used a razor to cut through the plastic.

The two men left, and the door locked on its own.

I was in a space no larger than a closet, a white room with a metal bed and a single sheet on it.

Some type of military holding cell.

There was a toilet completely made of plastic, and just seeing it made something in my stomach turn. At first, I thought I was going to vomit, but it turned out to be number two.

So there I was, in some secret military prison, shitting and sobbing.

Some fucking life.

What was worse, the space was very small, so when I finished, it stank, and I had to wallow in my own filth, *literally* – no matter how many times I flushed the toilet, the smell lingered.

I hated myself and my weak digestive system.

I hated the bright lights glaring down on me, the camera in the corner …

I glanced around the room, and a sense of utter savageness came over me. *Nothing to break the camera with.*

All I could do was pace back and forth, aware they were watching me, reeling as pure hopelessness washed over me.

I don't know how long I paced for – minutes, hours, no idea – but my feet hurt when I finally finished. Time had come to a standstill for me, and since there was no light coming in from outside, I had no idea if it was morning or night.

It has to be night, I thought. I pressed my ear to the door, hoping to get a sense of what was happening in the hallway outside.

Utter silence.

Grace! Grace! Grace! Grace!

"Wake up," I whispered, sobs welling up in my chest.

Ashamed to have the camera watching me cry like a little bitch, I sat on the floor and turned my back to it, brought my knees up and wrapped my arms around them as I let it all out.

There were legal words for the trouble I was in, but I preferred the colloquial term: I was fucked, royally fucked. My life was as good as over.

I have to get word out, I thought, staring at the white wall. *I have to let people know I've been captured.*

Then again, who would really give a shit if MercSecure got me? Sure, I had some readers, but I'd be long gone, sent to a black site in Egypt or Timbuktu by the time they learned what had happened to me. My parents? They didn't even know I'd left Connecticut. Luke? Definitely, but he was thousands of miles away.

Grace and Veronique. They'd care, but they were just as screwed as I was.

So I decided to rest. I still had that. I still had my dreams and my imagination. I don't know how long I ended up sleeping for, but the dreams I had were worth it. Dreams of Grace, Veronique, all of us in Louisiana, driving along the highway, sharing a meal in Austin, the hotel room in Stamford, the cherry blossoms.

The good times.

Never mind the fact that unknown enemies waited on the periphery, ready to strike and stop us from being together. Ready to retire Grace and Veronique and bury me.

Never mind those enemies.

Gideon, wake up.

Grace's voice was far away, a distant whisper, a gasp of fresh air.

Grace? I sat up, suddenly on high alert.

No response; it had likely been a figment of my imagination. I slapped my cheeks a few times. *Get it together.*

A slot on the door opened up and a pair of eyes peered in. "Get up, or we'll get you up," a man growled.

"Why?" I asked.

"Because she's ready to meet you now. Get on the floor, on your knees, with your hands behind your back."

She? I did as instructed. Once I was in place, two men came into the room. One immediately cuffed me and once they pulled me to my feet, still facing away from the door, the second one bagged my head.

"Is it really that big of a deal if I see things?" I asked them as they shoved me into the hallway. "I'm already fucked."

"Looks like you're finally starting to understand what's going on here. Now keep your mouth shut," the first man said. I recognized his voice. He was the one with the mustache and green eyes who'd put me in the holding cell to begin with.

They walked me through a few rooms and eventually we stopped. After a series of beeps that sounded like some type of scan, we were allowed into another room. Still blindfolded, I was shoved into a chair, and my cuffs were attached to a chain on the floor.

At least that was what it sounded like they were doing.

"She'll be here in a moment."

The fuckers left me in the room, my head still covered.

I sat there a good fifteen minutes, my thoughts lost in the black fabric covering my face, my shoulders hunched back slightly due to the way they'd cuffed me.

The door opened and I heard the click-clack of high heels.

"You may remove his head covering," a woman said, "and leave us alone."

The black bag was ripped off my head and my eyes twitched as they adjusted to the light. Like my cell, the room was completely white with no features, aside from the table and two chairs in the center.

But that was beside the point.

The woman sitting before me was tall and thin, with brown hair, high cheekbones, and hazel eyes.

A briefcase sat on the table between us.

"Mother?" I asked after the security guard exited the room. My throat was parched and clenched up as I spoke.

"I see you are aware what they call me." She crossed one leg over the other and shook her head. "I still can't believe you're the one who did it."

"Did it?"

"Turned 'Grace,' as you call her. And somehow Veronique too. I have to admit, I'm surprised someone like you would be able to do that."

"Someone like me?"

She casually wiped her hands together. "You're nothing; you have no influence, you're a nobody, and you certainly don't have any special abilities. We've already discovered that. You don't have the propensity to be superpowered."

I bit my lip. I honestly didn't know what to say to her, and my only response at that moment was to yell for Grace in my head.

Grace! Grace! Please hear me!

Grace is not listening, Mother said in my head.

I gasped. "You have the same powers?"

Then I remembered Veronique saying something about this. I soon found out she'd also been right about Mother's other powers.

Mother squeezed the edge of the table, and the metal began to morph under the pressure.

Snap!

She broke off a corner of the table. Blood oozed from her fingertips as she began crumpling the metal the way one would ball up a piece of paper. Blood smeared on the sharp metal ball she was constructing. Once she was finished, she threw it over her shoulder and showed me the palm of her hand.

Not only had the cut healed, but the blood had reabsorbed. Now there were just slight outlines of red in the lines on her palm.

I never thought much about how a healer would work in real life, and this would have been a great introduction … if it weren't for the fact that I was being held in some type of black site and the woman sitting before me wanted to kill me, the urge evident in her dark eyes that reminded me of Veronique.

"I get it," I finally told her.

"I don't think you do. Your actions have severely taken our operation off track and caused a major distraction. I'm expecting. The new subjects will be born soon."

Mother wore a tight black dress under a lab coat, and there was no indication that she was with child.

She smirked at the look of disbelief on my face. "You really are one of the stupidest men I have ever come across. Of course I am not *physically* pregnant. You must have known that Grace and Veronique were grown in a lab. How could you not know that?"

A feeling of animosity bubbled at the back of my throat. "You know what? Why don't you lighten the fuck up?" I snapped.

"Excuse me?"

He's back! I don't know how long 'Breaking Bad' Gideon would be around, but I let him say his piece.

"You haul me on a helicopter to wherever the hell we are, put me in a cell for god knows how long, and suddenly you expect me to piece together small hints based on facts I can hardly comprehend? You're a psychic, you know what's going on in my mind." I leaned forward like a badass. "So why don't you fucking read it?"

If I could have given myself a high five and a slap on the ass at that point, I would have. But that's in retrospect. What mother did next was one of the more unpleasant things I'd experienced up until that point.

A whispery scream rang out inside my head.

At first it was subtle, static even, but then it increased in volume, followed by something that sounded like a million people biting into a million apples all at once, and then the sound of metal scraping against metal, only amplified.

The cacophony continued, compounding exponentially until I cried out in pain.

"I guess you aren't as tough as you think. Funny, you put on the tough guy act with Angel once or twice and you think you're one of us." She laughed. "You actually think you have power. Don't you realize what's going on here – what's been happening since you kidnapped Grace and Veronique? It's *their* power, not yours. *You are nothing.*" And then, to drive home the insult, she added, "You're not even a good writer."

She knows everything that's going on in your head, she knows your weaknesses, she knows your darkest secrets, I reminded myself.

That's right, Gideon and this ends now, Mother thought to me.

"Ends?"

She walked over to my side of the table, her heels again clicking on the hard floor.

"I'm most pissed about Grace," she said, leaning over me. It felt like every hair on my body had stood up, grown two inches, and was trying to pry itself from my skin in an effort to escape her.

"My little Grace; she would have been the most powerful of them all, and you had to go and destroy her mind, take her virginity, show her the life of a pathetic normal like you. I might have let you live if it had only been Veronique. I never liked her much. Too cocky. But Grace … I loved Grace."

"Loved her?" I looked up at her in astonishment. My lips quivered as I took a deep breath to calm myself. "You kept Grace in solitary confinement her *entire* life. You're a piece of shit, you crazy fuck. You didn't love her." Anxiety made it hard to get the words out without sounding like slobbering coward. "You … you are the scum of the earth – you and all these fucking people here!"

Her hand wrapped around my neck.

"It's funny, isn't it?" she snarled. "Even if I weren't superpowered, I could kill you right now. My abilities will only make your death that

210

much quicker. And you know what, Gideon Caldwell? I think killing you would be one of the highlights of my year. Do you know how much bullshit I've had to go through because of what you did in New Haven?"

Fight back, Gideon.

Grace?

Mother tightened her grip around my neck as I called Grace's name again inside my head. *Grace! Please!*

Fight back, Gideon!

Her voice was miles away, light years away, in a completely different galaxy. Yet I could hear her perfectly, I could feel her, I knew she was there.

As Mother squeezed my neck even harder, I jerked my feet back and somehow managed to fall sideways, even with my wrists still chained to the floor. She kicked me in the stomach, brought her foot back, and kicked me again.

I was wheezing now and tasted blood in my mouth.

"It seems your little cries for help have woken Grace up. She imprinted on you. I can't *believe* she imprinted on you. *You!* She's only able to imprint on one person and she chooses you!"

I still wasn't sure what it meant that Grace had imprinted on me. The first time she'd used that word, I thought it meant that she could just speak inside my head, or that we had bonded over sex. It was shortly after we'd become intimate that she first mentioned the term.

But could it mean something more?

Mother grabbed me by the back of the neck and lifted me up, seat and all. "You really think this is going to work out in your favor somehow, don't you?"

"I don't know what I think, lady, I'm just taking it one day at a time."

I wish I could have been Clint Eastwood saying that last line, but I was Gideon Caldwell, and it didn't sound nearly as tough as it should have.

Mother offered me a placid smile. "I guess I shouldn't be so angry. We have you now. We have Veronique and Grace, and neither of them will be around much longer. Grace, we still need for a little while, at least until we can replicate her, but as for Veronique … goodbye."

I opened my mouth to speak, but nothing came out. Macho Gideon had quietly let himself out of the room; Writer Gideon was back and ready to piss his pants.

"How would you like to die? Have you ever thought about that?" she asked as she walked around the table and sat again. "I've been thinking of how we should get rid of you. We have complete jurisdiction over you, and there really is no point in trying you before a court of your peers. Or even a military court for that matter. It takes too much time. That's one thing you'll know about me – well, you won't know me for very long, but you'll recognize this about me for now: I don't like to waste time."

I swallowed hard.

"I suppose putting you in a room with Angel and letting him finish the job would be good. But first, we have to get those books unpublished. I'm not stupid enough to think that the people who have downloaded it already won't still have them on their devices, but at least we can prevent future people from reading it. So, let's do that."

"What?" I mumbled.

She pulled a small laptop out of the briefcase on the table. "Do I need to say it again? Books. Unpublished. I figured you could help me log in and do it."

The laptop powered up and Mother turned it around to face me.

"Oh, that's right, you can't use your hands. Well, I'll do it for you then."

She moved to my side of the table again and placed a hand on my shoulder. Her eyes flashed white and …

Something *came over* me.

It felt like someone was playing tug-o-war with my brain matter. Mother's power would advance, then another force would respond, pulling it back the other way.

213

The shriek of a thousand violins playing different notes all at once came with each pull of my psyche. The noise would dissipate and then reappear as it moved to the other side of my skull cavity.

By the time she took her hand off my shoulder, I was completely exhausted, my thoughts like hot knives as they began to repopulate. I gasped, looked up at her, and saw her white eyes fizzle out.

"In that case…" She closed the laptop and tucked it under her arm. The door popped open, and Angel stepped into the room.

Chapter Twenty-Two: Incest is Best?

"He's being difficult," she told Angel as he approached. She placed a hand on his cheek, and Angel moved in to kiss her. It was a long kiss, a fucking gross and sloppy movie kiss, and by the end of it, I was left wondering what the shit was going on.

And that was when bad boy Gideon decided to return. I didn't know what it was about Angel that triggered the ballsy version of myself, but my mouth came unhinged pretty quickly. "So that's what went wrong with you," I told the scar-faced fucker.

"Come again?" he asked as Mother stepped aside.

"You're her offspring – lab-grown, sure, but you're related to her."

"Yes?"

Mother shook her head. "You wouldn't understand my relationship – nor my fascination – with Angel."

I laughed. "Maybe, but I do know the definition of incest, and now I know the definition of *motherfucker.*"

Angel dropped his hand to Mother's ass and patted it. "Should I handle him for a bit?"

She smiled. "Sure, but don't kill him yet. I still need to deal with his little self-publishing empire. Keep his brain intact. And don't beat up his face too much. That's gruesome."

She left the room, heels clacking against the floor as she walked away. Just the sound of that pissed me off.

Angel turned to me and cracked his knuckles.

I glared at him, still not sure where my sudden confidence was coming from but running with it.

"I have to admit, Gideon," he said, walking over to the table. "You've made it much further than I thought you would."

He placed a single hand under the table and flipped it up, smacking me in the face. My nose gushed blood, and before I could try to wipe it on my sleeve, he grabbed the chain linking me to the floor and broke it in half. Then he gripped the back of my chair and threw me into the wall. The impact knocked the wind out of me, and my chin hit the floor as the chair skidded out from under me.

Hang on, Gideon.

I didn't know if the voice was Grace's or mine. I was too shaken up, especially when Angel wrapped one arm under mine, and tossed me up to the ceiling. I didn't break through or anything, but fuck, if cracking my head on the hard surface didn't rattle my brain.

"More?" he asked, when I crashed back down.

Wheezing now, I still wasn't able to get a full breath in. My body ached, and my nose continued gushing blood. I spit some of it out; a graffiti splatter of crimson.

"Are you ready to help Mother, or should I continue?"

"You still call her Mother even though you're fucking her?" I considered that for a moment. America once had a vice president who did that. "Okay, that's okay, I guess." I wiped more blood on my sleeve.

"You don't know when to shut up, do you?" He put his foot on my throat. "Last chance."

"That's enough, Angel," Mother said, re-entering the room. "We'll have to work on Grace before we work on him. She's the one preventing me from going any further."

"Are you sure I can't do it?" he asked, his foot pressing harder into my neck.

"That's a primitive way to kill him, darling." She moved over to us and took his hand. Angel removed his foot and stepped beside her, wrapping an arm around her waist. "I promise you'll be the one to kill him, but not before I get the information I need. Think of a better way though; something that will last longer and hurt more. Snapping his neck is too quick."

"You two are some sick fucks," I whispered through the blood dripping from my nose.

217

Mother turned to me. "He's good with insults, but not much else."

She walked over to the door and knocked on it twice.

"To be continued," she told me as the mustached merc entered the room with a black bag. He moved over to me, sat me up, and shoved it over my face.

Another man joined him and together, they took me back to my cell.

Once I was there, they had me stand with my back to the door so they could uncuff me. They kept the black covering on my head and left the room, slamming the door behind them.

I took the covering off and found a tray of food on the bed – an apple with a bite taken out of it, and a piece of bread with a loogie on top.

There was also a glass of water that looked suspiciously yellow, so I poured it out, flushed the toilet twice, and waited for the toilet water to fill up.

Yep. I drank toilet water and used some of it to clean the blood off my lips and face.

It wasn't too bad and since I was hungry, I devoured the apple and even ate around the glob of snot and spit on the bread.

I was probably going to die soon.

"You are probably going to die soon."

There, I said it. And I was ninety percent certain at the time that it was going to happen. So the question then became: How did I want to go out?

Gideon from a few weeks ago – hell, Gideon from a few hours ago – would have curled up on the bed and cried until he had to drink more toilet water to replenish his tears.

"And what good would that do?"

So, I decided to accept my fate. If this was my last day on earth, and I was likely to die today or tomorrow at the hands of a superpowered motherfucker …

I laughed.

Angel really was a *superpowered motherfucker*, in every sense of the phrase.

That got my author brain rolling.

Would that make an interesting story? I thought as I lay back on the bed. A superpowered child who came from the seed of a kinda hot – not going to lie, not on my deathbed – woman who groomed him into becoming her sex object.

It would definitely rile some folks, that was for sure. If the sexes had been reversed, it would almost be a gymnast in a controversial Olympic coach biopic. But making it a woman as the older figure changed the dynamics.

Oedipus as a superpowered guy struggling with the fact that he's tagging his mom?

Damn, I thought as I lay there, *I really need to get this idea down.*

I'd definitely add stats to the book and some type of game mechanics. That was my schtick. Maybe every mother he fucked gave him more power and he could level up.

"That's one powerful motherfucker," I whispered, cracking up at my own joke. What I wouldn't give to share the idea with Luke, just so he could give me a WTF-are-you-talking-about face.

I could see it now.

The book begins from young Angel's perspective. Let's call him Angel Rex, in reference to Oedipus, of course. I'd put a *Hamlet* reference in there too, but shit, I would have probably lost half my audience on just the Oedipus reference.

Or maybe.

I didn't know how many sci-fi fantasy readers are big into archetypes.

Anyway, it didn't matter. This was my vision, and it would start with young Angel training.

I pictured him training, kicking ass, beating up MercSecure, then mommy dearest coming and patting him on the head, rubbing the muscles on his neck and chest, maybe putting some conditioner in his hair.

She waits until he's older, of course, … well, old enough to get a decent-sized boner. So, let's say fourteen. No, fifteen – don't want to gross people out too much or turn them away.

"This is such a stupid story," I whispered.

Go on …

Nope, not Grace's voice, just my own dumb ass.

Plot the story, escape from here.

"Grace?" I opened my eyes and looked around the room. "Are you there?"

Are you there? I thought.

Please, just think something for me.

It *was* her!

Grace!

Please, just think something for me.

I got a sudden feeling that they were hurting her, somewhere near me, and that my crazy thoughts were soothing her in some way.

In that case …

I envisioned a scene in which Angel first learns to fly. He's sitting with Mother in his room – no, her room, on her bed, and it's the first time she touches him.

"You are one bad mother …" I whispered.

Well, fifteen-year-old Angel gets a raging boner and that's just about the time his flight abilities take shape. The superpowered motherfucker comes with just one touch on his inner thigh and blasts off Mother's bed, through the ceiling, and out into the stratosphere.

He hovers up there for a bit, looking at all the lights below and realizing he didn't have pants on and that he'd made a sticky mess of his pubes.

Got to trim those, Angel thinks.

Yeah, I'd definitely put that line in, something a little funny and awkward.

This is such a funny story.

Grace again.

It's dedicated to you, Grace.

So I thought some more about the story, hoping to entertain her as best I could.

Who was the bad guy? Child Protective Services? For sure. They have guys in black – because what police state doesn't have guys in black? – trying to take him from Mother. Thing is, CPS is also planning to exploit him, turn him into a worker at the secret gloryhole they run in Malaysia.

Why Malaysia?

And why a gloryhole? No idea. Just seems like a good twist.

As for the location, it could be any Southeast Asian country, could be anywhere. Just want to keep it interesting, right?

So CPS is trying to take Angel away from Mother so they can turn him into a sex worker. *That's it!* CPS, while they seem like the good guys, are actually the bad guys. The twist!

And where are the stats? I imagine Luke asking me.

Well, like I said, he gets a point for every mother he fucks, but since he only fucks his own mother, she has to change forms to trick the game into giving him stats.

Wait, the game doesn't know?

Dammit, Luke, I'm making this up as I go along, don't complicate things for me!

And she's a shifter?

You bet your ass she's a shifter, as shifter as American Pie, whatever that means. Just like Grace.

Just like you, Grace.

I yawned. I didn't know how I could get so tired working out my own story, but I was definitely starting to drift off. I stretched on the hard bed, trying to get comfortable.

Damn, did my body hurt.

I was just about to imagine how Angel frees himself from CPS and is rewarded with a little ass play from Mother when I saw a flash in the room.

Dorian appeared, a look of abject fear on her face.

"It worked," she said.

"Dorian?" I gulped, unsure if I was dreaming or not.

"We need to go, Gideon, now."

"Why should I –"

But Dorian didn't answer. She reached out, touched my hand, and we disappeared.

Chapter Twenty-Three: Back and Forth

Note to reader: teleportation is not for the faint of heart. It literally feels as if every fiber from your body is being stripped away, shot through some type of intergalactic portal, gargled by a guy who's missing a couple of teeth, and reassembled on the other side.

All this to say, Dorian and I materialized in what looked like a hotel room.

My first reaction was to run to the nearest restroom and vomit up the apple and bread I ate earlier. But I kept it down, my urge to vomit replaced by sheer anger at Dorian.

"You betrayed us!" I shouted, my voice wavering. No, I hadn't put two and two together yet, and I still wasn't sure if this was real or not.

It could be a dream, I thought. *It must be a dream. Kill her!*

Dorian raised an eyebrow at me. "I just saved you."

"I know what I saw," I told her, raising my fists. Not that trying to strike her would do any good; still, the gesture felt right.

"Try it," she said, lifting her paintbrush to her mouth. "But before you do, think about what I just did."

"I ... I ..."

Maybe she was right. Why would she have teleported me out of there if ...

"But I know what I saw," I finally said, lowering my fists.

We were definitely in a hotel room; another look around confirmed that for me. But I didn't know where the hotel was, and weakness from either the teleportation or the fact that Angel had pretty much handed me my ass had started to set in.

"Just hear me out," Dorian said. She took a step closer to me. There was something behind her dark eyes that I instantly trusted, even though every instinct in my body was screaming for me not to believe her.

I saw what she'd done. End of story.

"I know what you're thinking."

"You don't know anything."

"You don't play the best tough guy, did you know that?" She let her ponytail out and studied me a moment. Then she flexed her fingers, widening the elastic band and swiftly tied her hair into a new ponytail. She was still in her post-goth punk rock getup: a leather jacket, black shorts over fishnet tights, and black boots.

"I go back and forth between being convincingly aggressive and not at all," I said with a sigh. "But that's beside the point. What happened back at Butler's house?"

"It was Veronique and Grace's idea. We'd already discussed it."

"Discussed what? No one told me shit!" I kicked the bed for emphasis, which only served to hurt my foot. Damn, I wish I had superhuman strength.

"If for some reason they came for us, I was to act like I was on their side, that you three had kidnapped me. And that's what I did. When they start attacking us, I teleported to one of the upstairs rooms. I waited for a moment and then burst out through the window. Why did you think I was bloody?"

Was she bloody? I tried to remember if I'd seen blood on her but couldn't recall. The only thing I could remember was Veronique's bloody face as Dorian presented her to me.

"Why did you burst out of the window?"

"I thought it would look more convincing. As soon as I got to the ground, I started fighting on their side. There was nothing I could do."

"Why didn't you teleport us out of there?"

"Do you know how much energy it takes for me to teleport? I can only do it in spurts, and by spurts, I mean it's usually one or two times before I get burned out."

I thought of her stats. "I wonder if that's something I can adjust …"

Then another thought came to me: All of my stuff – all of my life, pretty much – had been at Butler's place, which meant they'd most likely taken it as evidence.

That meant they could get my laptop ...

But if that was the case, they wouldn't have needed *me*.

It must have been destroyed in the attack. It made sense; there'd been walls crumbling down and explosions inside the house.

My laptop had been on the table. I remembered that happy moment we were having when we were attacked. It was like we were a family or something, and then suddenly the world exploded, and the men came running in with their weapons, and the helicopters and the flying motherfucker appeared.

Damn, it felt good calling Angel a motherfucker.

I wasn't normally that vulgar, but the nickname just fit so damn well.

I sat down on the bed as Dorian continued her story. "I promised them I would get you out first. That I would go for Veronique next, and then Grace."

"Are you serious?"

The look of conviction on her face told me that she was indeed serious. The thing was, why would she go to all this effort just to double cross me again? It didn't seem viable.

I relaxed a little. Boy, did I relax a little. I'd been on swords and razor blades for the last twenty-four hours at least.

"I think you could use some rest."

"I need some food and a shower and … I need a phone."

"I still have a phone," she said.

I asked for her phone, and she pulled it out of one of her jacket pockets. I turned it off and took the battery out.

"Why did you do that?"

"If they haven't already found out that I'm gone, they'll find out soon. And they'll know there's only one person on this earth who could get me out of a room like that, and it's you."

She laughed a little. "There are more than one."

"More than one who can teleport?"

"More people with superpowers who could probably get you out. That's what this is all about, right? You're going to expose them. Grace told me, you told me, and even Veronique believed it. Veronique never believed in anything when I knew her; she was a nihilist's nihilist."

"I don't know if I'd call her a nihilist, but she was definitely pretty stiff when we first met. Okay, so let's see where we are. I need to get my bearings straight."

She sat on the bed next to me. "I'm guessing you have questions."

"I have a ton of questions, but I'll keep it simple. First of all, where are we?"

"Austin."

"And where did we come from? I mean, where is the military base that we are at?"

"Camp Mabry, also in Austin."

"And Grace and Veronique are there as well?"

Dorian nodded. "But I don't know how long they'll be there. We need to get Veronique first; that's what they told me to do."

"When were you all having this conversation? I don't seem to remember it ever happening. And why Veronique first?"

"We had it while you were upstairs going through the guy's stuff after I killed him. And Veronique is more helpful to us than Grace would be, that's why."

"I beg to differ, and I'm not saying I'm having déjà vu here, but I literally just went through this a couple days back."

"When through what?"

"A breakout. We rescued Veronique. Just Grace and me."

"Did you rescue her from a military facility?"

"No, not exactly, but paramilitary forces showed up. And that's another thing – I don't want to have to rescue anyone again after this. I think it's taken twenty years off my life trying to bust people out. We have to be smarter. We're not supposed to be captured by these people."

"If we had been smarter, we would have left Butler's place."

It dawned on me at that very moment: It was Butler's death that triggered the assault. *It had to be.*

If Dorian didn't say anything …

"Before we continue, I just need to clarify something. Was it Butler who triggered that assault? Did it have something to do with his death?"

She nodded. "We should have thought about that. The men I left with were talking about it, and yes, he had a fingerprint scanner that he pressed every night near his bed. He didn't press it, and that was supposed to trigger an alarm and a release of all the data he'd accumulated. But the lawyer who held the data for Butler was also working for them – for Mother. So the lawyer told them about it, and they made their assault."

I exhaled slowly. I had no idea how this was going to play out, but our prospects looked worse with each passing minute.

231

"I have a little money in cash," she told me. "Actually, I have a lot of money. One of the things I did when I went upstairs during the attack was take some of the cash you guys were hoarding. I think it's about five thousand dollars, maybe more." She reached into her pocket and took out a large roll of cash bound with a rubber band.

"Good, that should help some."

"I need some time to rest before I teleport again, and you look like …" She smiled, showing her dimples as she did so. "You know what? You look bad, but I'm surprised you're even alive. I wanted to come sooner. I even tried to teleport there and back, but I hit the wrong cell, and I had to recharge. It takes a lot more, if not all, of my energy to teleport. If I could just paint dinosaurs with gun arms out of kinetic energy and send them off, I would; I'd be able to do that all day. But teleportation is hard."

"How will we get Veronique then?"

"She'll be easier to get than you because you were in a long holding block. There were other cells, and as I said, I exhausted myself checking some of them. Back and forth. It was brutal. The hardest part of my teleportation was getting into the complex, and then I moved through some of the cells and got out before I lost energy. I got lucky this last time when I found you."

"You aren't the only one," I said, cracking a grin at her. "Angel had just beat the living shit out of me, and Mother and Angel were planning to kill me not long after."

I explained to her what had happened. (Don't you just love it when books do that so you don't have to reread everything?)

Dorian's face scrunched up. "Damn, I didn't know they were fucking."

"You and me both. Anyway, they wanted to get into my publishing account and take down my books. But they weren't able to because Grace intervened. I don't know how she did it, and …" I took a deep breath. "Never mind. First, Veronique. That's our first target."

"She'll be easy to find. In fact, I already know where she is on the base. They only have one holding cell made of plastic and it was recently constructed just for her." She stuck her paintbrush in her mouth and quickly made a schematic of the base, drawing a big 'X' where they were holding Veronique. Her map fizzled as it moved to the wall and burnt into the wallpaper, filling the room with a sickly sweet stench. "We'll get her out; just give me a couple hours of downtime."

Chapter Twenty-Four: YOLO

The first thing I did was take a long, hot shower. It wasn't the nicest hotel, and I hadn't yet looked outside to see where we were exactly. Not quite a roach motel, but there was definitely something in the way the room looked overall (the walls, the furniture, the carpet) that told me it was pretty run down.

But it was better than my cell back at Camp Mabry. No doubt about that.

I made a mental list of things we needed: a mini USB cable, food, and clothing. I still wore the vomit-stained Houston Texans T-shirt I'd picked up back at the mall in Longview. I definitely had some swamp ass going on, and my jeans were stained with my own blood.

I looked like I was auditioning for a role in a HuluFlix dystopian movie.

So as soon as I got out of the shower and got dressed again in my dirty clothes, I asked Dorian if she was ready to go out.

"Yeah, for sure," she said from her position on the bed. "I'd love to eat and get some new clothes."

Dorian had more of a personality than Veronique, and she wasn't as naive and innocent as Grace. My guess was that she'd been out a lot more, especially since it would be hard to keep a teleporter locked up.

"We could both use some new clothing," I told her, looking down at my shitty jersey.

"Here." Dorian tossed me the rubber-banded roll of money. Damn, it looked gangster.

"I'm the bank manager now?"

She raised an eyebrow at me. "That's how it worked with Veronique and Sabine – I mean, Grace – right?"

"Something like that, but only because I had more experience on the outside."

She stood, smoothed her hands over her black jacket, and said something about the temperature in the room.

"I thought it was hot too," I told her. "But that jacket must make it worse for you."

"Yes, but I'm wearing it as a disguise … sort of," she said.

"A disguise?"

She took off her jacket to reveal full sleeve tattoos on both arms. You name it, she had it – skulls, dragons, dice, Japanese waves, Sailor Jerry's iconography – and somehow, she'd managed to fit it all on both arms, but there was nothing past her wrists.

I'd never noticed it before, likely because she was always wearing that jacket.

"You don't like them?" She pulled the jacket back on.

"They're hot as hell. I've never been brave enough to get tattoos."

"It's not that painful." said the super hot punk rock goth emo you-name-it sub-genre chick in the leather jacket, tank top, and fishnet stockings. "Only problem is, I'm a little more obvious when I'm showing them off,"

Sure, it's the tats, I thought.

"What?" she asked as I gave her a funny look.

"You know what? Never mind. Keep the jacket for now. We'll get a long sleeve shirt or something when we go shopping. Or maybe a lighter jacket. I know it's hot as balls out there. I never thought I'd miss New England so much."

"Hot as balls?"

"An expression about testicles and how spicy they can get in the heat. At least I think it's about testicles. It could be about actual balls. Beach volleyballs are pretty hot."

Rather than go down that rabbit hole, I busied myself making sure the door was locked behind us and we headed downstairs. It was a creaky old hallway, and we passed only two other rooms before we hit the stairs.

The receptionist, an older Mexican woman with gray streaks in her hair, greeted us with a grunt. She gave me a double glance, having not remembered seeing me go up to the room.

"You were in the restroom," I told her. Satisfied with my answer, she shrugged and went back to her smartphone.

Which gave me an idea.

"Hey, so I'm going to be honest with you," I said to the receptionist. "We're kind of off the grid and we need a cable." I reached into my pocket and pulled out forty dollars. I knew the mini USB to mini USB cable couldn't cost more than five bucks, but I wanted to give her an incentive to cooperate.

"Okay," she said, looking at me suspiciously.

"All I need is for you to order us a mini USB to mini USB cable," I told her. She was a Millennial, which meant she was in her 50s or 60s, which meant she definitely knew how to quickly order something like that. "Do you have EBAYmazon?"

She snorted. "Who doesn't?"

"Yeah, that's a good question. Okay, just type in 'mini USB to mini USB.'"

She pulled up the app and did as I instructed. When she tapped the purchase button, a notification popped up telling her it would be delivered within two hours.

"Perfect," I said and slid the money over to her. "Also, do you know where we could go shopping and get some food?"

She eyed me skeptically for a moment, then finally said, "You're on South Congress Avenue. We're about a mile away from more expensive food and shopping. If you want something cheaper, you can go to South First Street."

"Can you call a cab for us? Sorry for the inconvenience, we just don't have phones."

"Do you need a phone too?"

"Actually, that's not a bad idea," I said and plunked three hundred more dollars on the counter. "Anything that doesn't require much registration. A smartphone and a couple of prepaids too would be best."

She found what we needed online, verified that it would serve our purposes, and ordered it. "Now, about that cab …" She whistled and a heavyset Mexican guy with dark eyes came from the back room. "Listen, mijo, I want you to drive these people around and they will pay you."

"Sí, Abuela," he said.

"Make sure to take good care of them."

"Sí, Abuela."

"Does he speak English?" I asked.

238

He looked at me like I was an idiot. "Sí."

I glanced at Dorian and back to the grandmother behind the counter.

So that was how we ended up with a chaperone that looked like a member in a drug cartel.

He led us out to his car, which I wish I could say was some type of badass lowrider, but it was actually a Honda Civic with aftermarket hubcaps, and like a gentleman, he even opened the door for Dorian. She got in the back seat and I scooted in next to her. I would have tried to sit in the front, but he had a garbage bag full of something up there. I couldn't tell if it was closed, and it definitely wasn't food, so the back seat would do.

"You want to go to South Congress?" he asked me.

Having no idea about Austin or what was available, I just nodded. "As long as some food's there, that's fine by us. Also, I'm Gideon."

"I'm Diego," he said with a grunt, not unlike his grandmother's.

"My name is Dorian."

He looked at her in the rearview mirror for a moment, "So, you want cheap food or expensive food?"

"Cheapish," I told him. "What do you recommend?"

"Torchy's Tacos, not too cheap, not too expensive, very good."

I noticed he had a Longhorns ball cap sitting on the dashboard. "Hey, do you mind if I wear your ball cap?" I asked. "I'll be honest with you; I'm trying to keep a low profile."

He started the car and shrugged. "Fine by me, but don't mess it up; don't get it all sweaty." He tossed the hat into the back seat.

His car smelled like burnt vanilla, mostly because of the Little Trees vehicle air freshener hanging from the rearview mirror. Abuela was right; it really wasn't very far from the hotel. And looking over my shoulder at the place we were driving away from, I wondered how Dorian had found it anyway.

The hotel was completely run down on the outside, its parking lot filled with potholes. It was across from some private Catholic university called St. Edward's University, and seemed incongruous to the manicured campus across the street.

If I'd had my smartphone, I may have looked some of the stuff up just to see more about where we were, but my little research binge would have to wait.

I put the Longhorn hat on, and we continued down the street to the sound of Tejano rap.

I was starting to like Tejano music, and a little rap in there really added something to the mix. It was upbeat, and even though I had no idea what they were talking about, it made me feel happy, a little positive. True, I'd disliked it on our drive to Austin, but my little stint in military prison had made everything on the outside *radiate* with positive energy.

And boy, did I need some positive energy at that moment.

We stopped in front of Torchy's and got out of the car.

Diego pointed to a side street, told us he'd park there and wait for us. The shopping district was about a block away from Torchy's, so I told him that would work.

With the baseball hat covering as much of my face as I could get it to cover, we entered the hip Mexican restaurant.

Their logo was a cute devil with a yellow pitchfork. All of their tacos were named, and I ordered two Trailer Parks, which were tacos with fried chicken, green chilies, and poblano sauce on a flour tortilla. Dorian went with a taco called Brushfire, which was Jamaican jerk chicken with grilled jalapeños, mangos, and sour cream. It looked yummy as hell.

"Order two," I told her. "Actually, three. Fuck, I'm hungry. Chips and queso too. Two drinks," I said to the bearded and tatted dude at the counter.

The food came, and by the time it reached our table, my mouth was watering. I practically inhaled the first taco. It was the taste of freedom. Just a few hours ago, I'd been served a half-eaten apple and a loogied-up slice of bread. Now I was eating like Pablo Escobar.

I hadn't even been a prisoner for more than two days, and I suddenly had a hatred for the prison system, even though I understood its purpose. I guess experiencing anything will do that to you; it levels you, makes you realize how much you have in common with other people.

But the tacos. Goddamn, they were good.

Dorian ate one and a half of her tacos, and I finished the other half, apologizing for eating like such an animal.

"It's fine, I'm sure you weren't fed very well in there."

"Let's get some new threads," I said.

I used a spoon to scoop what was left of the queso into my mouth, and we left Torchy's Tacos, heading down the street.

I wasn't one to shop at high-end boutiques, but right now I could use anything, including some new underwear.

We entered the first shop and started looking around. There were some douchy shirts here, so that wasn't going to do, but they did have a pretty extensive collection of undergarments. Unfortunately, the only underwear I could find cost twenty bucks a pair.

"They're made of Lenzing MicroModal," the female sales associate told us. "It's so soft!"

"I want some too," Dorian said. I watched as she chose two thongs and a pair of boy shorts.

"Yep, get whatever you want," I said as I grabbed three more pairs myself. So I spent nearly one hundred and fifty dollars on underwear. Sue me.

We went into the next boutique, which mostly had women's clothing.

"Get whatever you'd like, and get a few extra shirts," I told her. My fuck, did it feel good to say stuff like that. I'd never gone into a store before and just told someone to get whatever they wanted. Yet this had happened several times now since meeting Grace.

It really felt good to be rich, even if I was hood rich.

She picked out some T-shirts and asked me which ones I liked.

"RIP Willie Nelson is pretty sweet. The Leslie shirt too."

Apparently, Leslie was a cross-dressing Austin homeless man who died just around the time I was born. The shirt just had a silhouette of him (her?) standing over the words 'Local Hero.'

She showed me a shirt that said 'Magnolia Cafe, Sorry We Are Open.'

"Get that one too."

I had a feeling we'd need to get clothing for Veronique, so I wanted to have extra shirts around.

"My jacket is so hot," she reminded me as she went to the jacket section.

243

The female sales associate had heard what I said earlier and started telling Veronique about a form-fitting, light ribbed sweater. "It was designed for summer weather in mind," she said. "For people who like to cover up. And the buttons on the front allow for a little air, if you get my drift."

Dorian got that one too, as well as a shirt that said, 'Keep Austin Weird.' Four shirts, a ribbed sweater designed for summer weather (whatever the hell that meant), and two pairs of black form-fitting jeans later, we were down about five hundred dollars.

Next stop was a men's shop, and while I wasn't going for the dapper-mustache-in-tweed-jacket look – of which they had plenty of options – I was able to find some T-shirts and some good Levi's. I chose one T-shirt that paid homage to the short-lived hockey team Austin once had, the Austin Ice Bats.

I decided to get two pairs of jeans, knowing full well that I might not be able to get clothes for a while. I also got some fancy-schmancy socks – argyle, with the word YOLO written on the heel, for some reason.

If ever there was a word to define my life choices …

The clothing cost about two fifty, which was at least cheaper than Dorian's purchase, but still pricey. We were burning right through that five thousand.

But, YOLO, right?

Dorian and I were just about to head back to our car when I saw the candy store. I had to partake, and I was glad I did because the candy was delicious. We got about fifty dollars' worth of candy, which was a joke, and which no man or woman should ever purchase.

But I needed *something.* Yet as much as I tried to hide my anguish from earlier with shopping, I knew retail therapy wasn't going to cure the after-effects of what I had just gone through.

Candy would help though.

Diego took us back to the hotel. I tipped him sixty dollars and gave him all the candy. We'd already eaten enough to get the shakes. As we passed his abuela at the counter, she told me that the USB cable and the phones had arrived. I took the package from her, and we hurried up to our room.

"Glad we're back," I said after I shut the door and locked all the bolts. "I know you need some rest, so why don't you just lie down for a moment, and I'll plug in and see what I can fiddle around with?"

Dorian set her packages down. "Do you mind if I change?"

"No, definitely, do whatever you'd like."

Little did I know that meant she would take off her pants and jacket right in front of me. I started to look away, but she only laughed. "It's not like you haven't seen a woman naked before, right?"

"I ... sure, do whatever."

"You already said that." She peeled her underwear off and changed into one of her new thongs. Then her top came off and I gulped. I didn't know when I'd become such a horny bastard, but what could I do?

She put on the RIP Willie Nelson shirt and lay down on the bed.

"Good, I'm glad you're comfortable."

"I thought you'd like that."

"Yeah, sure, who wouldn't? But let's get down to business here."

I plugged into her neck, and the password screen came up. "Shit," I whispered as she turned on the TV. I was just about to panic when I saw that the password had autofilled.

Thank you, autofill.

Passwords were such a bitch.

Due to an increase in cybercrimes, everything these days required some intense password that involved at least ten digits, and companies had started rolling out a rule that you couldn't use the same password for another login. There was even a group that had been put together that checked to make sure you weren't doing this – of course, it was all part of the FCG's six-billion-dollar war on cybercrimes.

Point is, I hate passwords.

I went straight to her abilities folder and opened up the teleportation subfolder, creating a shadow box with four dials.

I looked at the options for a moment, wondering if I could adjust the Recharge Speed down a little bit and increase the Restoration Speed. Hovering over the option told me that it decreased the amount of time she needed to recharge from teleporting. Also, we would possibly have to increase the radius of her teleportation ability, especially if we needed to move a larger object.

At first, the options looked like this:

Tele-Sphere Radius: 2

Conscious Spatial Awareness: 10

Recharge Speed: 6

Restoration Speed: 6

By the time I had finished, they looked like this:

Tele-Sphere Radius: 3

Conscious Spatial Awareness: 10

Recharge Speed: 5

Restoration Speed: 6

"I feel a lot warmer." Dorian looked at me. "Touch my head and you'll see what I mean."

I did and noticed it was a little warmer than it should have been.

"My heart, too." She moved my hand down to her chest, directly over her heart.

It was thumping rapidly now.

"Okay, just breathe for me and let me play around a little bit longer."

I selected her energy ability and took a look at it.

Main: Ergokinesis

Overcharge: 6

Charge Capacity: 4

Charge Integrity: 3

I was about to close the shadow box when I remembered that her Overcharge was at two the last time I saw it. Now it was at six.

So, either adjusting the Restoration Speed or the Tele-Sphere Radius had increased her Overcharge, which was affecting her vitals.

Of course, I tried to turn down Overcharge just to see if it would work, and it did not. I then turned down Charge Capacity by one point and asked her how she felt.

Main: Ergokinesis

Overcharge: 5

Charge Capacity: 3

Her eyes lit up. "That's a lot better. What did you do?"

"I decreased the amount of time it takes you to recharge so you can teleport larger objects. Doing so caused your Overcharge dial to increase on its own, which is akin to heating you up, from what I can tell. To fix this, I decreased your Charge Capacity, which means you won't be able to make objects as large as you had been."

She considered that for a moment. "But making larger objects may be able to help us more," she finally said.

"I agree, and adjusting either the Charge Integrity or the Charge Capacity up could also help us, but if we do that, we have to adjust all your teleportation abilities down. Right now, *those* are the abilities we need to get Veronique out. That's why I wanted this cable, so I can adjust in real time."

"So, can we rest now?"

"Sure, I'm bugged out as it is. Long day, right?" I looked awkwardly around the room.

Dorian rolled her eyes. "There's room on the floor … or you could just rest on the bed with me."

"Also a good call."

Chapter Twenty-Five: Up and Away

Dorian woke me five or six hours later. It was around two in the morning, but I felt surprisingly rejuvenated after the rest. Even though the bed wasn't great, it was a lot better than the one in my holding cell, and hearing the faint hum from the television had actually helped me sleep better.

Background noise, don't leave home without it.

"I'm going to go soon." She stood from the bed and put her jacket on. The room was cold; the window air conditioning unit was working pretty well now.

"Okay, let me get ready real quick." I was in my new underwear as well, having changed into it after taking a quick shower. I liked to go to bed clean, so when I'd lain down earlier I figured I'd better scrub a dub a little bit before I actually dozed off.

She raised an eyebrow at me. "I wasn't aware you were going."

"Why wouldn't I be going?"

"What exactly are you going to bring to the table here?" Dorian asked as she fixed her hair. She checked to make sure her paintbrush was with her and put it in her front pocket.

"You need a holster for that thing," I told her.

"A paintbrush holster?" She considered it for a moment. "That could be handy. But stop changing the subject."

"I can be more helpful than it seems," I told her. "But, to be honest with you, I figured Veronique may need to feed. If anything, I am food to her."

"What if we run into people?"

"I thought you were just going to appear in her room, grab her, and go."

"That was the plan, yes."

"Then I'll go with you, and she'll probably need to be fed, and she can drain me some. I've been useful in that way before, when we first rescued her."

"You're going as food?" she asked skeptically. Damn, if Dorian wasn't hot in her ribbed sweater and tight black pants, which were low cut and revealed a sliver of her midriff when she moved her hips.

It was an incredibly stupid outfit to wear when trying to rescue someone from a military facility, says the guy who was currently wearing an Austin Ice Bats shirt.

"Yep, I'm the food."

"Why do I get the feeling this is a bad idea?" She placed her hands on her hips and cocked her head at me.

"It probably is a bad idea, but I was under the impression I would be going with you, and … Well, it's totally your call, but I think I could be useful. I don't know how, exactly, but … well … Yeah, I already told you how I thought I could be useful. Especially if we run into any issues. Having Veronique with some power is always helpful because she'll probably be exhausted."

"Don't make me regret this," she said and reached out to touch my arm.

"Wait! I'm not ready yet – I still don't have pants on."

She started to laugh. "I was hoping we could surprise Veronique."

"She wouldn't be surprised to see me in my undies."

"Why's that? You two fuck or something?"

"Ha! Not exactly," I said. I slipped into my shoes and new jeans. "But that's a long story."

I wasn't apprehensive in the least to go back to the facility. And I totally should have been.

Maybe it was the rest.

Before I could talk any more shit, Dorian touched my arm and we flashed out of existence, reappearing in a long, dark hallway.

My heart jumped into my throat; this was not the holding cell.

"I thought you said …"

Dorian's eyes went wide.

My stomach wasn't as topsy-turvy as the last time we had teleported, but as we became more cognizant of the fact that we were standing in a dark hallway, it started to churn.

A red light flashed at the end of the hall and Dorian's paintbrush went into her mouth. A blazing circle of energy appeared as she moved her hand in the air. She held the circle of energy at the tip of her paintbrush as we walked down the hallway.

"I swear this was it," she whispered to me. "I even double-checked it."

"We should go back to the hotel," I said, overcome with nervousness. "They must have known we were coming ... this was so stupid."

The glass door at the end of the hallway lit up from the inside. A man moved by wearing all black armor, and before he could turn to us, Dorian put out her small beacon of blazing energy.

We would have left right then if we hadn't seen a plastic pod open and the man look down at Veronique's nude body.

"What are they keeping her in?" I asked.

"Just follow my lead," Dorian said, steeling herself. "There can't be that many men in there, and if there's just one or two ..."

She stuck her paintbrush in her mouth and pulled it out again, this time painting a man in the air. She also painted a gun, which the man took, its form three-dimensionalizing as his hand touched it.

We stayed where we were as Dorian sent her humanized energy creation forward. As he walked, he lifted his firearm at the glass and began shooting at it.

The glass was thick, but it didn't take more than two shots to completely shatter, and for his next act, energy man shouldered through the glass and slammed into the security guard.

By this point, alarms were going off, and Dorian was making another man.

She created this one to stand guard behind us, wisps of energy licking off his body as he stood strong. As we moved toward the broken glass door, her free hand on my wrist, Dorian created a floating fireball of energy.

We entered the room and she instantly flung the fireball into another man, who'd been waiting in ambush. He cried out as it sizzled through his body armor and burned into his skin.

The smell of burning flesh made my stomach churn, so I returned my focus to Veronique. She was in a sarcophagus, the top part encased in glass. I could tell just by placing my hand on it that the rest of the sarcophagus was made of plastic, and I quickly searched around until I found a button that opened the top.

"Veronique," I said as the top clamshelled back.

We heard activity in the hallway that we'd spawned in, and Dorian went to work with her paintbrush. The tailless energy wolf she'd just created tore off down the hall.

"Get her out of there," Dorian said, worry spreading across her face.

"Working on it!"

"Veronique," I said, lightly patting her face. "Veronique, can you hear me?"

There were some cables plugged into her neck, so I figured those needed to go. I pulled them out, and as soon as I did, she sat up violently, her eyes filling with hate.

She gasped when she saw me and lifted her arms around my neck.

"Thank you," she whispered.

"Drain me, *now*," I told her. "We need you."

She placed a shaky hand on my neck, and as red energy swirled around her fingertips, I began to feel weak in the knees. I stabilized myself against the sarcophagus as she continued draining my life force.

I started to get lightheaded and was glad when she finally stopped.

"Is everyone ready?" Dorian asked, and I heard more shouting down the hall.

"I think we are," I said. She placed a hand on my shoulder and her other one on Veronique's forehead. She closed her eyes, and …

Nothing happened.

"What's going on?" I asked.

"Shit, it's not working, it's …"

Veronique looked toward the door we'd busted through. There was no metal around that she could use, but soon there would be men who had metal … in the form of bullets.

"I'll hold them off," she said, as she got out of the sarcophagus, nude as the day she was genetically created.

"Good," I said. I pulled out my smartphone.

Dorian and I moved to the far side of the sarcophagus and I instructed her to sit. I smoothed my hand over her neck and found the port. Once I plugged in, I quickly located her teleportation stats.

Main Second: Teleportation

Tele-Sphere Radius: 3

Conscious Spatial Awareness: 10

Recharge Speed: 5

Restoration Speed: 6

"I'm going to crank up Restoration Speed as high as I can by turning down Recharge Speed and Tele-Sphere Radius," I told her.

I heard a burst of gunfire, and then I heard a man cry out as the bullets were reversed and punched through his skull. At least I assumed it was his skull; all I could see was Veronique's naked ass in the doorway – hunched over slightly, but still in control.

More gunfire. Dorian looked at me with true fear in her eyes and nodded.

"Just trust me," I said, and no, she shouldn't have trusted me because I had no idea what the fuck I was doing. But that never stopped someone from trusting an idiot.

I decided to crank it all the way up, and in doing so, noticed it wasn't a one-for-one exchange as it had previously appeared to be.

Tele-Sphere Radius: 1

Conscious Spatial Awareness: 10

Recharge Speed: 1

Restoration Speed: 10

A pulsing vein appeared on her forehead.

"Gideon," she said as her face turned red.

I had confused Restoration Speed and Recharge Speed.

Recharge Speed was the time it took her to recharge, duh. Restoration Speed was the time it took her to reform after teleporting.

Fuck!

In my haste, I'd gotten the two mixed around in my head. I started making quick adjustments and was able to bring Restoration Speed way down, and Recharge Speed up.

"Whoever made these labels did a bad job," I muttered under my breath. *Or whoever is messing with them isn't the sharpest spork at McStarbucks,* I thought and saw with relief that her face had lost its redness.

Tele-Sphere Radius: 2

Conscious Spatial Awareness: 10

Recharge Speed: 8

Restoration Speed: 2

If I was hoping for a sigh of relief from her, I wasn't going to get it.

The pulsing vein remained on Dorian's forehead, and I could tell by touching her skin that she was overheating.

I removed the cable and stuck it back in my pocket. "You think you're ready?" I asked.

"I ... I think so," she said as I helped her up.

There was a short break in the gunfire and I called out to Veronique. She fell to the side, and like a hero I would never be, I actually caught her.

Dorian put one hand on my shoulder, the other on Veronique's head.

We were gone in a flash.

Chapter Twenty-Six: A Much-Needed Shower Scene

We slowly reappeared back in the hotel room.

I don't really know how else to describe it other than that; our bodies reformed in slow motion. It wasn't exactly painful, but it was weird seeing our heads take shape, and then an arm or two, then a torso or three, followed by each leg. Some Harry Potter shit.

"Drain more," I told Veronique, who was still in my arms.

"I need clothes," she said.

"I already thought of that – and really, I had no idea you'd be kept naked, but we wanted to get some clothes anyway."

Dorian exhaled audibly and sat on the floor next to the bed, her knees pulled to her chest. "That was …"

"The point is, we got out," I said with a sigh.

"Clothes," Veronique repeated.

"We'll get you dressed in a moment, but first, you should probably drain more of my energy. You look like you're on your last leg." I glanced at Dorian. "And I'll mess with your stats in a bit. Are you feeling overheated or anything?"

She nodded, the vein pulsing on her forehead. "But, it's getting better. I think the change you made created less Overcharge. I can't say for certain, but I don't feel as warm as I did back there. Still hot though."

Yes, you are, I thought and then felt guilty for such a stupid comeback.

"Adrenaline probably hit you too," I told her. One glance down and I noticed that my hand was shaking. "You aren't the only one."

Veronique placed her hand on my arm. Instantly, I felt myself losing energy, to the point that I grew sleepy, the edges of my vision blurring. She was draining more than she had drained back at the military facility. I could tell in the time it took me to lay down in … Dorian's lap?

"Relax, Gideon," Dorian said, her fingers pressing my eyelids down.

My brain sparked and fizzled.

On one hand, this was incredibly sexy, and I was still male enough to realize that. On the other hand, I was scared. And then on the third hand – because who doesn't have three hands? – I was *so* weary, barely able to keep from falling asleep.

Veronique suddenly stopped. I blinked my eyes open to see that she was sitting up and touching Dorian's cheek.

"Drain me," Dorian said softly. "It's fine."

Is this the start of a fucking orgy?

A quick email exchange happened between my two heads.

Dear Gideon Caldwell's Dick's Brain,

I fucking hate you sometimes. She's just trying to be helpful. No, this isn't the start of a threesome. You are a horny idiot.

Love,

Gideon Caldwell's Actual Brain

Dear Gideon Caldwell's Hypersensitive and Overly Concerned Snowflake Brain,

Why do you always let your moral pedantry get in the way of me and vaginas? This could totally turn into a vampiric orgy with teleportation highlights if you'd just calm the fuck down, stop overanalyzing, and let the heavy petting begin. Touch me again, Veronique! There's energy left down here!

Kind Regards,

Gideon Caldwell's Dick's Brain

"What's going on?" Veronique said as she removed her hand from Dorian's cheek. She glanced down at the tent I was pitching.

Dorian caught wind of it too. "Looks like there's still some energy there."

"Don't ... it's nothing! Dicks have minds of their own, as do most world leaders. Sorry, that doesn't make any sense, but really, just keep doing what you do. Please don't kill me!"

Veronique placed her hand on my member and laughed. "I guess I haven't drained you enough."

"Apparently not!" I said. I tried to stand, but my knees buckled and I fell forward, which hurt like a bitch when I cracked my boner on the floor.

Shit!

"Don't mind me," I mumbled as Dorian helped me up.

"Just relax, Gideon," she said. "You've done enough for tonight."

"What about you? Are you overheating?"

She sighed. "I think I'll be fine."

"No, just … let me handle that first."

Weak as I was, and partially guided by Veronique's helping hand while ignoring my raging hard-on, I plugged into Dorian and adjusted her Teleportation Recharge Speed down so it looked like:

Tele-Sphere Radius: 3

Conscious Spatial Awareness: 10

Speed: 5

Restoration Speed: 6

I checked to make sure her Overcharge had also gone down, but I really didn't need to; as soon as I dialed the Speed down her face lightened and she started to breathe more easily.

"Now relax," she said as she helped me to the bed.

I'm pretty sure they ended up watching more fucking home and garden shows after that. Then again, there's no telling. I was out.

Fade to black. Literally.

It only took another second of Veronique's touch to completely put me out. I was trapped in utter blackness, swimming through an endless pool of dark crimson, my mind moving forward toward a bright light.

The light seemed so familiar, so warm, so real.

As I swam closer to it, I watched it begin to change into Grace, starting with her long blonde hair and quickly forming her face and voluptuous, soft features.

"Grace!" I called out to it.

But I was too late, it was now too far away. Something was pulling me backward, deeper into the cool water.

I awoke in a cold sweat.

It was morning now, and I was lying on the bed between Dorian and Veronique, both of whom were cuddling me in some way. Veronique had put on the Willie Nelson shirt and a pair of panties. Dorian was in her thong and black bra, tattoos covering her arms.

Rather than have another heated epistolary exchange with my little trouser snake, I slipped out of bed and lugged my ass to the bathroom to drain the lizard.

After I finished, I looked at myself in the mirror and saw I was a little worse for wear. My beard was unkempt, the scar on my face had started to darken, and my hair was thickening as it grew out.

Worse for wear? Shit, I looked hard as fuck, but it felt like I'd been hit by an eighteen-wheeler.

After a couple of poses, just to see if I'd grown any more muscle (I hadn't), I decided to take a shower.

The water took a moment to warm, but it eventually got there, and I was able to ignore the lump of hair sitting where the soap should be. Shitty seedy motel.

Damn, did the water feel good on my sore muscles though. Once it got to the point where it was too hot and my skin had turned pink, I took a step away and just relaxed in the steam for a moment.

I actually heard the door open this time, and sure enough, it was Veronique.

"We meet again in the bathroom," she said, taking off the shirt and panties.

"It seems to be the place for us to meet …"

She stepped into the shower and kissed me. She kissed me again and again, and I was definitely into it, but I could also tell that … well, I don't think she'd ever kissed someone before. Grace hadn't been the same, likely because she'd read my mind on how to kiss. Not that I was an expert or anything, but I'd had my fair share of make out sessions in high school.

So I let Veronique experiment on her kisses for a while, to get used to it.

Eventually, she turned around and bent over, beckoning me forward.

I shouldn't have had enough energy for an erection, but there was a time and place for everything. And this was the time and place for me

266

to swallow the fact that I'd been drained pretty hard last night, I was hungry, and to forcibly send all my energy toward my nether regions.

Not that I needed to do much begging. My member had already grown to full size. I approached her, my hands on the shower wall and water spraying off my back. It wasn't too hard to slip in.

She was incredibly tight, but the water and the fact our juices were flowing soon made things a little easier. She looked at me over her shoulder, her hair partially covering her face as she got into her rhythm.

"Gideon," she whispered, and even though the shower was beating down upon our bodies, my ears were completely tuned into her words. "Gideon," she whispered again. "Gideon."

I just kept going, trying my damndest not to come too soon. I got the sudden feeling – like I had with Grace in the past – that this would be the last time I had sex. This thought only inspired me to get more into the motion, grunting as I went at it as best I could, forgetting all the things that were out to get me.

She raised one leg and placed it on the side of the tub to stabilize herself. It was then that I noticed the door had cracked open, Dorian standing on the other side.

I blinked as she stepped into the bathroom, nude from the waist down. If Veronique cared, she didn't show it.

In fact, she became more aggressive when Dorian entered.

Thank you, God, I thought as Veronique turned to me and wrapped her arms around my neck. She climbed up onto me, and I leaned against the bathtub wall for leverage, aware that one false step and I would crack my ass pretty hard. I don't know where I got the strength for it, but I definitely wasn't going to let her down now. Once we were in a steady position, she lowered herself onto the luckiest dick this side of Richard Branson and started going at it again.

Meanwhile, Dorian closed the toilet lid and sat on top, her legs spreading wide until one knee pressed against the sink and the other against the side wall. She made eye contact with me as she started fingering herself.

It wouldn't be long now; I should be considered a superhero for how long I'd already lasted with all this going on. And to think there were some people out there who encountered these things in their normal life!

I'd never met a swinger. Well, no one had ever introduced themselves to me as a swinger, but I imagined this was what life as a swinger would be like, except the women wouldn't be as hot.

As much as I kept trying to tell myself to shut down my inner monologue and enjoy the moment, my inner monologue was the only thing keeping me from blowing the top off my penis. The more I rambled in my head, the easier it was not to blast off into outer space.

With Dorian in front of me, touching herself and moaning, and my arms growing tired and sore from holding Veronique, something had to give.

So I set Veronique back down, turned her against the wall, and started up again. Keeping my eyes closed this time so I could concentrate.

But my eyes didn't want to stay shut; they wanted to watch Dorian, so that's what they did. Now three parts of my body had minds of their own – my brain, my eyes, and my dick – and all were screaming for me to come.

And as Dorian moaned and Veronique found the perfect groove, I couldn't take it anymore.

Damn you, male orgasm! I was done in a matter of seconds, finished, ready to jump off a cliff if someone presented one to me, and just as I was about to pull out, Veronique's pussy clenched around my penis, draining me even more.

My legs got weak, my arms started to shake. Veronique was *orgasming and draining my life force,* the metal of the towel holder bending in her direction, the sink's faucet starting to rattle.

She came and released me. I fell backward and just barely stopped from cracking my ass open.

Dorian started to laugh, still lightly touching herself. I started laughing as well, and as Veronique turned back to me, I saw that she too had a crooked grin on her face.

Boy, were we all fucked in the head.

Chapter Twenty-Seven: Ken Kim Calls Again

The shower to end all showers? Maybe. I hadn't expected Dorian to join in the fun, even if her fun only meant she was watching and touching herself, but that was what happened. And now that the three of us had that out of our system, it was time to get down to business.

Once we got Grace, I'd have a full-blown harem going and there was nothing society could do to stop me.

Society isn't trying to stop you; besides, you could just move to Utah, my inner voice said. *And what about Grace? Isn't it an insult to her to do what you've just done?*

I'm going to save her, possibly today, I told the bitchy, retrospective Gideon. *Damn you and your societal norms! And don't you dare tell me to move to Utah!*

The voice didn't reprimand me after that.

As I put my clothes on, a feeling of intense hunger came over me. I checked my smartphone to find the nearest place to grab a bite. Curiosity led me to my email inbox, and while Dorian and Veronique got dressed, I started reading through my messages.

A rep from EBAYmazon had contacted me, asking if they could speak to me more about my first two *Mutants in the Making* books. They wanted to feature the first book in a deal that would go out to their incredibly large mailing list of readers. They also wanted to republish everything once I got a third installment out.

Republish everything? I nearly did a backflip.

My first instinct, rather than run around the room high-fiving and slapping asses, was to message Luke, and I would have done just that if I hadn't seen an email from Dr. Ken Kim.

Gideon,

Please email me your phone number. I know about what happened over the last two days. We need to talk. I can help.

Ken Kim

I considered the message for a moment.

"What's up?" Veronique asked and moved to sit next to me. Her face was still a bit red and her eyes were still incredibly dark, even though there was something soft behind them that I hadn't seen before.

"Ken Kim. He wants me to call him."

Dorian and Veronique exchanged glances. "He's still contacting you?"

"For the last several days," I said. "He's even given me a code to put in your systems – yours and Grace's – if you remember correctly. But I just don't know if I can trust him."

"Well, you bought the prepaid phones ..." Dorian said, referring to the phones Abuela had ordered for us.

"I did. Fine, let's have breakfast, then call him. But let's go somewhere like thirty minutes away or something, just in case we're being tracked."

"Teleportation?" Dorian asked.

I thought about it, then shook my head. "Nah, let's use Diego's services again. Keep things low profile for now. We'll see what Ken has to say."

I put the Longhorn cap on and stood. "Also, I need to give Diego his hat back."

After I set up the prepaid phone and made sure it had a charge, the three of went downstairs. The abuela at the front desk didn't say anything about the fact that Veronique had joined us, despite never seeing her come through the front door last night. "Mijo," she called to her grandson, "I think they need a taxi."

Diego came out of the back room, towering and intimidating as ever. He nodded when he saw Veronique. She returned his gaze with just about the coldest look possible and he glanced away.

"Where to?" he asked me.

"A breakfast restaurant, maybe a diner. Only stipulation is that it needs to be somewhere not here."

"Not here?"

"I mean, somewhere else in the city. Not in the vicinity of the hotel."

He looked at his abuela.

"Take him to the Jim's in Oak Hill," she said with pure grandmotherly finality. "Your tia used to work there."

And so we went to the Jim's in Oak Hill, wherever the hell that was.

It took about twenty minutes, going from South Congress to 71 to a suburban nook surrounded by rocky cliffs, oak trees, and a complex traffic grid. The Jim's was smack dab in the middle of the shopping center, near a gym – yep, Jim's near a gym – and across the road from a McStarbucks. Diego waited outside as we went in and got seated.

We ordered. Pancakes, sausage, and gravy for me, the same for Dorian, and each of us had a coffee.

My phone buzzed. It was Luke.

Luke: Are you alive?

Me: Barely. I'll be frank. Our little MC was taken hostage by government forces, put in a military jail, rescued by a teleporting hottie, and nursed back to health with Mexican food.

Luke: Damn, I could use some Mexican food. 😵 *Wait, did you say put in a military jail?*

Me: FML. The MC then teamed up with the teleporter to rescue the vampire. The following morning, he hooked up in the shower with the vampire while the teleporter watched. Now he's eating pancakes.

Luke: LOL. This. Is. The. Best. Message. I've. Read. All. Year.

Me: Please do not share this with anyone.

Luke: You got it. Just let me take a mental screenshot. Sometimes, I would hate to be you. Other times, I'd trade my left nut.

Me: You keep your damn left nut because you don't want to be me, trust me there!

Luke: But back to the military jail. Tell me about that.

Me: They attacked us. We were captured, they put me in jail and attempted to interrogate me. It was terrible. I don't want to relive it.

Luke: Okay then. Tell me about the almost threesome.

Me: It started when I took a shower. Vampire came in. Teleporter came in after. I don't understand my life. It wasn't a threesome, but two of us had sex while the third rubbed one out.

Luke: I thought 'rubbed one out' was just for guys, no?

Me: Yep, women can do it too. Apparently.

Luke: I've seen videos of that!

Me: Stop trying to cheer me up with your humor because it's working.

Luke: LOL. Your life is the stuff of legends, man! So what's next? Where's the psychic?

Me: Still need to rescue the psychic. I'll update you later. I don't know how this is going to go down just yet.

Luke: Well, shit, stay safe.

Me: Also, EBAYmazon contacted me. They want me to write another novella so they can publish all three into a full book.

Luke: Wow! That's great news!

Me: It is. Shit pancakes are here. I'll hit you back when I know more.

Luke: Shit pancakes? Is that an American thing?

Me: Shit COMMA pancakes are here.

Luke: Hey man, whatever you're into. No judgment. #grammarnazi

I cracked a grin at my phone. If I were British, I would call Luke a cheeky bastard.

Dorian didn't finish her pancakes, so I finished them for her. We had another cup of coffee, the three of us discussing a number of things, mostly centered around what they knew about Ken Kim –

which wasn't much – and what Veronique had experienced once they took her.

I also told her what I'd gone through, and for once, I saw true concern in her eyes.

"But back to what happened to you. What was that vat that they had you in? Sarcophagus? Maybe that's what I should call it."

"I don't know," she said, finishing off her third cup of coffee.

"Well, we'll just have to figure that one out. Or not. Who knows?" I paid the bill and we stepped outside. Dorian and Veronique formed a small perimeter around me. They were on edge, Veronique more than Dorian. I motioned to Diego – who was still waiting in his car – that we'd be a moment. "Time to call Ken," I said.

I had already sent Ken Kim my phone number back in the restaurant, and I figured it wouldn't take him long to respond.

I was right; my throwaway phone rang a few minutes later.

"Gideon."

"Ken."

"Okay," he said cautiously, "I don't know how you've managed to do it twice, but kudos. Really. And now the tough part begins."

"Do it?"

"Escaped. I mean, you were in a high-security military prison that was set up at Camp Mabry just to house you and the other supers."

I smirked at the ground. It was already hot in Austin, and the sun was glaring down on us. "I got lucky," I finally told him.

"I can't believe Dorian Gray flipped! I've been reading the inside report …"

"How do you have access to that, Ken?" I asked, sitting on the curb. "I need you to be honest with me because what you say next will decide if I ever speak to you again."

"Look, I know you're suspicious, I get that."

"More than suspicious," I said. I pulled the phone away from my ear and put him on speaker so Dorian and Veronique could hear.

"Okay, more than suspicious, fine, but I'm on your side. I want you to succeed. I want them to be defeated. The … the fuckers!"

Dorian and Veronique glanced at each other when he said this. I couldn't tell if they bought it or not, but I certainly didn't.

"Tell me every reason why you're helping me. Get on your fucking soapbox and dance, Ken."

I watched Veronique as a small smirk formed on her face, lifting her sharp features.

"Well?" I asked after Ken had been silent for a moment.

"I … look, I'm a coordinator of the program – senior coordinator in charge of subjects and their well-being. That's why I met with Sabine so frequently. And yes, I know the person you have referred to as 'Mother,' and to be honest," he paused, "I'm a dead man. Once she sees me in person again, she'll know what I've done. I can hide in New Haven, but I can't hide once we actually meet. So I'm trying to get out before she comes back. Point is, I want to help. What's so bad about that?"

"There's nothing bad about that. But how can I trust you?"

"I've seen shit that I can't … the things they did to other subjects … the decommissioned ones. And there are more that will be coming for you soon. Mark my word."

I stared at the phone for a minute. They hadn't actually sent many after us, just Angel and Dorian, which was odd.

"Why are they holding back?"

"They haven't been authorized to leave yet, but they're coming," Ken said, not quite answering my question. "I want you to know everything I know. Fuck, I'll say it. I loved Sabine just as much as Bobby did. That's the goddamn truth. I want her to succeed, to have some semblance of a life, dammit!"

So, it's about Grace then, I thought.

"You've done something I don't have the balls to do, Gideon. You're my fucking hero."

Dorian looked at me and raised an eyebrow. I shrugged, giving her the 'I'm nobody's hero' look.

"You've risked it all for a few people you barely know," Ken blurted out. "I wish I had your courage."

"It's not courage as much as it is utter stupidity," I said. *Mixed in with bouts of misguided horniness,* I thought.

Might as well be real about it; Grace, Veronique, and now Dorian had changed me. They'd brought me incredible success, opened up realms of possibility I never thought possible, and given me a life aside from a failed sci-fi writer working at a gift shop. They had become my companions.

"Well you asked, and I'm answering. So that's who I am, and it's why I'm trying to help. Did you activate the code yet?"

I shook my head at the phone. "No, you never told me what it did, and I was afraid it would turn on GPS tracking or whatever. So I figured it was a bad idea. Plus, I forgot the code."

"Grace would be with you now if you had activated it. And I'll send the code in an email."

"What do you mean she'd be with me now?"

"For Sabine, the code unlocks an ability to make people's nightmares become reality. Let me rephrase: She can dip into someone's mind, take the thing they fear the most, and make them see it. It's an incredible power, and she could have ... fuck ... she could have even taken down Angel with that."

"Did you know Angel has sex with Mother?" I said. "A real motherfucker."

Dorian and Veronique snickered. I placed my hand over the receiver and told them I'd explain later.

"I had a suspicion they were having relations."

"Sorry, it was irrelevant to our conversation, but I thought you should know." I cleared my throat. "What does the code do for Veronique?"

"Have you noticed that Veronique can only use her body metal consumption ability if she can physically touch someone?"

I thought about last night and, well, parts of this morning. "Go on," I finally said.

"Activating the code allows her to use her ability at a distance of up to twenty feet."

"She can absorb long distance?"

"She can indeed," Ken said, "and it's a game changer. She used to be able to before they took the power away from her. It stopped her opponents before they even met her."

I looked up at Veronique and saw her nod. Even though we'd had sex now and continued to grow closer, I still feared her. I don't know

281

what it was; maybe the fact that she could kill me at any time. Then again, so could Dorian.

But Dorian didn't have that 'vibe.'

Odd to think of it that way, but Dorian was just less threatening. Maybe it really was the fact that I equated Veronique with a vampire in my mind. Maybe what I really needed was to redefine her.

"What?" she asked, her eyes narrowing at me.

"This brings me to my other dilemma, Ken. What do you know about Dorian's teleportation ability? It's causing her to overheat. For someone who teleports, she can't do it very efficiently without having issues. I played with the dials a little bit, but I think that made it even worse."

"I know exactly what it is. It was a stop measure put in place to prevent her from constantly relying on teleportation." I heard some clicking in the background as Dr. Kim typed on something. "Yep, that's what it is; they had these functions from her main stat folders. Like I said, the point was to prevent her from relying too heavily on it, so she could enhance her energy-wielding ability. I guess they never switched it back. You can do it if you have a cable with you right now."

I always carried the USB cable now; it was small enough to fit in my pocket and I never knew when I would need one.

"I'll send screenshots of how you get to the file location. The thing is, these drives in their necks can be a little wonky. It's a terrible interface – I mean, scrolling through folders to open shadow boxes with dials, really? – but the screenshots should help, especially since you'll have to find the folder in the picture I'm sending you. Go to options, set all options as visible, and once you've done this, backtrack to a different folder to re-add her full teleportation abilities to her main system. This will also require a reboot."

"Seriously?"

"The reboot will only take a matter of moments, but have her sit down when you do it. Did you get the email?"

I tapped my screen and saw that I had indeed received a message from Dr. Kim with screenshots. "I've got it."

"Great, that should really change the game for her."

"Thanks for your help, Ken," I said and started to hang up.

"Wait! More info for you. They're moving Sabine tomorrow morning to California, and they know you'll be coming for her. So, if that is your plan, well, you need an actual plan. I mean, I'm all for you doing this, and I hope to God you get out of it alive and that you can get Sabine out of there. Poor Sabine. But you need a real plan because Angel and Mother will be there."

"They're moving her tomorrow? Shit." I thought for a moment. "Do you happen to have any more info about how they're holding her? You said it was a makeshift installation?"

Ken hesitated. "I believe I can get more information. If I can, I'll forward it to you. Good luck, Gideon, and don't be a stranger. I don't know how much longer I'll be able to aid you, but until they catch me, I'm here to help."

"Thanks, Ken. I look forward to your email."

As soon as he hung up, I popped the back off the phone and took the battery out. I threw the battery in the bushes in front of the restaurant and tossed the phone itself into a trash can.

Better safe than sorry.

"Ready to have your stats adjusted a little bit?" I asked Dorian.

"Here?"

I took a look around the parking lot. "Yeah, maybe you're right, this isn't the best place for that. Let's get our supplies first, and then we'll mess with it after. Also, there's a video I need to show you."

Chapter Twenty-Eight: A Texas Gun Show

Our next stop was the hardware store. We were lucky that the one in South Austin was near several retail outlets. As Diego waited for us in the parking lot – to the tune of twenty-five dollars an hour, mind you – we hit the retail store called Marshall's TJ Ross Maxx, which was a terrible name that most people just called 'M TJ Ross'em,' after an advertising campaign in 2023.

Damn it, I did not want to be having déjà vu right now, but I couldn't help but recall our situation with Chip Parker in New Haven; how he had gone around gathering supplies for us. (I hated narratives that did this repetitive stuff, but what was I supposed to do?) Grace needed rescuing, and I was the one that would rescue her, hook, line, and sinker. It wasn't like this was a book … well, yet.

Or should I say, *they* were going to do the rescuing. Not that I wasn't going to help. It wasn't my intention this time to sit back and idly watch things play out. I wanted to get involved, even if it meant I may get hurt.

After checking out the clearance aisle for some goddamn reason, we bought two backpacks and three fanny packs. I chose a larger backpack, and Dorian chose a much smaller one, almost like a preschooler's backpack but made specifically for women to look cute while wearing it.

I never really understood women's fashion, and I probably never would, but she did look cute with it on, so let's leave it at that.

We went to the men's section next and got as many XXL black T-shirts as we could find – thirteen in total. Lucky us! A few of them were even on sale.

Once we made our purchases, we went to the home improvement store. Dorian lead the way as Veronique and I hung back a few steps. It was hot outside, and even though we only had to walk a few stores down, I'd already worked up a sweat by the time we reached the store.

We entered and were greeted by a friendly Texas woman with a southern drawl. "Welcome! Now, ya'll let me know if you *has* any questions."

"Thanks," I told her as we passed by.

Damn, were these home improvement stores intimidating. The rows of tall aisles only made me feel like a very small man. But I wasn't here to build a wall between Texas and Mexico; I was here for IED equipment.

I didn't know much about building things, unless it came with instructions from Ikea, but I did have a fair idea about what we could use to make frag pouches.

So that's what we went for.

We purchased several dozen packs of nails, all the circular saw blades under seven inches in diameter, countless nuts and bolts, three pairs of shears, and bundles of thumbtacks.

No, I didn't take an IED 101 crash course from the latest extremist group out of Baghdad. I simply wanted to provide things Veronique could work with; I wanted to be part of what was going to happen.

I also wanted to test something we hadn't tested before. I had asked Dorian if she could charge objects, and she said she couldn't. But I wondered what would happen if she licked her paintbrush and charged them that way ... or perhaps licked the object itself?

It was worth a shot.

Once we had our items, we asked Diego to drive us to an open field. We got out and took a walk, realizing that we weren't actually in an open field, but more likely the outskirts of a golf course.

Didn't matter, it would still work.

As gnats and mosquitoes buzzed around me, I took out some of the nails and handed them to Dorian. "Let's try something."

She understood what I meant almost instantly. "Should I lick them?"

"Do you mean you really never tried this before?"

"No, honestly, I've always just used my finger or a paintbrush." She popped her finger in her mouth to demonstrate what she meant. "Sounds stupid, but … I didn't really want to lick random objects." She scrunched up her face in disgust.

I laughed. "Yeah, I didn't think about that part. In that case, lick your finger, lift a nail, and see if you can charge it. I'm envisioning something like Gambit here."

"Gambit?" Veronique asked.

She was on my other side, keeping an eye out to make sure someone wasn't coming for us. I wanted to tell her to relax a little, but it was better that she was at least prepared. Because god knows I wasn't.

"Sorry, disregard the reference. It's not even a good reference, to be honest, because she's neither from Louisiana nor a dashingly handsome superhero. Beautiful, of course you're beautiful, Dorian, but Gambit was handsome. Sorry. Sidetracked. Let's try this."

I gestured to an old oak tree. "See if you can hit that."

Dorian licked her finger and thumb and picked up one of the nails from my hand. As soon as she touched the nail, it began to turn pink and boil with energy.

She pulled her arm back and brought it forward, flinging the nail at the tree.

"Whoa!" I said, clapping my hands together after it slammed into the trunk like a bullet, spraying out chips of wood.

"Oh, shit yeah! Try this." I took one of the circular saw blades out of its packaging.

The blade was about three inches in diameter, and as I handed it to Dorian, she licked her finger and took it from me.

The foliage in the top branches shifted when the saw passed *straight through* the oak tree. The top of the tree fell, crashing to the ground.

Even though there wasn't anyone around, I glanced about, just to be sure no one was watching us take down trees in Austin. Based on what I knew about the city, I had a feeling the people here wouldn't like it.

"Let me try," Veronique said.

I gave her one of the small saw blades, and it began to fold once it was in her hand, almost as if I had handed her a pancake. It straightened immediately, and she pulled her arm back, then let it go, spreading her fingers wide as she did, forcing the saw blade farther.

Veronique's saw cut through *two* trees. Now we had even more branches and foliage on the ground.

"This is a good idea," she said.

"We needed something we could use against them, and since I don't know how to use a gun, and don't have time to learn how in order to go up against MercSecure, this is our next best option. Also, we need bulletproof vests. All of us."

I got out my smartphone and did a little searching.

It was Texas; guns practically sprouted out of the ground here even if the state was in a perpetual drought. And sure enough, I found a gun show taking place this weekend.

"Only an hour away," I told them.

Now that I had my phone out, I remembered the message Ken Kim had sent. I found a large rock and asked Dorian to sit so I could plug into her port. She did, and Veronique scooted in next to her – which seemed like kind of a strange place to sit considering the size of the rock, but I was beyond asking questions about these two, especially about after what happened this morning.

Best morning of my life? Without a doubt.

But that's not what mattered at the moment. I needed to plug in and follow the directions Dr. Kim had given me.

This turned out to be a pain in the ass because I only had one smartphone, so I had to keep minimizing the screen and going back and forth between the different windows.

Damn you, technology, how I love you so.

It took me a bit longer, but I followed his instructions, and then rebooted Dorian's system, reminding her to just relax while I did so.

"That was strange ..." she said, taking a deep breath.

As we waited for the reboot, bees and hummingbirds zoomed in the air around us. There was a sprinkling of flowers in the grass, and I watched a particularly chubby bee collide with one of them, nearly knocking it to the ground.

Fucking fat-ass bee.

Once Dorian's drive was back up and running, I went to her teleportation abilities folder and the shadow box with dials opened.

Main Second: Teleportation

Tele-Sphere Radius: 3

Conscious Spatial Awareness: 10

Recharge Speed: 5

Restoration Speed: 6

Teleportation Rapidity: 1

Teleportation Distance: 10

Empathetic Teleportation: 5

Banishment: 1

Overcharge: 8

"Hell yeah, everybody!" I said. I started reading what the additional abilities allowed for.

Teleportation Rapidity increased the speed in which she could teleport over short distances, usually covering a hundred yards or so.

Empathetic Teleportation allowed her to teleport to someone she has strong feelings for, which I assumed meant someone familiar to her.

That's helpful.

I checked what Banishment did. By placing my finger over the listing, I saw that it allowed her to touch someone and teleport them away to a place she'd visited recently.

"That's badass." I quickly turned Overcharge down. The only reason I could figure they'd put that on her dials was as a type of governor and to handicap her if necessary. Still, I had to be careful not to trigger it.

With a few adjustments, I had her teleportation ability rearranged in a way I thought would work best.

Tele-Sphere Radius: 3

Conscious Spatial Awareness: 10

Recharge Speed: 5

Restoration Speed: 6

Teleportation Rapidity: 7

Teleportation Distance: 10

Empathetic Teleportation: 6

Banishment: 3

Overcharge: 1

The added options really allowed for customization.

I wasn't able to bring Overcharge lower than one, nor was I able to modify Teleportation Distance. I could see, by touching its dial, that she could move upwards of two thousand kilometers at a time, or roughly thirteen hundred miles.

Not bad at all. If I kept Dorian around, I'd never have to get groped by TSA agents again.

"You feel alright?" I asked her.

She nodded. "I feel pretty good."

"Now it's time for you to see what you could be capable of."

I unhooked the cable from her neck and went to TwitchTubeRed. I knew the exact scene I wanted to show her, and while the movie *X2* had been released three years before I was born, it still held up. I remembered watching it as a kid and being pretty impressed.

I typed 'Nightcrawler White House Scene' in the search box and the scene came up.

Again, damn me for having no other reference point for people using superpowers, but sometimes you have to stick with what you know.

"This is what you can do now," I told her as I started the three-minute clip. "And I don't mean kill the president. Because that's what he's trying to do here. I mean … just watch."

One of Dorian's eyebrows raised, which caught Veronique's attention, who moved closer to watch the clip as well.

"The blue creature should have stabbed him," Veronique said after the Nightcrawler scene ended. "It seems useful to have a tail, though."

"Do you see what I'm suggesting here?" I asked Dorian.

She disappeared in a flash, reappeared fifteen feet away, her paintbrush in her mouth, flashed again, reformed alongside a fireball made of energy that slammed into a tree as she zipped away and materialized next to a tree stump, touched it, *freaking exploded it,* and disappeared again, finally reforming behind me.

"That was so awesome," she said between gulps of air. "It's like running, almost. A little different. I don't know how to explain it."

"That's going to be very helpful," Veronique said.

"Do you feel like you're overheating?" I asked.

"Not in the least bit."

"Try again, go for longer this time, and see how it goes."

Dorian jumped forward and – *poof* – she was at it again. She bounced back and forth, her form taking shape and disappearing, leaving a cascade of brief afterimages each time she flashed away.

It took her a moment to really find a groove, charging things, using trees and rocks as targets, and her paintbrush to paint objects into existence.

Thank you, Dr. Kim, I thought when she finished.

"Where to now?" Diego asked.

"Dripping Springs. We need to go to a gun show there."

"Damn, you're a crazy white boy, you know that?"

"I fucking know it."

The drive to Dripping Springs was uneventful. As we'd done on our way to the breakfast restaurant, I sat in the front, the two superpowereds in the back. Mostly I just stared out at the open road, at the beautiful wasteland between hubs of civilization in Texas.

It was quite different from Connecticut. Most of the cities in my state were separated by trees and rocky cliffs where gray skies often hovered, signaling rain to come or rain that had recently passed.

Texas cities were separated by large swaths of parched land, land peppered with dying shrubs, the occasional tree, and a constant blue sky overhead that seemed as endless as it was foreboding.

Most of Connecticut had unrestricted access along highways, whereas Texas had barbwire that screamed of autonomy and anti-government sentiment, which got me thinking of my favorite quote from *It's Always Sunny in Philadelphia:* "The government of today has no right to tell us how to live our lives, because the government from two hundred years ago already did!"

Ha! What a quote.

We arrived in Dripping Springs, drove past a couple churches and a Dairy Queen, waited at a traffic light behind a big dually truck with chrome exhaust, and found the gun show at the convention center.

"Keep an eye on everyone," I told Veronique as we got out of the car. "There's no telling who we'll encounter ... On second thought, just be cautious. Don't use your powers in here. There will be tons of metal. Dorian, be ready to teleport us out just in case something happens."

Dorian nodded. She wore her long sleeve ribbed sweater, which perfectly accented the contours of her body. I could see her paintbrush sticking out of her pocket, almost as if it were a wand.

I had an idea of what to expect once we got inside, and I was not disappointed.

The first booth we ran into was an NRA table with bikini-clad women taking signups. Their bikinis were, of course, made of fabric that looked like the American flag, and each of them had a pink AR-15 across their backs.

It was awesomely bizarre, sexy in a female Rambo way. Damn, those Lady Rambo movies of the early 2020s were the shit.

That was the first time I saw Natalie Johansson, back before she was a household name.

"Where are we going?" Dorian asked.

"Sorry, I was having a flashback."

"Do you normally announce that to people?"

"He does," Veronique said.

We continued our way through a diverse crowd of mostly men, many of whom took second glances at Dorian and Veronique. I couldn't blame them there; aside from the bikini-clad gun hawkers at the front, there really weren't many hot ladies here.

Focus, I had to remind myself as we waded through booth after booth of death instruments. Everything from a handgun to a grenade launcher was present, and one guy had every grenade that had ever been used by US forces cut in half and displayed, showing their inner workings.

"Anyone have good body armor?" I finally asked a man in a leather vest with skin the color of a maple leaf in late October. He squinted at me for a moment as he scratched the mole on the side of his nostril, glanced from Dorian to Veronique, and then used his chin to nod me toward the booth next to him.

"Nick got the best stuff," he said in a gruff, Texas voice. "Custom shit too. Stuff for your ladies. Fits the curves of a woman. Not being no sexist here, just saying they have curves. Even them thin ones like you two." He started cackling. "Boy, you don't see many folks from Austin out here gun shoppin', but I'm glad to see it!"

"Thanks," I said as we turned to the next booth.

"Wait a dang minute now. You cain't just stop at mah booth without takin' a look. I got all sorts of exotic shit," Maple Leaf man said. "After you," he told Veronique, extending his hand to her.

I gulped as she took his hand.

Don't do it, I thought to her, and as if she were as psychic as Grace, Veronique looked at me with a wolfish grin on her face.

I was pleasantly surprised when I entered his booth to find vintage guns and martial arts weapons. The centerpiece of the booth was a golden dragon above a wood statue of a naked woman holding a katana.

"See here, I got muhself a Japanese wife," he said. "Two actually. Well, divorced the first. Ha! But the second misses is still with me.

Imagine that. Old country guy like myself. Can't help but love an Asian woman – no offense to you two, but they just get the job done for me."

Veronique picked up a throwing star and showed it to me.

"How many throwing stars do you have?" I asked him.

"How many? Well, I got nicer ones than that. That's just one for kiddos. Edges ain't too sharp. Those are five bucks a piece, and I gots me about twenty."

"We'll take them," I said, pulling out a Benjamin.

He chuckled as he filled a bag with the throwing stars and handed it to me. "Shit, if you want that, maybe I can interest one of you purty ladies in a katana."

I exchanged glances with Dorian and Veronique. Dorian shrugged.

"I think we're good," I said, and we moved on to the next booth.

The body armor guy was pretty chill, and he let us look around without trying to sell anything. I found a ballistic helmet for myself – got to protect the money maker! – and a light bulletproof vest.

"That's the best I have right there," Armor Guy finally said as I took the gear over to him.

"I also need vests for them. Helmets too."

The man had salt and pepper hair, wore a plaid shirt and an Iraqi war vet hat. As he moved over to a rack of body armor, I saw that one his legs had been replaced.

"These are some of the best vests available, used by Israeli forces and designed to give breathability – which is important if you're moving frequently – range of motion, and provide the protection you need. It's comfortable and lightweight. Form-fitting too."

He handed Veronique the first vest and pointed out armor specs as she started to put it on. "Interior front and back padded zonal panels, oversized air channels, holds ten by twelve and eight by ten plate sizes, but I've got the ten by twelves in this model. Along the right side you'll find a one hand quick release escape system, and let's see … what else can I tell you? It's the best on the market, plain and simple."

How anyone could look sexy in body armor was beyond me, but Veronique pulled it off, and Dorian soon would as well when she tried on her own model, which was larger than Veronique's due to her bust size.

"I also have it in desert camo, if that's what you're looking for."

"Black will work," I told him and got out my roll of cash. "And helmets for them."

He raised an eyebrow at me.

"We're shooting a movie in … San Antonio. Our prop guy didn't get the right stuff, so the director sent me out to pick this stuff up. The actresses," I said, nodding at Dorian and Veronique, "wanted to come along because they'd never been to a gun show."

He laughed. "Yep, I thought there was something interesting about ya'll. I bet Hollywood types don't get out to too many Texas gun shows. What are your names? Been in any movies I've heard of?" he asked, pulling out his smartphone to use the calculator.

"Veronique Caldwell," said Veronique.

I gulped.

"Dorian Gideon," said Dorian with a flirty smile, "But people call me Grace."

"Grace and Veronique," Armor Man chuckled again. "Boy, if that doesn't sound like trouble."

I smiled. "If you only knew. What's our total?"

He showed me his calculator and then added a ten percent off discount. We were down another twelve hundred dollars or so, but it was necessary. I counted out the cash and handed it over.

"You need anything else?" he asked.

"Not unless you have some EMP weapons."

"Damn," he snapped his fingers. "All sold out."

"Could we wear this stuff out or would that be too much?" I asked.

"Hell no, it wouldn't be too much," he said. "You're at a gun show; half the people in here have body armor and the other half are carrying heat. Not me. I only sell armor, not guns. Guns make me twitchy, but I like the culture, and a gun show is a damn good place to sell body armor."

"Great, thanks again." I waved to him and we left his booth, Dorian and Veronique in their armor with their helmets tucked under their arms.

Chapter Twenty-Nine: Grand Theft Auto ATX

We arrived back at the motel and I paid for another night. Diego hadn't said anything about the girls wearing body armor, and aside from commenting that he was ready for a beer, he was quiet most of the ride back to the motel.

Once we were in our room, I laid out the supplies on the bed and got to work. After admiring themselves in the bathroom mirror, Dorian and Veronique took off their vests and joined me where I knelt at the foot of the bed as I worked.

If either of them sensed I was thinking about their proximity, they didn't let on. Instead, they began cutting the black T-shirts into squares of fabric and placing thumbtacks, nuts, bolts, and nails inside before twisting the ends together and tying a knot.

I wanted to make weapons I could throw and Veronique could then wield, as well as weapons Dorian could quickly charge and toss.

Each pouch was about the size of a golf ball, and by the time we finished using all the fabric, we had at least a hundred of the little pouches. We stuffed them in our backpacks and fanny packs.

Veronique put the smaller circular saws in her fanny pack, and Dorian kept the larger ones in her backpack. They had other ways they could take someone down, but this gave them something extra to wield.

Which reminded me.

I checked my email to find that Dr. Ken Kim had sent me the code again as promised, with instructions on how to activate it.

"You ready to try?" I asked Veronique. I indicated what I meant by placing my finger on my neck.

"Sure," she said as she lay down on the bed. I found the USB cable and got my smartphone ready. I needed to charge it, especially because of what was going down tonight, and I figured having an extra phone for communication purposes would help too.

"Dorian, will you plug in the other phone?" I asked. She plugged it in and walked over to the picture she'd been slowly burning into the wall. It was a stunning piece, a Tibetan mandala if I'd ever seen one. To get started again, she lightly touched the tip of her paintbrush against her tongue.

I could smell the paper sizzle of the wallpaper almost immediately.

Focus, I reminded myself. A shadow box appeared on my smartphone and I cycled to the bottom, following the directions Ken gave me. A few more folders later I arrived at a place where I could input a command.

I took a deep breath in. I trusted Dr. Kim more than I did a few days ago, but I'd also proved with David Butler that my instincts could be wrong.

I hesitated, and Veronique noticed I was stalling.

"If they come for us, we'll be ready," she told me.

After another deep breath, I keyed in the code and a pop-up box told me it had been accepted.

"Feel anything different?" I asked.

"No," she said, but by this point, I was already scrolling back to her main abilities list. I found her Metal Absorption and Modification skill and saw that an option had been added.

Main: Metal Absorption and Modification

Wielding Capacity: 5

Adaption Speed: 6

Alloy Integrity: 4

Blood Metal Conversion: 6

Blood Metal Absorption Proximity: 10

It's at ten now? I moved a few steps away. Her head turned to me, the muscles in her neck quivering slightly.

"Try from here," I instructed her.

She lifted her hand and red energy swirled around it. Soon, I was feeling that increasingly familiar sensation of weakness in my knees.

"It works," I said, gasping as she let go.

She unplugged the cable and sat up, a smug smile on her face.

"This is what Grace's holding area looks like," Dorian said. I glanced over to see that she'd made an entire schematic on the wall next to her mandala.

"How did you ...?" I moved over to it and she reminded me not to touch the piece.

"It might still be hot," she said. "But this is what I remember it looking like. I walked around it once, just to get a better picture in my mind. This is where we'll spawn." She touched the image with the tip of her paintbrush.

There was nothing unique about where they were holding Grace.

It wasn't like the place back in New Haven, Connecticut, which was attached to the main facility by a hyperloop pod. There were three rooms, and Dorian had suggested we spawn inside Grace's room, rather than risk any type of altercation in the others.

"It's big enough for us to spawn there?"

"It is," she said, "and we'll spawn in a way that keeps you toward the back."

Way to make me feel useless, I thought, but she was probably right.

"They're going to try something, I just know they are. The faster we can get her and make it to the getaway car, the faster we can get going and switch vehicles somewhere along the way. And switch again. And switch again."

"We still need a car," Dorian said.

"That's our next step, and we're going to rely heavily on Veronique for that. Let's take a walk."

We put the laptop, money, and spare clothes in the empty shopping bags we had. Then we went downstairs to find his abuela on her smartphone, smacking gum. She barely acknowledged us as we left the motel and crossed the street to the university.

St. Edward's University seemed like a pretty nice place, and as we walked up the curving road, we saw a large parking lot full of vehicles.

It was fucking hot outside, even with the fact it was past five. I don't know how people down here did it, but I would take New England weather over this any day. Wiping sweat off my brow, I found the vehicle we wanted, a convertible Mercedes, and we started the waiting process.

We stayed under a nearby tree for a moment as I scanned the parking lot for a different convertible. I wanted the convertible just in case Veronique needed to do some fighting while I was driving.

I couldn't believe that was one of the considerations I had to take in my life, but …

"What if we trigger the alarm?" Veronique asked after we'd waited for about twenty minutes.

"Actually, that's not a bad idea. The driver probably has their alarm set to their smartphone. Everyone does that nowadays. Yeah, let's trigger the alarm."

As birds chirped overhead, I left the shade of the tree and walked down to the car. I placed my hand on it. That didn't do anything, so I reached across the door and started fumbling with the rearview mirror.

The Mercedes beeped at me.

"Making progress …" I said as I started fiddling with the door handle.

The alarm finally went off.

I went back to the tree and picked up our shopping bags, which I'd set on the ground. We waited for the driver to come out. A female college student exited the art building, and by the way she was walking, I could tell it was her vehicle.

She was a light-skinned black woman with curly hair dressed in jeans and a black tank top with the words *Stubb's Barbeque* on it and a silver necklace that hung over the upper edge of her top.

"That's her," I told Veronique.

Before the woman could pull out her keys and stop her car alarm from going off, Veronique began draining her. Dorian moved to catch the woman just as she fell and guided her back over to me. I asked her for the car keys.

"Who …?" The woman tried to scream, but as soon as the sound came out of her mouth, Veronique placed her hand on the woman's head and drained more energy.

Damn, we really needed Grace in this operation. It was a lot cleaner.

You never know how much you need a psychic until the psychic is gone.

I glanced around nervously as Dorian opened the woman's purse and took her keys. We helped her into the back of the Mercedes just as another student came out of the art building.

With the key in the ignition and our life and funds in a couple of shopping bags in the trunk, I started the vehicle up and peeled out of the parking lot.

Veronique was in the front, Dorian in the back with the student.

"She's okay, right?" I asked as we got onto the highway.

"Seems fine to me," Dorian said without checking.

I would have chuckled if it weren't for the fact that this was a somewhat serious situation. We had kidnapped someone and stolen their car.

Shit had just gotten real.

After a little confusion, we ended up driving to the parking lot outside of Jim's. It was a familiar place, and we could easily get on the road heading west from here. Once I parked, Dorian placed her hand on the woman. She instructed Veronique and me to hold hands, and when we locked fingers, she clasped her hand around ours.

We reappeared in the hotel room.

"How's your charge going?" I asked her after the butterflies in my stomach settled.

"Better; it's like you got some of the kinks out."

We set the college student down and propped her against the wall. Veronique drained energy from the woman until her skin started to shrivel.

I didn't know how long she would be out for, but we needed it to be until at least tomorrow. We'd be long gone by then.

So we relaxed.

Later that evening, we would order tacos and go over our plan again, but for now, we all needed to rest.

That was something they never covered in action movies or action-adventure books. The good guys had to rest sometime. Well, we weren't quite the good guys, but we weren't quite the bad guys either.

Truth of the matter was, and it applies even to this day, I still didn't know what we were. But I do know, and I did know at the time, that part of our identity was held by Grace, and that she was a very important key to this puzzle.

Just as important, and maybe selfishly so, I missed the hell out of her.

Chapter Thirty: Taking Down Helicopters is Fun

We knew we were heading into an ambush. It was an unsettling feeling, but there was nothing we could do about it now.

Veronique wore the black bulletproof vest, her ballistic helmet, and the fanny pack filled with frag pouches.

Dorian wore the same thing, and also had a backpack full of saw blades and more frag pouches.

I too had on my vest, helmet, and carried frag pouches, both in a fanny pack and my backpack.

"Let's do our best to get in and get out," I said for the sixth time since we ate dinner. "Mother and Angel will be there, for sure, and I don't think anyone can withstand Mother's telepathic attacks. That's why we need Grace. So, let's get in, and get out. Sorry, I just said that. And sorry for the pep talk. This is fucking scary."

Dorian nodded. "We will make this work, Gideon, just stay low. Ready?"

We got into position, Veronique at the front with her hand in her fanny pack, me in the middle, and Dorian behind us both.

We flashed away and appeared inside Grace's holding cell, my stomach somersaulting twice as our forms took shape.

It was an unlit concrete space, easily forty by forty, with a low ceiling and a sarcophagus in the center, similar to what had been holding Veronique.

Only problem was, *the sarcophagus was empty.*

"Gideon!" Dorian grabbed my arm and teleported away, just as Veronique unleashed several of her frag pouches. Nuts, bolts, thumbtacks, and nails buzzed around the room, assault weapons firing as Dorian and I appeared on top of the building.

"Stay," she told me, pulling out some of the frag pouches, and then she was gone.

An explosion threw me off balance and cut holes through the roof, letting out the frenzied noises from inside. The building creaked as metal was stripped from the wall, as more men died, as more shrapnel tore out of the roof.

I could now see into the chaos below, and what I could make out, mostly from muzzle flash, was that my team was winning.

Dorian was teleporting mayhem, Veronique orchestrating metal chaos.

From the north, another group of men were advancing on the compound, two black Humvees in their mix.

Shit!

Dorian reappeared and placed her hand on me, both of us teleporting away in a flash. We reappeared on the opposite roof.

"More are coming," I told her before she could disappear again. "There!"

"Got it. There are just a few more left with Veronique."

"Keep one alive," I said quickly. "And …" I handed her my backpack, "charge this, teleport next to the group coming from the north, and toss it."

Dorian licked a finger as she reached for my bag. It began to charge purple and pink and then she was gone in the blink of an eye, returning just a few seconds later.

Fuck, I thought as an explosion rocked our quadrant of the base. I was behind the parapet now, and as I moved to look over the side, an incredible force struck me in the chest.

I spun backward, Dorian's hand landed on me, and we were gone before I could figure out what hit me.

We reappeared on a different rooftop and I toppled over, gripping my chest.

It felt like someone had smacked me with a baseball bat ... like I'd been punched with an iron fist. I was still trying to catch my breath when Dorian took down two snipers, both of whom had turned toward us and pulled their handguns.

To take them out, she'd appeared between the two snipers and tossed one over the side of the roof, disappeared to the other one's right, and tossed him as well. She then charged two frag pouches and threw them down onto the men's bodies as they hit the ground below.

Most of that I pieced together after the fact.

My chest was pounding; I'd never been in such pain. But adrenaline took over and I was able to ignore it some.

A bullet, I told myself as I tried to catch my breath. If I hadn't been wearing the vest, I would be dead by now.

Dorian popped back beside me. "Stay here," she said and flashed away again, my backpack in her hand, charging with pink and purple energy.

Still trying to breathe normally, I peeked over the parapet just in time to see her reappear next to the incoming paramilitary forces, toss the backpack, and disappear before it could explode.

The explosion vibrated in my chest. I had to turn away once it struck, not prepared to see the bodies fall and the people scream in pain. My hands naturally went to where I'd been shot, feeling the indention in the vest, again realizing that my life had just been spared.

Before I could start doing some Hail Marys, Dorian reappeared, the vein on her forehead slightly visible.

"Let's go," she said, grabbing me.

"Keep one alive," I reminded Dorian as we disappeared again.

Our bodies reformed next to Veronique and I lost my dinner.

"Sorry," I whispered to them both. Vomit finished, I wiped my mouth and saw that Veronique had mopped the floor with the security detail that had been waiting to ambush us. The violence was almost something out of a Dark Horse comic with its stack of bodies accented by pools of blood.

Grim.

The room was lit by bodies that were smoldering – for some godawful reason – and the skylight that Veronique had opened up when she brought the ceiling down onto the rest of the men still standing.

"Tell me you kept one alive," I asked as the strength returned to my legs.

"I did," Veronique said, nodding to my right.

Fuck me ...

A man was crucified to the wall with large metal shards, blood forming a straight line from his impaled hands and reaching all the way to the floor.

Veronique didn't say anything as she walked over to him. A downed female soldier gasped in pain, still alive. Veronique stopped before the woman and drained her energy until she shriveled up and died.

"What are your questions, Gideon?" she asked, turning back to the man. Her hand flared red and he cried out in pain.

"Where is she?" I asked, or more appropriately, *I growled.* It's amazing how leverage can change one's demeanor.

"Don't know ... who you're talking ... about ..."

"Yes, you do," I told him. "It's the reason you were in this room. Now where the fuck is she?"

"Honest, I don't know!" the crucified man cried.

"You've got to know more than that," I said. I huffed out a breath. "All right, this is the last time I ask. If you don't tell me where she is, I'm going to have her," I gestured at Dorian, "teleport you to a point in the sky above the freeway. She'll teleport away before you hit the ground or are killed by an eighteen-wheeler. I'm not fucking around. Tell me what you know, and we'll let you live; you'll get some type of severance, extreme combat package. Dunno, I'm not a mercenary, but I'm sure there's something in it for you. Oh, and your life. You'll keep that. It's that simple."

I had to turn away for a moment. The person who'd just said that was not me, or better, was not the old me. This was the new me – the me that had decided to take everything into his own hands.

What have I become?

I gritted my teeth and turned back to the man. "Now, what do you know?"

"You're not going to make it out of here alive," was his answer.

"We'll see about that."

"They're waiting for you," he said through gritted teeth.

"Just like you were waiting for us. See how well that worked?"

"Near the track, in Barrack A," he blurted out. "That's where they moved her. The helicopter should be moving them … now. Really soon. They thought you'd attack later. May have already gone … I have no fucking idea."

Veronique looked at me. "Leave him." I turned my back to the man and approached Dorian. "You know where that is?"

"We can take a point on top of a rooftop and then go from there."

Veronique stepped up beside me. "Good job," I told her, taking one last look at the carnage. "Remember, we get Grace, and we go. And I drive until we see a gas station and then we get another car. In and out. I don't want to take them on without Grace at full capacity."

The crucified guy cried out to us as we flashed away.

We appeared on a rooftop, not far from where the snipers were. I was still surprised there were only two snipers, and I had a feeling we'd run into more.

I still couldn't believe I'd been shot. If I hadn't been wearing the vest … I touched my chest again and gulped. It would leave a bruise, but shit, that was the least of my concerns.

"Someone's there," Veronique said, pointing to someone at one of the cross streets.

The streets separating the barracks reminded me of the ones in New Haven, not a lot of wiggle room on the side. Sure enough, there was a person sitting in a wheelchair at the intersection of one of the streets.

"Are you two ready?"

Dorian pulled two frag pouches out of her fanny pack. I saw that Veronique was running low, so I handed her several from my own pack.

"You two are awesome," I said as they both looked at me. "If I die tonight, I'm proud to have died by your sides."

Dorian grinned. "You haven't known me for that long."

Veronique laughed. "You've known me for a bit longer but …
yeah, I'll miss you too. If you die. Don't die. Who will I shower
with?"

The two exchanged glances and started laughing.

"Yeah, about that …"

A pair of helicopters appeared in the distance.

"Shit. To be addressed later."

Veronique grinned. "Taking down helicopters is fun."

"I'll bet. Keep an eye on them. Once they get too close, see if you
can use them to our advantage."

She snorted. "And I thought I was the one who had military
training."

"I think it was both of us," Dorian said.

"Just trying to be helpful."

Veronique placed a hand on my cheek "Stay alive. You are most
helpful to us alive."

After the two got in front, I touched their shoulders and we
teleported to a spot just in front of the person sitting in the wheelchair.

I gasped when I saw it was Grace, her hair covering her face, her
skin sagging off her chin. She was naked, her body in spasms, unable
to do more than silently nod at me. I could see that her eyes were

completely white, shining through the shadows cast by her long hair. And just as I was about to scream her name like an idiot, Angel zoomed down from the sky and landed behind her, Mother in his arms.

The standoff had begun.

Angel let Mother down, and she dusted off the front of her black bodysuit, similar to what Veronique wore when she first came after us.

One of the helicopters' spotlights landed on Mother, giving her the stage.

"Gideon Caldwell, you have quite the reputation." The choppers were high enough in the air that we could hear her speak, but I had to strain a little. "You actually got out of here, and then you came back, now for a third time. Had I known you'd be so resilient, we wouldn't have kicked you out of the program all those years ago."

I glanced at Veronique. *Out of the program?* Damn, I wished she could read my thoughts! Was this why my picture was on Grace's drive? It had to be!

Mother continued. "You are now responsible for the death of … I don't know how many American soldiers you killed back there."

"They're from a private security company," I told her through clenched teeth. "Not quite soldiers, so don't try to guilt me there."

Dorian lightly touched my wrist. She was on edge, but if Veronique was as well, I couldn't tell. She'd actually stepped forward, valiant as ever as she sized Angel and Mother up.

321

"They are whatever we say they are," Mother finally said, her expression souring. "And you'll be charged with their murders. Dorian Gray, I really thought you were one of our more unique creations. But you aren't. The ones on the East Coast, *they are.* And the one in my womb *she is.*"

She's pregnant? Mother had mentioned during our interrogation that she was planning to create others, but those were test tube babies, according to her. I didn't think she was actually pregnant, especially because she'd specifically said she wasn't. But now I could see it, especially because of how tight her outfit was. She had a slight motherly bump, just a hint, maybe four months pregnant or less.

"You got your mom pregnant?" I asked Angel. "Damn, man."

I knew he could crush me in an instant. But for some reason, seeing his greasy long hair covering his perfectly chiseled yet slightly burnt face just got to me. If I'd had a chance to go back and make the joke better, I would have said something about how we were in Texas, not Arkansas, where inbreeding and child marriages were accepted, but I always had better jokes in retrospect.

Angel ignored me as Mother continued speaking.

"Dorian and Veronique, you both disappoint me, and you will both be retired after this, but not before we do some experiments on you. I would really like to watch you suffer. Especially you, Veronique. And I know it'll be a little hard considering your power, but we could just let you starve. That may be the way to go; lock you in a plastic room and let you starve."

Grace! I called to her in my head. *Are you okay? Focus on my words!*

I'd heard enough of the supervillain bullshit talk. I didn't think what she was going on about would actually happen in real life, but it seemed like every time Mother came around – or Angel for that matter – they wanted to talk about their evil plans or how inferior I was.

If there ever were real supervillains, they would just kill everyone and not say anything about it. There would be none of this banter, and there wouldn't be any movies about superheroes either because the villains would kill all the good guys.

Mother rambled on and on about how I was inferior and how Dorian and Veronique were doomed, and as she finished her diatribe, I began to think about my book, *How Heavy This Axe.*

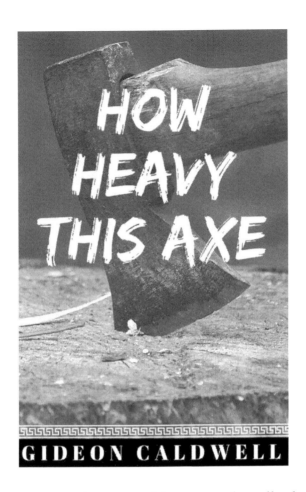

GIDEON CALDWELL

Damn, that was a good cover, and damn, people really should have gotten into that one more. But I mean, transgendered dwarves were still a controversial topic, and no one liked to see the Hero's Journey upended. Still, maybe I should republish it with a forward and an updated cover …

From there, I thought about a spin-off of *Mutants in the Making* that I'd call *Hot Mutant Adventure.*

Talk about keyword stuffing.

I would make it a harem because, let's be honest, sex sells, and guys like to think that having control over multiple women somehow ups their masculinity.

And shit, I didn't even like most of the harem books or anime I'd consumed. Too corny and unbelievable, and the covers on the books! How many times do I have to see a guy surrounded by two impossibly beautiful semi-nude babes to get past the sexual undertones and see the book for what it really was?

Then again, maybe it was better to lean into it, really get that shit going. *Hot Mutant Adventure: A Superhero Harem Adventure.*

'Adventure' twice? I thought as Mother kept yammering about the different ways she was going to torture us. Change it to thriller. *Hot Mutant Adventure: A Superhero Harem Thriller.* Circle jerkers, we have a winner! Wannabe alpha males rejoice!

"I'll get Grace, and then I'll come for you," Dorian said suddenly, interrupting my train of thought. "Cover yourself."

"What?" I asked.

Dorian was gone in a flash. She appeared in front of Grace, grabbed her, and disappeared again. Veronique tossed her frag pouches at Mother and Angel, just as I dropped to the ground to cover myself.

Veronique was full-on raging now, trying to cut one of them down before Angel could reach her or before Mother's powers could take effect.

Predictably, Mother won.

Just as Veronique was about to throw one of her circular blades, her eyes flashed, and she staggered forward.

"Veronique!"

"Get down, Gideon!" she managed to get out before her eyes turned white.

Angel, who had just protected Mother from a barrage of shrapnel, shifted his weight to his heels and burst into the air, bits of metal and blood flying off his body as he tackled Veronique.

But Veronique wasn't finished.

Even as Mother tried to control her, she lifted a hand to Angel's throat, and the flying motherfucker suddenly started losing steam. Veronique's hand flaring red, the energy moved up her arms as she overpowered him.

Damn, I wished I could do something. Damn it all to hell! But I had other problems, including the fact that Mother was approaching me, now ignoring the struggle happening between Angel and Veronique.

The thing was, when Angel hit her, they flew about forty feet to the right, but Mother had naturally focused her attention on me during this time.

A stupid move on her part, bad luck for me though.

The mangled symphony of screams began in my mind again, whirling waves of neuronal debris scraping across my brainscape. It felt like Mother had put my head in a microwave. My knees were curled to my chest, and I spasmed, trying to break free from her hold.

Then the twisted orchestra grinded to a halt.

Gideon.

Grace! I knew it was her, and even though I was on the ground twitching like a beached eel, just hearing her voice sparked courage in me. I pushed myself to my feet just as Mother stepped over me.

My god, had she taken every move out of the supervillain playbook. She actually lifted me by the throat, holding me in the air, a sinister smile on her face as she began to squeeze.

"You've have made it far, I'll give you that."

Dorian popped into view behind Mother and punched her in the back of the head with one of the circular saws. It was clear she hadn't charged it, evident by the fact that Mother's head didn't blow off. But the attack did take her off guard, and she dropped me.

By the time I hit the ground, Dorian was next to me, her hand on my wrist.

We reappeared beside Grace, who was sitting with her back against one of the buildings, her head hung low, hair in her face.

"I have to get Veronique, and then we need to get out."

"Yes, yes," I said quickly. "Be safe!"

She was gone just about the time Mother screamed out. We weren't very far away, maybe a hundred yards, and it wouldn't take Mother or Angel long to reach us.

I heard the sound of metal being pulled from the building and the whir of the helicopters being operated by clearly confused pilots, since they hadn't started shooting – *because who do you shoot at?*

One of them lifted to try to find where Dorian had taken us.

I pulled Grace into my arms, aware that it wouldn't do anything but needing to feel like I was helping and protecting her in some way.

Gently, I wiped her hair out of her fucked-up looking face, saw that her skin had sagged along her jowls, that the middle line of her face was now a different color than the rest, that one of her eyes was open, flickering white and black, and one of her hands was two times as large as the other.

"You'll be fine," I told her. "We're here now, dammit, we're here now. So just stay with us; we'll be gone soon." I kissed her forehead. "Just stay with us, Grace, I know you can do it."

Her head sank forward, and I tried to speak with her telepathically.

Grace, please, respond.

Silence.

I was startled when Dorian reappeared with Veronique slung over her shoulder. Dorian was breathing heavily, her face red.

Veronique was completely passed out, her eyes rolled up under half-closed lids.

Before I could say anything, Dorian placed her hand on Grace and spread her fingers so that she was also touching my skin.

And we were gone.

Chapter Thirty-One: Kidnap or Kill. The Story of My Life.

Our bodies took shape outside of Jim's in Oak Hill and fortunately, our Mercedes was still there. The moment our forms solidified, Dorian dropped to her knees, barely able to keep hold of Veronique.

I could tell she was overheating. I was sitting on the ground, in the same position I'd been in back at the military base. Once I adjusted to my surroundings, I unlocked the car and put Grace in the back.

Then I moved to Dorian. "I've got her," I said as I took Veronique from her arms.

I removed Veronique's helmet and body armor and set her in the front seat. As I did, she opened her eyes and looked at me. "It's going to be all right," I told her. She looked pretty bad off; her skin pale, a bruise already forming over one eye. "Just relax."

"I need …" She nodded and lifted a hand to the side of my cheek.

"Just a little," I warned.

Instantly, I felt a shift in the energy of my body. Her hand reddened for only a moment, and then she let go.

"Thanks," she whispered, her skin lightening some.

I moved to Dorian and helped take off her bulletproof vest and helmet.

I looked back at the car and realized it would be better for Veronique to sit in the back so Dorian could sit in the front with the A/C blasting her. "I'll be right back," I said, and after I moved Veronique to the back, I helped Dorian to the front.

We hit Highway 71 heading west, our fast-paced drive all but a blur to me. Dorian to my right, Veronique in the back, next to Grace … I didn't know what the fuck my life had become, but I couldn't lose any of these women.

And damn, if we didn't need to get Grace some clothes, but the few clothes we had were in shopping bags in the trunk.

I bit my nails as I drove, the lights from the road casting horizontal orange arcs across the inside of the vehicle. No music, stars overhead, my heart still beating fast even though we were moving far away from the violence.

I hadn't become desensitized yet, but I was getting close.

In my mind, I could still see the men Veronique had killed. I could still feel the bullet as it struck me in the chest. Hell, I still wore my bulletproof vest, which I'd forgotten to take off back at the restaurant. My helmet too. I was seriously driving a convertible Mercedes in a ballistic helmet and bulletproof vest.

Fuck my life.

But I was alive; it was the most alive I'd ever been. Even though Veronique had drained some of my life force, I felt rejuvenated, powerful, safe. Thank you, adrenaline! And I shouldn't have felt safe; if we had been attacked at that moment, we would have been done for. Dorian was down, Grace was in la-la land, and Veronique needed to feed.

Still, we were together, safe enough. Yeah, safe enough.

And I was the getaway driver. Some fucking superhero skill to have: I can drive a car! But it was useful. And sure, if we ever got out of this alive, later we could alternate between teleporting and driving, but that remained to be seen. So much had happened between us, and I felt it in that singular moment.

But like Italo Calvino said, "The past is like a tapeworm."

I set the vehicle into auto drive and took out my smartphone. I sent an encrypted email to Ken to tell him all was well and that we needed to talk soon. I started to send a message to Luke, but I didn't want to get into everything that just happened, so I kept it under wraps.

Sometimes it was better that way. And besides, once I had time to unpack everything that had happened, I could give him the lowdown in a series of quick texts.

Staring out at the endless highway, my *Mutants in the Making* naturally came to the forefront of my mind. I needed to write the third part, put them all together, and release it as a proper book.

But where to begin? And how could I continue writing without incriminating myself more than I'd already done? I should have published it under a damn pseudo; my vanity will be the death of me.

"Are you feeling better?" I asked Dorian after we'd driven for about thirty minutes with the cold air blasting against her face.

She nodded. "That was ... I don't know."

"We need another car, and I'll need you and possibly Veronique to help. Also, Grace needs clothes. Can't have her just sitting naked in the car."

"I can help," Veronique said from the back seat. "Just get me close enough that I can feed. Regarding her clothes, once we stop, I can try to dress her. We still have the Leslie shirt and Dorian's shorts. I believe."

"Sounds about right," I said. But listen, and seriously here – we can't leave a body trail this time." I thought of the college student we'd left back at the hotel; how frightened and confused she'd be when she finally recovered enough to wake up. "That's why we need Grace ... What are we supposed to do with the person after we drain them and steal their vehicle?"

"I could teleport them to the desert somewhere," Dorian said.

"I'll file that under 'body trail.' We should try to set that up as our MO: the less killing of innocent people, the better. I'd like that number to stay at zero going forward. The security personnel, private military soldiers, other supers – those are our targets."

"I'm sure we'll figure something out. If not, just let me feed." I watched in the rearview mirror as Veronique closed her eyes and laid her head back.

"Remember, *no body trail.*"

I pulled into a gas station about an hour later. It was the largest gas station I'd seen in my life, easily the size of a WalMacy's back east.

"Bucky's," Dorian said as she read the sign. "There are a lot of cars here."

She wasn't lying. The place was packed, and since it was open twenty-four hours, it didn't show any signs of slowing down. There were at least fifty pumps and sitting outside the entrance was a large collection of towering roosters made of corrugated metal.

Only in Texas, right?

Our goal was Santa Fe, damn near ten hours away. Grace had mentioned she wanted to go there. It was near one of the secret facilities, and once we got her up and running again, we could continue our assault.

The question of our endgame came to me and I swallowed it down, as I'd done multiple times over the last few days. *But what happens if you actually succeed?* a voice at the back of my head asked.

A memoir? was my answer.

I hated to laugh at my own answer, but I did, and Dorian gave me a funny look.

"Sorry," I told her, "my brain is a mess, scrambled like eggs, poached, boiled twice, burned around the edges."

"So, it's an egg? I'd love to eat."

"Funny. Veronique, can you walk?" I took off my helmet and worked on removing my vest.

She nodded.

"Let's get in, get some food, get back to the car, get our bags in the back, and then get another vehicle." I found a spot away from the bright lights of the entrance.

"I think I'll just stay here while you two feed." Veronique got out and retrieved our bags from the trunk. "Conserve energy."

"Good call," I told her, and Dorian and I turned to the supersized convenient store.

I was going to be driving all night, and I needed to get lit as fuck on energy drinks. Bull Bean was my go-to choice; I found their twenty-hour energy cans and grabbed a six-pack. I also picked up a pulled pork BBQ sandwich, a bag of chips, and a freaking forty-eight-ounce cup of coffee. Dorian got a sausage wrap, a sixty-four-ounce Dr. Pepper, and a pint of Blue Bell ice cream, which came with its own spoon.

We headed outside and found Veronique still leaning against the Mercedes, a sly look on her face. She watched as a man got out of a sporty two-door Mustang.

"We need something a little larger," I reminded her. "There's four of us, and we'll still have an extra body to deal with."

Nope, I hadn't come up with a solution as to how we were supposed to steal a car and not kill or kidnap the person. Since I'd already laid down the 'no killing' rule, we were going with the next best thing: kidnapping. I'd tried to come up with other options, but they all led back to these two choices. Kidnap or kill, the story of my life.

"Ah, there. That's more what we're looking for," I said as a Toyota Four Runner pulled into a space a few spots away from us.

"On it," Veronique said, and before I could really say or do anything, she approached the driver – a short woman in a pair of overalls – and drained her. She started by draining her long distance but moved in closer until the woman had all but shriveled up.

Veronique used her powers to transfer the woman's keys over to me, and after making sure no one was watching, we quickly placed the woman in the back of the Four Runner. I checked her pulse. *Whew,* she was still alive.

We then moved the naked mess that was Grace into the newly acquired vehicle, and once we put her in the back as well, Veronique began dressing her.

A car pulled up, clearly wanting our spot, but we waited for a moment. Dorian leaned against the trunk of our Mercedes, giving the country guy driving the other car a pretty good view of her rear. He focused on this for a moment, licked his lips, and moved into another spot not too far down.

"Let's go, Dorian," I said before he could approach us.

Yes, he stood no chance against her, and I'm sure Veronique wouldn't mind feeding again, but I didn't want to cause a scene. She followed my lead, Blue Bell spoon in her mouth, drink in hand as she sashayed to the front passenger side of the Four Runner.

With a smile on my face (because who doesn't like seeing someone walk like that?), I grabbed what was left of our bulletproof gear, and kept the Mercedes keys in my pocket.

"Good job, everyone," I said. I adjusted the seat in the Four Runner and started it up. We got back on the highway, and when we were about thirty minutes away from the gas station, we pulled over and I buried the Mercedes keys.

By this point, Dorian was sleeping, her hands on her distended belly, and Veronique was awake in the back seat, sipping from the big ass cup of coffee I'd bought.

"What are we going to do with her in Santa Fe?" she asked.

"Which her?" I looked at Veronique through the rearview mirror. "The owner of the vehicle?"

"Grace."

"We're going to contact Ken. But first, we're going to see what we can do on our own."

"And the woman in the back?" she shifted her weight so she could look behind her at the unconscious owner of our new vehicle. "I could drain her some more," she said, red energy radiating up her fingertips.

"Veronique, don't kill her. We're going to drop her off at a hospital. Take her ID first, make sure we aren't on camera. Better yet, maybe we'll just drop her off in front of a McStarbucks or something. No, that's too visual. A hospital. We'll figure it out. Maybe Dorian can teleport with her to the front and teleport away instantly. Yeah. Then they won't see the vehicle."

I was thinking out loud, two Bull Bean energy drinks down, my heart thumping in my chest.

More driving. Minutes became hours and every now and then Veronique would check on me to make sure I was still awake. But I'd never been more awake in my life. It wasn't so much because of the energy drinks as it was a determination to save Grace. We'd made it this far. We would see this to the end.

At some point we stopped, refueled, used the restrooms, and got more coffee.

Kept moving.

Texas became a tumbleweed blur.

I set the SUV in auto drive and relaxed a little. Damn, was auto drive nice, and as the Toyota drove itself, I took a deep breath and finished another energy drink. I felt a hand fall on my lap and I took it, squeezing tightly. I looked over to see Dorian smiling at me.

"You're doing well," she whispered.

"You'll get us there, Gideon," Veronique said from the back.

"Why are you two still up?" I asked, half-jokingly.

"We're keeping watch," Dorian said, her hand still in mine. "Let me know if there's anything else I can do." She flicked a finger at my pocket.

"And I'm making sure she doesn't wake up." For the third time that night, Veronique drained the woman we'd taken hostage.

"Careful," I reminded both of them.

We neared the Texas-New Mexico border.

I'd been driving for hours, and after we reached a small, semi-forgotten town, I saw a sign pointing to a hospital. We drove to the hospital, stopped a few parking lots away, and Dorian disappeared with the woman, returning seconds later empty-handed.

The mind-numbing journey continued.

I drank another Bull Bean and felt a surge of faux energy.

The sun was starting to come up, adding a touch of pink to the horizon.

I suddenly felt like crying. I suddenly felt like jumping into the air and clicking my heels together.

I suddenly felt like driving the SUV off a cliff.

Relax, Writer Gideon.

It wasn't Grace. It was my own subconscious, but I was fine with that.

Long story short: We somehow made it to Santa Fe. And when we did, I pulled up to the first hotel I could find and got a room with double beds.

The sun was up, the air was cooler, the altitude higher, and I was exhausted.

Chapter Thirty-Two: A Golden Shower in Santa Fe

It wasn't quite a golden shower, but as I carried Grace into the hotel bedroom in Santa Fe, she pissed in my arms and all over the front of my shirt.

I was too exhausted to care, but rather than lay her in the bed, I put her in the bathtub, figuring she may go again. I took off my shirt – so long, Austin Ice Bats – and realized then that I didn't have any other clothing.

The gift shop.

It was about eight in the morning, and the gift shop would be open soon. Not at all concerned with the fact that I was a bearded shirtless man with a gnarly scar on his cheek, I walked back to the hotel's reception area and told them I needed a shirt.

The clerk looked at my bloodshot eyes with alarm, and her manager came running. I told them I'd had a problem with my other shirt and that I'd like them to open the gift shop so I could buy one of those kitschy New Mexico shirts.

"In particular," I told the manager, "I'd like the one with the wolf jumping in front of the moon."

"The gift shop opens at ten," he said.

"Please give me something, or …"

I glanced over my shoulder, assuming Veronique or Dorian had followed me.

They hadn't, but I didn't need to press any further. The manager saw the crazy look in my eyes, opened the gift shop, and handed me a medium.

"Make it a large," I told him, "I need some room to breathe."

If ever there was an understatement of the year …

He returned with a large wolf shirt and I meandered my way back to our room.

"I need to message Ken," I mumbled when I stepped inside.

Dorian, who was resting on the bed, flashed away and appeared behind me.

"You need to rest, Gideon," she said, placing her hands on my shoulders. Veronique was already out, cuddled up under the blankets on the bed farthest from the door.

"I need to shower too," I said.

"Relax."

342

"Grace," I told her, and with that, I entered the bathroom.

Grace's skin had melted away even more, but I wasn't bothered by it in the least bit. I knelt by the tub and started smoothing her hair out of her face.

"Gideon," Dorian said, stepping into the room behind me. "You drank too many energy drinks. You need some rest."

"There's no such thing, goddammit!"

But by this point, I was stripping down to my boxers and getting into the tub with Grace. I positioned myself behind her, wrapped her in my arms, and looked up at Dorian.

"I'll rest here."

And rest I did. For hours and hours, I slept with Grace in my arms. She was breathing, and I could feel her lungs expand with each breath in, but other than that, she was pretty much dead to the world.

Or so I thought.

I woke up hours later to Grace's voice in my head.

Writer Gideon.

I tried to move out from under her, but my leg was asleep.

Grace? I thought and tried to shake my leg out. It wasn't easy, especially because she was on top of me. As I woke up, I saw that Dorian was sitting with her back against the door, also asleep.

I'm here. I don't know what Mother did but ...

We're in Santa Fe, I thought to her, *where you wanted to visit.*

Is it beautiful?

Don't know.

You drove here last night after rescuing me and haven't seen the city.

That's right. I only saw some Pueblo-styled buildings. George R.R. Martin once lived here. That'd be a nice life, living in Santa Fe and writing fantasy.

It would be very nice. Dorian, Veronique, and I could live with you and we could redesign the home.

I would love that.

We would too.

I swallowed hard. I never pictured myself as the type to have a polyamorous commune with beautiful women, but then again, Mormons did it ...

Why are you thinking about Utah again? Grace thought to me.

Sorry. My brain is an onion that shouldn't be unraveled.

Your brain is more like a dog that chases its tail and sometimes catches it.

Hey!

I don't know how long I'll be like this, she thought, changing subjects. *And I'm sorry for my appearance. It must be gruesome.*

I don't care about that. What I care about is getting you back to your full operating level.

It may not be possible. Are you prepared for that?

We will do it, Grace.

I wanted to ask your permission before I did something.

What do you mean? The blood had returned to my leg and I was able to shift myself to a more comfortable position, waking Dorian. She nodded as she wiped the sleep out of her eyes, smearing a bit of her eyeliner.

I want to transfer my power to you.

"You want to do what?" I asked aloud.

It would be temporary, but before I did it, I wanted to ask your permission.

"Why would you want to do that?"

Dorian looked at me this time, realizing almost immediately who I was talking to.

Please be prepared for what I'm about to tell you, Gideon.

What do you mean?

I know the picture you found on my drive has been on your mind.

Yes, you never told me what that was about.

A series of flashes came to me. I saw myself going to the Rose-Lyle facility, my parents dropping me off, being led down a hallway, staying overnight in a sterile room …

I gasped. *Are you serious?*

Yes, it's really what happened.

More images, these containing my parents picking me up from the facility, a discharge letter handed to my mother, payment, looking over my shoulder at the place one last time.

They tested local children to see if Mother could give her power to anyone else, aside from me.

Aside from you?

It's how Mother gave me my abilities.

You weren't born with superpowers?

No, I was the only one in my batch who didn't have a power. So, Mother gave me some of hers, as she was the only telepath at the time. Like Dorian's teleportation, the shifting part of my abilities grew later.

I looked from Grace to Dorian, who had no idea of the drama playing out in my head.

You were one of the children they tested, around the time you and your family moved to Hamden. You made it to the second round; only a few others made it that far.

So, I'm a mutant?

No, but you aren't far off. They actually stopped testing the children who made it to the second round; they were more susceptible to the procedure, and there's no way of telling if it would have actually worked for them if they had continued. This is why I believe I can give my power to you. I'm almost certain, and I also believe it's why I found you that first night. It wasn't just fate; some part of me sensed you.

This is a lot to process ...

There's no time. They are coming. They activated tracking devices in our drives.

"Come again?" I asked aloud.

Grace repeated the thought in my head.

"Shit, shit, shit! Dorian, tell Veronique to expect company. They're tracking us!"

"How soon?" she asked.

"No telling, but we should ... Fuck, okay, I'll handle what I can. Shit! We've wasted hours. My fault, totally my fault."

Writer Gideon, I will give you my power.

347

"You can't do that," I told Grace, confusion setting in. *Would my parents really do this to me?*

It was a long time ago. We're your family now, and Grace and Dorian will need you.

A thousand thoughts came to me and I compartmentalized them all. Panic rose in my chest and I forced that shit down.

Now was the time to act.

The first person I needed to talk to was Dr. Kim. He'd know how to disable the GPS tracking. I scrambled to get out of the bathtub so I could get my phone, which was in the pocket of my pants that I'd tossed haphazardly on the floor.

You haven't given me permission about transferring my psychic powers.

"You have my permission, but I only want you to do it if we're attacked."

There may not be much time.

"Just let me get things in order first," I said. I scrolled to my inbox and fired off a message to Ken Kim telling him to call me immediately.

There were also messages from Luke. While I waited for Kim to call, I read through them and started to reply.

Luke: Update me. I haven't heard from you.

Me: I'm in the southwestern part of America. We have Grace. She's comatose. I'm preparing for an attack. I may be a mutant.

Luke: WTF.

Me: WTF X 2.

Luke: You never get a chance to rest, do you? Well, I don't know what to say. I'll be honest, I haven't known how to respond to any of this since I realized the truth. I hope that's okay.

I put on my shirt, slipped into my jeans, and returned to our conversation. "Come on, Kim," I whispered as I looked back at my phone.

Me: I'll be able to talk about it more later. It's just too much right now.

Luke: Let me know if there's anything I can do. Sounds dumb to say, but you know what I mean.

Me: Thanks, man.

Luke: Update me once all this settles down. You really need to set up a file of info I can publish or get to the Canadian authorities if something happens.

Me: Seriously.

My phone rang, and I answered it immediately.

"Ken, they're tracking us, and I need a way to stop them from doing that. *Now.* Actually, *yesterday.* I needed this yesterday. They're probably on their way here now. Fuck! Sorry, it's been a long thirty-six hours, and for at least ..." I checked the time on my phone. "For at least seven of those hours, I was sleeping. I just found out I was tested on and almost became a mutant."

"What? You're talking too fast. Calm down and tell me what happened."

I repeated pretty much the same thing but slower this time.

"Damn, okay, so they've activated their GPS locators. And you're just now figuring that out."

"Why weren't they active all the time?"

"Because the girls weren't supposed to escape; Dorian and Veronique were part of the team that existed for real-world extractions. I don't think you realize how uncanny it is that you were able to convince them to join you."

"It wasn't as hard as it sounds. We can discuss that later." I glanced over at Grace's melted form. "I need to handle this now. And something is wrong with Grace, but I'll get to that later too."

I heard Ken typing on a keyboard. "Shit, just what I expected," he finally said after a few bated breaths.

Veronique and Dorian came into the bathroom wearing their bulletproof vests, fanny packs, and helmets. Dorian handed me my gear, and I put Ken on speakerphone.

"Getting dressed," I told him as I slipped into the vest. "What's going on?"

"The GPS fix can only be done with a manual override."

"How do I do that?"

"I'll need to plug into one of their ports and do it. It requires a special key, and you don't have the key."

I looked at Dorian, who also wore the backpack we'd purchased back in Austin. "How long do you think it would take you to get to New Haven from here?"

"Alone?"

I nodded.

"How far is it?" she asked.

"Ken, how far is it from New Mexico to Connecticut?"

"Over two thousand miles. And she can move in increments of about twelve hundred miles a pop."

Dorian crossed her arms. She looked concerned. "I'll have to recharge," she said after a moment. "And eat something. It'll take me a moment to figure out a spawning location. Two thousand miles there and back. About an hour. I think it will take me about an hour."

Ken's voice piped out of the phone. "Have her go to Memphis or possibly Nashville. Teleport out from there. Come back the same way. I'll give her photos of my apartment. We can make the exchange here. The problem is: if they come for you while she's gone, you're down a member."

"We may have a solution for that," I said, thinking about Grace's request to transfer some of her power to me. "These keys, are they simply USB drives?"

"Something like that. I'll set this key to override GPS signaling upon manual reboot."

"Got it. Forward the photos to my email. I'm sending Dorian to you with my smartphone and then she'll come right back to us. I have a burner phone just in case."

Dorian nodded. "And I'll be able to find you because of what you've done with my teleportation abilities."

"That's right, Empathetic Teleportation. Please don't take long; I have a feeling we're going to need you."

I heard something land on the roof. Then another thump, followed by a much louder sound.

"We've got to go," I told Ken. "They're here."

"How did you find this place?" I asked Dorian as soon as our bodies took shape, Grace in my arms, Veronique and Dorian triangled in front of me.

We were on a cliffside near an abandoned Pueblo-styled house that looked like it had been decades since it was someone's home.

"I saw it when we drove into Santa Fe," she told me.

"And why did you choose this place exactly?" Veronique asked.

Dorian indicated the road below us. "I believe we're about twenty to thirty miles outside of town. There's only one way to get here, and it's on that road; the same road that we drove on yesterday – or was it today? It was today."

I had to laugh. "Fuck, do I feel you there, I don't know what day it is."

"Anyway, you'll be able to see them coming. And ..." she looked around. "Yep, over there's a pile of scrap metal. I saw that too."

"How did you have time to see all this stuff?" I asked. "I don't even remember driving on that road."

"It was the first house I saw that was shaped in this style of architecture they have here. And there was that metal trash heap next to it. Use it to your advantage." Dorian looked at Veronique. "I'll return as fast as I can, you have my word."

"We'll hold them off, isn't that right, Gideon?" Veronique asked me.

"Before you leave, there's something you two should know," I said suddenly. "Grace has asked if she could give me some of her power. Apparently, I was once tested for susceptibility to whatever superhero gene you three have. I believe it's only the psychic powers, not her shifting abilities, but it could be handy. Especially her Omnikinesis. So I'm going to say yes."

Dorian smirked. "Welcome to the club."

"The club?"

"You always wanted to be a superhero, didn't you?"

"I guess that's right," I said and handed her my smartphone.

Dorian disappeared, leaving me with Grace and Veronique. It was a cool evening, and as I carried Grace over to the shadows provided by the abandoned house, she spoke to me again inside my head.

Are you ready, Writer Gideon?

Will you lose any of your abilities by giving some to me? I thought back to her.

I don't think so, and I don't plan to give them to you permanently. Once I'm better, I will take them back.

I heard the clink of metal behind me as Veronique used her ability to move some of the metal around, so they faced in the direction of the road below.

Okay, if you say so, Grace; I trust you.

I trust you too.

As soon as she said that, a strange sensation moved up my body, stopping at the center of my skull. It felt like someone had constructed a pillar made of light inside me. My surroundings became clearer to me, the feeling in my hands lightened, my chest lost its heaviness ... it was almost what floating might feel like.

I realized that my eyes were closed and that the luminous landscape I saw before me was my consciousness expanding.

I opened my eyes with a gasp and saw Veronique continuing to use her powers to move metal.

There was something different about me.

I looked at a piece of metal and thrust my hand out like I was auditioning for a role in Star Wars. To my surprise, the metal lifted, twisted once, and fell back to the ground.

Veronique stopped what she was doing and looked at me. I could see her aura in the form of a strange, shadowy darkness hovering over her. I could see in her eyes that ... she really liked me.

She averted her gaze. "Do not use her abilities on me."

"I don't know how to turn them off," I said as I approached the edge of the cliff. I guess calling it a cliff was overselling it a bit, as it was more of a ridge, but that did give us a vantage point.

Plus, I was a writer. Everything I thought or experienced was cast through the gaze of hyperbole.

"I'll help you move metal," I told Veronique. "I need to practice this."

Veronique nodded, but she refused to look back in my direction.

The strange thing about the power Grace had transferred to me was that I could sense more than just humans. I sensed everything around me – blades of grass beating in the cool evening wind, a rabbit not far away burrowing into its hole, the life of the city miles away.

It was an entirely psychedelic experience.

I practiced swinging the metal bars, and as I got the hang of it, I heard Grace in my head again, only this time it was as if she'd descended from heaven and pressed her ethereal body into mine.

It was different than before, not just a voice … almost as if I were speaking it to myself, almost as if we suddenly had a hive mind.

Do you like it, Writer Gideon?

I think? It's just so powerful. I feel like I've always existed and that everyone has always been here, that our stories are all intertwined and replicas of each other. I'm sorry, it's just so strong.

You'll get used to it. They're coming soon, and you need to focus on getting ready.

Please come out of whatever coma you're in, Grace. This power belongs to you. We need you here, I need you here.

I can't yet. There's something stopping me. I can hear you, I can sense you ... I can almost feel you, and I can speak to you, but my body is not mine right now.

I continued to practice my abilities.

One of the first things I noticed was that I didn't need to make any cool Bruce Lee hand gestures to move things and that some of the changes happened almost before I could complete their thought.

Case in point: a partially crumbled brick wall. I walked toward it, focusing on it, wanting it to collapse, but it was only when it fell that I realized my desire for it to fall had come *after* the action.

It was entirely bizarre.

There had been vehicles traveling on the highway below us the whole time we were here, but the way some of the latest ones moved told me that we were about to get some company. The odd part about this assumption was that I intuited it when the vehicles were just specks on the horizon.

And as I watched, I *felt* them approach, sensed their impending arrival. I turned toward Veronique and told her this was it.

357

"Good luck," she said.

"Same to you," was the only comeback I could muster.

Veronique launched her first attack the moment the SUVs and Humvees started turning onto the dirt road that led to the house. Bars of metal rocketed down the hillside, straight into the windows, killing the drivers of the first three vehicles.

By this point, the vehicles had stopped and people were piling out. I didn't know the range of Grace's ability, and rather than test it, I held back, waiting to handle those who actually breached the barrier.

I recalled one of Grace's abilities that I hadn't had a chance to practice yet, mostly because I didn't have a target.

This was another reason to hold back, because if it worked …

The first two soldiers breached the front of the property, and as soon as I saw them, I took control of their minds.

Is this what it feels like?

Yes, Grace answered.

I smiled as the two men's consciousness appeared in my pane of vision. It wasn't like a video game with multiple perspectives, it was more like a dream in which I was someone else, yet also myself, our experiences playing out at the same time.

I imagined myself as the men, pointing their guns at each other and shooting.

358

Pop! Pop!

They fell.

"Holy shit ..." I whispered.

I heard a swoosh behind me. Angel had landed on the roof of the house.

"Angel!" I shouted to Veronique, telling her of his location with a thought that she clearly received.

She struck him with another metal bar just as he reached the ground. He flew to the right, smashed into a fucking cactus, and tumbled in the dirt.

"Bullets!" I warned Veronique, foreshadowing their arrival.

Bullets came, and she quickly stopped them, turning them back on the men moving up the hill.

Dorian had chosen an incredibly good spot to leave us, as the men could only fight going up. Even Angel was now standing on a slope.

I kept listening for helicopters, and sure enough, I heard some.

No matter, as long as I could see the pilot ...

That's right, Writer Gideon, you can do this! Grace's voice rang out in my head.

"I've got Angel," I told Veronique.

His hair in his face, the superpowered mommy humper stomped over to me, ready to put an end to this. "Something has changed about you," he growled, likely noticing the color of my eyes.

I could see Angel's aura, and I could see there was no way I would be able to overpower him and take over his psyche. Forcing him to do something like shit his pants and perform the chicken dance wasn't going to be an option.

I had to act fast.

I used my mind to swing one of the steel bars at Angel, bitch-slapping the hell out of him and dislocating his jaw.

Blood dripping from his chin, Angel wiped his face and prepared to fly into me. Just then a soldier came up around the bend. I took over his psyche and instructed him to fire his weapon at my adversary.

It was that fluid. Everything moved fast, but somehow, Grace's ability slowed things down. It gave me time to think, to move, to orchestrate an attack from the soldier, who began firing quick blasts at Angel as the superpowered man charged him.

Brrrrrat! Brrrrrat! Brrrrrat!

Rather than slamming into me, Angel smacked into the guy, grabbed him by the neck and threw him over the side of the ridge. Meanwhile, Veronique busied herself gathering a wall of bullets with one hand – which she turned toward Angel – while collecting more with her other hand.

The helicopter appeared, a spotlight shining down on us. Veronique tossed some of the bullets at it, but to no avail.

I heard the whir of a weapon, and just as the chopper was about to fire on us, and Angel was about to mop up whatever mess was left, Dorian appeared, out of breath, with a small case in her hands.

Veronique ran to me, and I scooped Grace into my arms. Dorian grabbed hold of us, and we flashed away in an instant, reappearing on the roof of the house.

I swear it happened in slow motion.

The helicopter pilot looked at us and I caught his gaze. In an instant, I had taken over the man's psyche and suddenly, I was *mentally flying the helicopter while still in my own body*, trying to come to grips with what was going on.

I tipped the fuselage toward Angel and crashed into him before he could zip away, causing an explosion that launched dirt, rocks, and hunks of steel into the air.

"Did you just fly the helicopter into Angel?" Dorian asked, the vein pulsing on her head. It had only been about forty minutes since she left; she'd hauled ass back here. "Gideon. Please. Gideon. Can you hear me?"

She touched my cheek and I snapped out of it.

"You've got to install this on Grace and Veronique," she said, handing me the key and my smartphone. "Do it on Grace first; Veronique and I will continue the fight."

"Are you okay to fight?" I looked over the edge of the rooftop. I didn't know how I was going to get down, but that was answered a second later when she teleported me to the ground.

"I'm ready," Dorian said, paintbrush in hand.

I took a deep breath, smoke, fire, and the taste of metal in my mouth.

Chapter Thirty-Three: Everyone Needs a Little Head

Dorian wasn't lying. As I plugged the key she'd given me into Grace's neck, the punk rock teleporter conjured up a man with a huge buster sword. She sent the sword-wielding energy creation running toward the next group of soldiers who were approaching with their weapons drawn.

They fired on it, and as they did, she conjured up a muscular, two-headed giant with an energy cannon on its shoulder. It was weird to see her construct something so tall; it was all in the way she used her forward momentum when making the creation. The more exaggerated she became, the larger it grew.

On the other side of the fight, Veronique was tossing anything metal she could get her hands on, figuratively and literally. She was also losing steam, and I saw her drop to one knee, pulling a downed soldier in her direction.

Dorian teleported in front of Veronique, covering her with more creations while she fed. When Veronique finished, she touched Dorian's hand, and the two of them disappeared, only to reappear down the hill behind enemy lines.

I returned my focus to Grace.

The key in her neck was still loading. There was a liquid crystal display on it, light blue, and of all goddamn things, it was showing me the hourglass symbol. If there's anything that has come to represent the shittiness of the twenty-first century and first world problems that many of us face, it was the hourglass symbol.

This would have bothered me less if it weren't for the fact that Grace and I were sitting ducks, and the smoke around the helicopter hadn't cleared, so I didn't know how Angel was doing over there.

"Come on, come on, come on," I whispered as the hourglass continued to load. A green light on the key flashed, and I took that to mean it was done. I plugged in my smartphone and did the reboot, just as Dr. Kim had instructed.

It was Veronique's turn.

I stood, hyper-aware of what was going on around me. I could still feel Grace's powers coursing through me, and I could still sense movement nearby. I turned just in time to see a female in MercSecure gear raise her assault weapon.

She shouted for me to raise my hands, and then her eyes flashed white. It had taken me a split second to completely take over her mind, and once I'd done so, I turned her back toward the fight, instructing her to take out anyone in MercSecure gear.

Dorian appeared beside me, her face red, chest heaving as she took deep breaths.

"Grace is finished. Now I need Veronique."

She wiped her face. "Okay, I'll bring her."

Dorian flashed away, and they were back in a matter of moments. I told Veronique to be as still as possible while I loaded the information.

She crouched, and I plugged the key into her neck port. Her eyes were trained on the horizon, ready for anyone and anything to come in our direction.

There was another helicopter approaching, but they didn't scare me as much as they used to.

It took a moment for the hourglass to appear, and I reminded Veronique to stay still while it did its thing.

As it loaded, I tried to focus as hard as I could on our surroundings, especially the smoke clearing near Angel's downed body. I was able to catch one of the men crawling toward us and turned him on his colleagues. There was some gunfire, the sounds of a few people crying out as they either died or Dorian's energy creations burnt through them, but the battle was winding down.

And we were winning.

"You did great out there," I told Veronique as she continued scanning for anything that could be construed as metal death coming in our direction.

The helicopter drew closer, but she didn't need to take it down. Dorian had already flashed inside the chopper and left a small energy bomb before bailing out, sending the bird crashing down into the cacti, debris, and bodies at the bottom of the hill.

She appeared next to me, completely out of breath, two veins now pulsing on her forehead. "That's all of them," she panted.

"Come the fuck on," I said to the damned hourglass.

"We have to make sure he's dead," Veronique said.

"We will. Just let this finish loading."

Once the program finished, I pocketed the key, ran the reboot, and we began searching the wreckage. We should have just teleported away, but if Angel was dying or dead, knowing that would aid us in the future.

This was something that usually isn't covered in comic books and superhero action-adventure movies: the aftermath. Sure, they pan across it or show it for a brief moment before switching to the next scene, but actually seeing the carnage firsthand is something that still gets to me, even after everything I've been through with the Cherry Blossom Girls.

But that wasn't on my mind as we searched the wreckage.

I knew that Angel may still be alive, and I was using every part of Grace's power to make sure we weren't blindsided by an attack.

There was a charred body not too far away, which I assumed was the helicopter pilot, mostly because of his helmet. I moved past him and saw another body under one of the helicopter blades, its legs still covered in flames from the burning wreckage.

Metal lifted off the body as Veronique finished moving debris to the side. She dropped to her haunches and began draining the rest of the life force from what I now saw was just another random private military operative.

I needed a new noun to call these guys, because they weren't soldiers – well, not soldiers in the traditional sense – but calling them 'private military operatives' or 'security detail' or 'security personnel' or 'paramilitary unit' or 'assholes with guns' didn't exactly roll off the tongue.

The search for Angel continued.

I found part of another body, which is gruesome to say and was gruesome to experience, and I found a clump of something that seemed like it used to be alive, but still no Angel.

His body shouldn't have melted away; even if he was burned to a crisp, there would still be something left, I thought as I walked around the wreckage site.

Veronique was just turning around when she was tackled by a man wearing a pilot's helmet.

The man was on his feet in a matter of seconds, ripping the helmet off and throwing it over his shoulder.

Angel.

His skin was blackened, and there was a large swath of his hair that had been torn away and was now scabbing up, but he was still formidable, and my fuck, was he pissed.

He brought his leg back to kick Veronique, but she rolled away just in time and struck him with one of the helicopter blades.

Dorian's form flashed to Veronique's left and she began drawing a lance in the air.

Angel recovered almost instantly. He brought both fists back, only to have his forward momentum thwarted by Dorian's energy spear. It struck him in the shoulder, burnt a hole right through him, and came out the other side. He cried out in anguish and flung himself into the air in an effort to escape, only to be slammed back down to the ground by Veronique's helicopter blade.

His muscles bulged as he lifted the blade off of him and threw it in her direction. She was able to stop it in midair, but by the time she did, Angel had reached her.

Dorian flashed behind him, one of the small frag pouches in her fist.

Boom!

She was gone before the pouch exploded, sending bits of shrapnel into Angel's back and throwing a nail right past the side of my head.

Goddamn, was I glad I was wearing a ballistic helmet!

Realizing what Dorian had done, Veronique reached into her fanny pack and came out with one of the circular saws. Neither of them had used much of our makeshift weaponry this time, so they were fully stocked and prepared to take on the superpowered motherfucker.

Angel recovered from Dorian's attack and pick up his speed, rocketing toward Veronique and grabbing her by the neck. He lifted her into the air and slammed her hard into the ground.

Dorian teleported behind him again and he swiveled around just in time to connect his fist with her chest as she zipped away.

She appeared on the other side of me, stumbled forward and fell to one knee, gasping for air.

"No!" I shouted.

Grace's ability surging through me, I swept Angel off his feet with a wave of telekinetic energy. My borrowed power pushed him back about ten feet, leaving a mark in the soil as he was dragged and scraped across scattered bits of debris.

Angel jumped to his feet and glared at me, his fists curling at his side.

And then his head flew off his body.

I watched in what seemed like slow motion as Veronique's circular saw continued on over the side of the ridge, and Angel's headless corpse tumbled to the ground.

Silence passed between the three of us. Well, four of us if you count Angel's head. Or, five of us if you count Grace's comatose body.

"What now?" I finally asked.

But Dorian had already staggered back to her feet and was moving toward Angel, unzipping her backpack as she went.

Chapter Thirty-Four: Cherry Blossoms

Our bodies took shape on the other side of Santa Fe. I mean, I guess it was the other side. It looked kind of like a neighborhood, so that meant it may have been near our last hotel. I really had no idea, but Dorian seemed to know where she was going.

She was exhausted, and her abilities were pretty much depleted. From what I could tell, we were in a cul-de-sac, which was a strange place to transport us, but I didn't think we were in any condition to try to check into a hotel.

By 'we,' I meant Dorian, Veronique, Grace, Yours Truly, and Angel's fucking head, which was in Dorian's backpack.

Look, there are a lot of situations I never thought I'd find myself taking part in, and carrying someone's decapitated head with me probably topped that list. No, it *definitely* topped that list, but as I would find out on this continued adventure, expectations and my increasingly demented reality rarely coexisted.

And even though she was relatively light, Grace was starting to get heavy in my arms. This was likely due to exhaustion and hunger.

But if *I* was exhausted and hungry, I could only imagine what Veronique and Dorian were going through.

"So here's the plan: We find a house, and I do Grace's thing with the owners; Veronique, you drain one of them; we sleep and shower in their place and leave in the morning."

"What about the people?" Dorian asked.

"We'll send them somewhere. How about Texas?"

She nodded. While she still looked like she was overheating some, she'd recovered from having the wind knocked out of her by Angel. Veronique, on the other hand, was still limping a little.

Dorian helped Veronique walk while I carried Grace. We made our way to yet another Pueblo-style home with a big truck in the driveway and an SUV next to it.

I walked up to the front porch, and a light came on. I rang the doorbell and waited.

We were in the South, and the chance of someone opening the door with a shotgun was high. I wasn't in the least bit surprised to hear a man call out on the other side of the door that he had a weapon, and he wanted to know what I needed.

"I was jogging in the area, and I found this woman's body."

I realized then that I was still wearing my ballistic helmet and a bulletproof vest. But maybe he couldn't see clearly enough through the peephole to tell. So I changed my story.

"Sorry, not jogging … biking, and seriously, I just need a way to contact the authorities. Something's wrong with her, and I don't have my phone with me."

"You just stay right there, and I'll call the police."

I looked over my shoulder at Dorian.

She flashed away and flashed back, the man now with her. Before he could raise his gun or figure out what the hell was going on, I had him under my spell.

Or, Grace's spell.

This was odd, because he was actually looking at us – or at least, Veronique and me because Dorian was at his side. I saw myself in that moment, even though I was also viewing him through my own consciousness.

And what I saw frightened me.

This was what I look like in a bulletproof vest, a ballistic helmet, a melty-faced shifter in my arms, and scratches and dirt all over my body. Veronique was next to me, also looking like she'd just been put through the wringer, her short blonde bob tangled and messy, blood on her forehead, and clearly suffering from pain in her lower back, evident in the way she stood.

But the man no longer saw that.

He let us into his house, where we found his wife standing with another gun. He told her to relax, even though he didn't need to because by that point I'd already taken over her mind as well, which added yet another perspective of us to my pane of vision.

I asked them if they had any kids and they said yes, in college. I told them to go ahead and pack their things, that they were going to visit one of their kids.

"Which one?" he asked me, a hint of white to his eyes now.

"Which one is closest?"

"Well, Michael is at the University of Colorado at Boulder. I guess he's closest."

I considered the distance. I was pretty sure Colorado wasn't too far away from here, so I asked him which one was the farthest.

"Lucy is at the University of Arkansas."

"Sounds like a great place to go," I said. "Pack your things and meet me down here before you leave."

"You got it," the man said as he and his wife went upstairs to their bedroom.

We cased the house and found it to be pretty damn comfortable. There were several bedrooms, but what really interested me was a huge, fluffy sheepskin rug in the living room.

Lots of pillows too. A perfect place to sleep, even if it was on a hardwood floor.

"I need to shower," Dorian said after we made our second sweep of the place. I'd already set Grace down in the living room on one of the leather couches. Angel's head was still in Dorian's backpack.

"By all means," I said. "And put that backpack in a closet or something."

The couple rejoined me in the front foyer.

Veronique drained one of them – the woman – until she was on the verge of passing out. I told her not to take the man's energy because he was going to be the one driving.

Once the couple left, we retired to the living room and collapsed onto one of the other couches.

"What a fucking day," I finally said.

"Yes, it has been a fucking day."

"I believe that was yesterday," I told her with a grin.

"Maybe your superpower is being clever."

"I wish!" I yawned, and as I did, I got a whiff of my armpit. "I need a shower."

"So do I."

We locked eyes and stood at the same time.

Figuring it would be a good idea to save water, we decided to use the downstairs bathroom together. No sex this time – both of us were too exhausted – but we at least cleaned each other, which was always a good experience.

We were blessed by the fact that this couple happened to be good hosts; there were actually bathrobes in the guest bathroom. I slipped into one, and Veronique donned the other.

We went back to the living room and found Dorian sitting with her legs crossed on one of the couches, also in a bathrobe, watching a home improvement show.

I laughed.

I laughed long and hard, thinking of how odd it was that one could act so leisurely after all that had happened.

I plopped down beside Dorian, Veronique sat next to me, and as if nothing had happened that night, we watched a couple purchase a fixer-upper and rebuild it from the ground up.

Toward the end of the episode, I decided to bring some pillows over and get down onto the sheepskin rug. Veronique came with me, and after getting a blanket from one of the bedrooms, Dorian joined us.

It was the best sleep I'd had in years.

I woke the next morning surprisingly refreshed.

My initial thought was to get on my phone and tell Luke about what happened and also let Dr. Kim know we were safe. But my phone was out of battery, and it needed to be charged.

So no phone for now.

The windows at the back of the house let in a nice view of rocky hills peppered with cacti. I decided to take Grace out there, even though she couldn't see it.

Another thought came to me. *Grace hasn't spoken in a while ...*

This was followed by the realization that I still had some of her abilities, evident by the aura I could see around Dorian and Veronique's bodies.

I took a second glance at both of them and noticed that the belts around their robes had come loose. "If you're reading my thoughts, sorry," I told Grace as I opened the glass door that led to a backyard patio.

I laid her down on one of the long wooden lawn chairs. Rather than pull another chair over, I simply sat next to her, my knees to my chest, and basked in the morning sun.

Why aren't you talking to me? I thought to her.

No response.

So, I just enjoyed her company for a while, even though there was no real company to enjoy.

The sun was on her face now, and she was still in the clothing we'd bought back in Texas.

As I stared at her, I was struck by an idea.

I don't know if the idea had somehow been planted by Grace, or if it was my own, but I had the sudden notion to try to *put* her power back into her.

I even had a vision of a Pentecostal possession, a curing of someone's illness.

Maybe I just need some coffee, I thought, but the image remained, and part of me felt like it could actually work.

As crazy as I knew it would look – and I was glad Dorian and Veronique were still asleep – I straddled the long chair, pressed both thumbs on her temples, and gazed intently at her deformed face.

Leave me, I thought.

And it was just about as effective as saying 'leave me' to a rock would be.

I began to think about the moment Grace appeared in my life and all that had followed. I remembered how much she liked the cherry blossom trees and how her appearance that day had signaled their blooming.

Thinking about them created more cherry blossoms in my mind, swirling red and white petals falling from the trees like I'd seen in Wooster Square.

"Cherry blossoms," I whispered, and more came to me, whirling in my head, taking over my body as if they were a pillar of luminous life force.

I opened my eyes and I *saw* the cherry blossoms between us. I saw them piling up on Grace's chest, melting into her skin, floating away with every exhale I made and drifting back when I breathed in.

They were everywhere, they were tangible, they were real, and as I realized this, I felt a sharp pain at the base of my spine. The pain spread upward, carrying with it blooming deep red cherry blossoms through my body. They began to leave my body, surging into Grace's misshapen, mangled form and transforming it, reshaping it ... *repairing* it.

Her features returned, her skin softened, her nose reformed, and color returned to her lips.

She gasped and opened her eyes – beaming white eyes that quickly regained their iceberg blue color.

"Grace!" I practically knocked the chair over as I gathered her into my arms.

"Gid ... eon?"

"How are you feeling?" I asked as I pulled away from her and swept the hair from her face. By now we were both standing, straddling the chair, and I had no idea how it happened.

"I'm … weak," she said as I helped her over to the banister that overlooked the yard.

"You'll get stronger again," I promised, a wave of emotion moving through me. "We'll lay low for a few days and … damn, there's just so much I have to tell you. Yes. Lay low. Let's start by just laying low for a few days. I can finish my book, you and the others can rest, and we can put together a solid plan. They won't find us. They can't track us any longer."

"A solid plan?" she started coughing, and I waited for her to finish.

"We're not far from Albuquerque," I told her, "and there's another facility outside the city. That's our next target."

"We can't stop now," she finally said, her voice scratchy. "They tried to kill me. Veronique too."

"Dorian and me too." I looked down at my feet, at our feet as they touched, felt the anger coursing through me. "And they're not going to stop trying to kill us. But we have a present for Mother next time we see her."

Grace's eyes flashed white as she read my mind, likely stopping on an image of Angel's decapitated head in Dorian's backpack. "She's not going to like that."

The end.

Made in the
USA
Lexington, KY